RELUCTANT WIZARD

BY

JEFFE KENNEDY

Only in an insane world would a young wizard find herself battling monsters and automatons one day and returning to Convocation Academy to cram for finals the next. But this is the world Alise Phel lives in.

Like it or not, Alise must face the consequences of ditching out a second time and dealing with the crushing workload assigned to her as a punishment. Worse yet, succeeding at the Academy means Alise must learn to master her powerful and unusual magic—the same magic that caused her to accidentally murder her own mother.

But graduating is her only way to protect the family she has left—and perhaps save the Convocation itself.

Cillian Harahel is a wizard of the mind. An archivist. A disciplined thinker. Thus, he absolutely cannot be in love with Alise Phel. Apart from the fact that he is faculty and she's a student—one destined for far more greatness than a lowly librarian like him—the provost has told him in no uncertain terms that Alise is off limits, which would be much more of a problem if Alise actually remembered he was alive.

Cillian has resigned himself to being Alise's friend and mentor, but when she cuts off even that much contact, in the coldest way possible, he suspects that darker forces than either of them imagined are haunting her. Alise has made it clear she wants nothing to do with him, but how can he abandon her to the demons clawing at her, from her House's enemies to the doubts plaguing her own heart?

DEDICATION

To David

My own personal cinnamon roll hero, who even cooks for me.

ACKNOWLEDGMENTS

Many thanks to Minerva Spencer for an early read and a final read. Also for long, boozy, talky afternoons at Jinja.

Tons of thanks to the librarians and library-adjacent friends who suggested their dream-list for librarian magic! These folks gave me wonderful suggestions. If I didn't use them yet, I might still!

- Jon Ajudah Barr
- Jeremy Brett
- Randy Brown
- David Burch
- Kate Chambers
- Jen Cilia
- Halley Ui Cinnsealaigh
- Laura Darnell
- Teresa Dennis Cummings-Rogers
- Lynne Facer
- Steve Harvey
- Amy Kay
- Stacey Knight-Davis
- Elaine Robson
- M.H. Townsend

The answer to a riddle I needed to solve came from Halley

Ui Cinnsealaigh, who suggested library hammerspace, and Jeremy Brett, Curator, Science Fiction and Fantasy Research Collection, Cushing Memorial Library and Archives, Texas A&M University—and archivist for my work!—who suggested the ability to create and move stacks at will. (He's also a total cinnamon roll.)

Much love and gratitude to the usual suspects: Grace Draven, Darynda Jones, Jennifer Estep, Megan, Mulry, Kelly Robson, and Jim Sorenson, who keep me afloat every day.

As always, immense gratitude to Carien Ubink and Sullivan McPig, for catching the details I forget and for All The Assisting.

Love to my mom, who is sleeping in a hospital bed as I type this. I won't dedicate this book to you because I promised you'd be all right.

And love to David, ever and always, for being there for me.

RELUCTANT WIZARD

~ 1 ~

F OR THE SECOND time in her life, Alise Phel returned to Convocation Academy with her metaphorical tail tucked firmly between her legs. Besides the humiliation of it all, she didn't even want to go back to school. Dark arts knew, both she and the academy had had quite their fill of each other.

And yet, here she was: literally kicking her heels outside Provost Uriel's office, in a chair too tall to allow her boots to touch the floor. She could be eight years old instead of eighteen. That was a nifty intimidation tactic there, making the students called to the provost's office feel like children in for a scolding.

It was enough to drive a person crazy.

Provost Uriel's familiar, who also worked as her aide, gave Alise a sympathetic glance, as if hearing her thoughts. He couldn't, naturally, as familiars were only able to supply magic, not wield it, but the aide didn't need psychic ability to read her glum expression. He no doubt saw a parade of downcast students waiting to discover the newest twist in the fates they couldn't control. Alise clung to her resentment, wallowing in that angry misery rather than in the wrenching guilt over having murdered her own mother.

A little interoffice Ratsiel courier buzzed in to sit on the aide's shoulder. "Provost Uriel will see you now, Wizard Alise," he said, giving her a bolstering smile.

"Thanks."

"You can leave your things here," he added.

"I remember," she replied wryly. He'd made the same offer the last time she was there.

Alise stomped into Provost Uriel's office, her big boots making a satisfying clomp of disdain on the lovely polished wooden floor. The waterproof boots had been perfect for the muddy, sloppy, and chilly-rain winter of much warmer Meresin, but not so much in frigid Convocation Center—nor in the beautifully furnished room that reeked of academia and storied tradition.

High in one of the turrets of the expansive connected buildings that formed Convocation Academy, the provost's office was ringed with a semi-circle of windows giving an expansive view of the snow-covered campus. The provost herself sat at a grand desk at the center of it all her platinum hair arranged in an exquisite twist, her skin dewy from the attention of grooming imps, a spiderweb of lines fanning out from her wizard-black eyes. Her House Uriel psychic magic waved impersonally against Alise's own wizard senses, an assessing multicolored field of well-crafted, exquisitely balanced magic of a high-level wizard. The provost raised a single brow as the imposing woman looked her up and down with keen insight.

Alise could just imagine what the provost saw, but she didn't care about her appearance. She wasn't at academy to look pretty. She was there to play obedient wizard, to graduate as quickly as possible—and possibly discover the root of a Convocation-wide conspiracy that went back generations. No big deal.

"Wizard Alise," the provost finally said in a musing tone, apparently finished with her cataloguing of Alise's many faults. "I'd rather believed, after our previous conversation, that you would not be in my office again so soon. Or ever again. In fact, I'd been fully convinced you were sincere about finishing your education—and in obeying the rules set forth for you here. I clearly recall fervent promises on your part to that effect."

Alise bit back a sigh, and a pointed retort. "I apologize, Provost Uriel."

The provost waited an expectant moment, then tipped her head slightly. "At least you don't attempt to offer excuses. I would, however, be interested in the tale of how a planned field trip with Archivist Cillian Harahel to access the archives at House Harahel—an excursion, not incidentally, approved by me, personally, and with the understanding that strict limitations would be observed—turned into you haring off to House Phel, *yet again*, where you became embroiled in highly illegal and contentious activities."

Put that way, it all sounded very bad, though the choice to rush to her family's aid had been very clear at the time. They'd been under a literal siege, their lives at stake. "Archivist Harahel *did* go with me," Alise offered weakly. "I was still under Convocation faculty supervision the entire time."

"I'm aware of Archivist Harahel's decision in this matter," Provost Uriel replied drily, "and I will be speaking with him also."

Alise jerked her chin up. Was Cillian's job in jeopardy? And all because of her. "It wasn't his fault. I insisted."

"Oh?" The provost raised a brow. "I can't say I think much of his 'supervision' as a faculty member if a minor student was able to sway him from the explicitly defined parameters of his assignment."

"I'm not a minor," Alise replied, trying to sound reasonable. "I'm eighteen now." Never mind that everyone had forgotten her birthday in the cacophony of events. She would be horribly selfish to even wish for anyone to think to celebrate that, given all that had occurred.

"You, Wizard Alise, despite your recent birthday, elevated birth, and estimable high-house connections, are but a *student* here," Provost Uriel said with stern emphasis. "That makes you a minor in the academy's eyes. Whereas Archivist Harahel is a faculty member, albeit a junior one and a librarian rather than teaching staff, and is therefore expected to adhere to binding regulations. Taking a student on an excursion unauthorized by the academy or her family is a severe breach of professional standards."

"We went to *save* my family!" Alise protested. "Lord Phel will—"

"Lord Phel does not direct Convocation Academy," the provost interrupted with a severe chop of her hand. "*I* do. And, despite what some high houses believe, Convocation Academy is an independent entity, not a political one. We do not cave to the desires of the individual houses nor to the pulling of rank by the scions of those houses. Not Phel. Not Elal. Not Harahel."

"I did not intend to pull rank," Alise said as evenly as she could, attempting to stick to the primary accusation. "I certainly never have called on the influence of House Elal. I've renounced the house of my birth, as we've previously discussed, Provost."

"Yes, about that…" The provost plucked up a missive from the many on her desk, this one on expensive stationery with the gold-embossed seal of House Elal. It soured Alise's stomach just to see it. "Any idea why Lord Elal is writing to me to withdraw you from Convocation Academy due to a family emergency?"

Alise had a pretty good idea, yes, but not one she'd like to articulate. Even if you hated your father, it wasn't good form to accuse him of vengeful and murderous impulses. "He can't do that. House Elal already disowned me."

"Not officially, he didn't. According to Convocation records, you are still a scion of Elal, and your father has been heard saying that he's considering you to be his heir."

That was news to Alise. According to her younger brother, Nander, the disowning had been done a while ago. And Nander had been equally certain of being their father's heir. He'd taunted Alise with the information, though Alise didn't care in the least. She wasn't fit to be a standard wizard, let alone the head of a high house, not with the terrible way she'd used her magic. She'd witnessed firsthand how power had corrupted her father and had no intention of following any further in his footsteps.

"House Phel pays my tuition, my room and board," she pointed out. "Papa—Lord Elal, that is, doesn't have the power to withdraw me," Alise tried, feeling more than a little desperate.

"To some extent, that's true," the provost allowed, dropping the missive onto her desk again. "As my previous remarks on Convocation Academy not being subject to the whims of the heads of high houses, even one as powerful as Lord Elal imagines himself to be, still apply. There is, however, the more than slight problem, Wizard Alise, in that your status here as a student is in question—entirely due to your own actions—no matter *who* is paying the bill. Surely you understand the problem?"

"Yes, Provost," Alise answered, sick at heart but unable to deny the truth.

"You were *already on probation.*" Provost Uriel smacked her palm on the desk, a psychic echo slapping Alise's mind with stinging emphasis. "Do you recall our conversation regarding your status here, a dialogue we conducted right here, in this very office, not three months ago?"

Alise winced. "I do recall, Provost Uriel."

"Would you please indulge me and reiterate the, what I thought were very clear, conditions for you to be readmitted to the academy following your *last* unauthorized excursion? Please begin with the part where I granted you a second chance when I did not have to and in truth had serious reservations about extending."

Well, this sucked even more than Alise had anticipated. She really hadn't expected to feel guilty. Not about this, anyway. "You graciously granted me the second chance I asked for, and—"

"That you pleaded for," the provost corrected.

"That I pleaded for," Alise agreed glumly, staring at the blunt toes of her boots. "I agreed to all of your conditions—the campus restrictions, the heavy course load, that I would apply myself diligently." She lifted her gaze, meeting the provost's. "I accepted the independent study you assigned me, Provost Uriel, and pursued it in good faith. If I may be so bold, I'll add that I followed through on all of those commitments. My grades were excellent."

The provost regarded her with pinched lips, then heaved a sigh of exasperation. "You being bold, Wizard Alise, does not seem to be in question. I should count my blessings not to have *more* bold Elal scions like you and your sister."

Alise noted with considerable interest that the provost didn't include Nander in that group. She also said nothing, choosing that course of action as the wisest in the moment.

The provost sighed again. "You *were* doing well. That's only one frustrating aspect of the problem you present. You had made impressive strides, particularly with what you'd uncovered in the course of your independent study."

Alise gave the provost a cautiously questioning look. The terms of her independent study had never been explicitly outlined. The provost had simply given her a full-access pass to the Convocation Archives—a rather dizzying amount of freedom for a mere student—and listed herself as faculty advisor. The provost, possibly acting in House Uriel's interest, given their long enmity with House Hanneil, had basically given Alise license to look for Hanneil interference in the official Convocation records, especially regarding the fall of

House Phel. Alise had sent regular reports to the provost, as her independent study advisor, but Provost Uriel had never replied, nor had she given any indication she'd read, or even received those missives.

Of course, Alise's "findings" had all been in the negative column: no records of House Phel remained in Convocation Archives. The real discovery had come about when she'd finally relaxed her pride, and justifiable caution, enough to ask for a librarian's help, which was when she met Cillian. He verified her findings—or, rather, lack thereof.

"That's why Wizard Cillian was taking me to House Harahel, to search the original documents there and…" She took a breath, decided she might as well say it. After all, the provost's office was privacy shielded. "And potentially petition House Harahel to investigate suspected tampering in the official archives."

The provost didn't exactly straighten, but her psychic magic focused on Alise with an intensity that communicated her complete attention, wizard-black eyes snapping with alert interest. "Librarian Harahel did not mention that information in his field trip requisition to me. A missive that, I might mention, did not request permission, but rather informed me of the expedition," she added with irritated distaste.

Oh, Cillian. Alise managed not to roll her eyes, but Cillian's special blend of absentminded professor and single-minded researcher nevertheless filled her with exasperation. "He likely thought he was being discreet, given the nature of our inquiry."

"Hmm." Provost Uriel tapped silver-pointed nails on the

desk. "I suppose I shall soon enough discover from the horse's mouth exactly *what* he was thinking, if he was at all."

Alise managed not to wince, but she did send a mental apology to Cillian for throwing him to this particular wolf. She didn't have a very high MP score in psychic magic, so he wouldn't get the message. Not to mention that meddling in minds even that much was highly unethical and absolutely illegal.

"Will Lord and Lady Phel be petitioning House Harahel in your stead?" the provost asked abruptly.

"Ah, erm, I don't know," Alise ventured. "There were a great many things to deal with in the aftermath of the battle at House Phel, injuries and property destruction, and then we received your summons to return to Convocation Academy and—"

"I see. No need to continue. I'll discuss with Archivist Harahel. He should be waiting outside in the anteroom. Please send him in on your way out."

"Ah…" Alise hesitated, surprised to be dismissed already, and the provost glanced up impatiently. "Where should I go?" Alise ventured.

"To *class*," the provost answered as if Alise were dense. She raised platinum brows in astonishment. "I'm given to believe you're substantially behind in your coursework. You have a great deal to do to catch up if you're to graduate on time."

"Yes, Provost," Alise breathed, rather startled by the immense relief she felt at being allowed to continue her studies. The sense of reprieve came as a stark contrast to her earlier unhappiness about being back at Convocation Academy only a short time before. "Thank you, Provost Uriel," she said sincerely, tempted to bow.

The provost flicked her fingers in dismissal. "My reward shall be penning a missive to Lord Piers Elal, explaining why he cannot withdraw his daughter from my school. I believe I shall enjoy tweaking his nose. Begone, Wizard Alise. Please consider a change of clothing before you return to class."

Alise flushed, surprised to be chagrined. "I was planning to, Provost Uriel," she replied with dignity. "Thank you for this second, second-chance."

"You paying attention to your independent study project would be thanks enough. And, I am begging you," the provost added with a glare and a ping of psychic reinforcement, "don't screw up again."

$$\sim 2 \sim$$

C ILLIAN HARAHEL WAITED in Provost Uriel's antechamber, a book in his lap as always, but for once unable to concentrate on it. He kept reading the same few lines over and over, until they began to seem like an acid commentary on his entire, until recently, sedate and disciplined existence.

Sylus raged over the loss of Lyndella. In his fury, he tore apart the contents of his arcanium, slamming loose objects against the stone walls to shatter to pieces as useless as his wits. How dare she refuse his offer? She was meant to be his, in every way, utterly and completely. Sylus wouldn't rest until Lyndella knelt at his feet. And when she did, he would make her pay. For kneel she would. He vowed to make it so.

Cillian didn't at all understand his fascination for these objectively terrible lines. He'd begun reading *The Saga of Sylus and Lyndella* in order to better understand romance. And yes, he was drily aware of the implicit commentary on his staid and scholarly self, that he'd approached the topic of romance as a research project. From his tenure in the Convocation Academy libraries, he knew how popular Sylus and Lyndella's story was. Among the many romance novels available, and then in the subset of those that dealt with wizard–familiar romances, the highly questionable and ultimately tragic tale of overbearing and controlling Wizard Sylus and the delicate, doomed Familiar Lyndella, could not be kept on the shelf. The archives contained multiple copies, enchanted to signal Ratsiel couriers to return them to the library after a set time, because so many had mysteriously vanished over the years.

So, to kick off his research into romance—an effort likely to be as doomed as this epic love affair—this afternoon Cillian had started reading *The Saga of Sylus and Lyndella* for the first time in his life. He hadn't even gotten past the first few pages, an unusually slow pace for him, because he kept sticking on various passages like this. *She was meant to be his, in every way, utterly and completely. Sylus wouldn't rest until Lyndella knelt at his feet.*

The kneeling, of course, his analytical brain informed him, was a reference to the bonding ceremony, in which a familiar knelt at a wizard's feet and accepted the binding enchantment that would tie them together until death parted them. That part wasn't relevant to Cillian's interests. He'd embarked on this research project to better understand his feelings for the lovely, prickly, and often remote Alise Phel, who was a wizard like himself. So, really, a wizard–familiar romance wasn't an appropriate model at all. Not to mention the reality that Cillian was unlikely to ever have a familiar as archivists typically never required that kind of magical boosting.

Alise was a different story. With her tremendous natural talent for, and growing skill in manipulating spirits, she would almost certainly bond a familiar someday. And she would need a familiar appropriate for her status as a high-house wizard, possibly even the head of a high house, as looked to be her destiny. Romances between wizards certainly occurred, but were rarely monogamous, unless the wizards were lower-tier types, like himself. Harahel, alone among the high houses, seemed to have more lasting, wizard–wizard marriages. The wizard–familiar relationship, however, was an intimate one, usually including erotic play, unless the bonded pair were siblings. Thus, many wizard–familiar pairs were also married or sexually exclusive. More, he understood that magical bond created an intensity of connection unlike any other.

Alise would have that someday. He wanted her to have that, and more. Alise deserved happiness and her heart's desire. And that would not be a wizard–wizard relationship, particularly not with the equivalent of a magical pedestrian, currently employed in an entry-level position at Convocation Academy.

Cillian didn't even know why he was thinking about anything but being Alise's friend, much less studying up as if he'd take some kind of action.

Well, strike that. He *did* know the why. The first time she'd walked into the library, clutching her pass from the provost to her slim bosom like a shield, her wizard-black eyes huge in her piquant face, his heart had lurched dangerously. With her warm, golden skin, and slight figure, she'd resembled a candle flame, lighting up the gloom of his dull night shifts at the reference desk. Something about her struck him hard and fast, hitting him with heady desire and something dangerously like love at first sight.

She was meant to be his...

There was no "meant to be," of course, outside of fiction.

No love at first sight, especially without an actual conversation—though he *had* known who she was.

His Harahel magic meant that he could recall anything he deliberately memorized, and he made a point of keeping up with the Convocation Academy student roster. So, he'd known that Alise Phel, née Elal, had returned to the academy after a great scandal in which she'd helped two lovelorn familiars escape. Good girl, heir-apparent to House Elal, early manifesting Wizard Alise had been the last person anyone had expected to aid in that rebellion.

Alise had returned to Convocation Academy to finish her education, to the delight of gossips and annoyance of those professors who considered her a lost cause. Cillian hadn't paid much attention either way. Until she walked into the library, catching his attention not unlike the way Lyndella had seized Wizard Sylus's singular devotion the first time he saw her dance. A trope that annoyed Cillian even as it resonated.

Cillian had been riveted by Alise, hit by lightning, her magic as tantalizing as the scent of roses on a warm summer afternoon. And she hadn't even glanced in his direction, just waved that pass at him, entirely focused on her search. He loved that intense, single-mindedness of hers.

He'd kept an eye on her, rationalizing that it was part of his job, though weeks passed without her asking for his assistance. She was a loner, wrapped in a cocoon of remote stillness. And, as he reminded himself daily, she was a student. She might be only four years younger than him, but he was faculty and in a position of power over her, even if it was only a laughably minor sort of power. Cillian was no Sylus, master of vast holdings and possessor of a telekinetic wizardry so devasting he could rend the very bedrock of the land.

Which, a salient point about Sylus, he'd eventually done, destroying his enemies and an entire land along with them in taking vengeance for Lyndella, who died alone and separated from him. At least, if the story was to be believed. *The Saga of Sylus and Lyndella* was a fictionalized account of a historical tale with murky provenance, at best. Probably ninety percent of the purported "history" had been embellished, if not created whole hog, over the centuries. The book was almost entirely nonsense. So, why was he reading it?

Because he didn't understand romance, he supposed, and he desperately needed to. He didn't understand this consuming desire for Alise nor what, if anything, to do about it. She'd been called to Provost Uriel's office the moment they disembarked from the carriage they'd shared to return to Convocation Academy, and he'd been commanded to attend shortly thereafter. He had no choice but to wait. And wonder. So he did what he always did: read a book to pass the time; bonus if it served as research. He snorted softly to himself in disgust, reading the same lines again.

How dare she refuse his offer? She was meant to be his, in every way, utterly and completely. Sylus wouldn't rest until Lyndella knelt at his feet.

Alise hadn't refused Cillian's offer, of course—because he hadn't made one. He wasn't even sure *what* he'd offer, even if he mustered the balls to do it and overcame all good sense at the same time. He didn't have much of anything, with no prospects of ever having much. And, when he allowed himself to indulge in romantic fantasies about Alise, none of them included her kneeling and capitulating to him. He wanted her by his side—and he had absolutely zero desire to be like Sylus, full of possessive rage. That wasn't him at all.

The problem was: he also didn't much want to be himself. Bookish, retiring, baker of cinnamon rolls, and apt to blurt out things he shouldn't. Probably Alise knew very well that he had a crush on her, as he'd foolishly said inappropriate things to her when she finally *did* approach him for assistance. She hadn't even known his name then, pronouncing it with a soft C instead of a hard one. That should have been humiliation enough to make it abundantly clear how delusional he'd been. He groaned in the back of his throat at the memory.

"Are you well, Archivist Cillian?" Priyan, the provost's aide and familiar, asked with a frown of concern. "You were making some... noises," he added when Cillian looked up in confusion. "Would you like a glass of water?"

"No, no," Cillian said, sharply enough to make Priyan's frown deepen. "I mean, I'm fine. No problem here."

"Provost Uriel should be with you very soon," Priyan said kindly.

"I'm fine," Cillian said, realizing he was repeating himself. "I have my book." He held it up in demonstration, feeling like even more of an idiot when Priyan smiled and nodded.

Just then, the doors to the provost's office flew open and Alise stalked out. She had a way of entering every room like she defied anyone there to kick her out. Her older sister, Nic, now Lady Phel, had a similar manner, though more confident and less prickly. Both Elal sisters took up a lot of air in the room, drawing the light to them. Alise just tended to look as if she'd rather that wasn't the case.

Alise's sharply black eyes fixed on him, and she nodded in greeting, formally, as if they hadn't just shared a carriage ride back from House Phel for two days. Not to mention all the time they'd spent together before that. Her short black hair stood out in tousled spikes, looking as if she'd been running her hands through it, and she hunched her shoulders inside the mud-spattered black raincoat she'd worn from Meresin, which wasn't really warm enough for Convocation Center in wintertime. A flush of emotion graced her high cheekbones, but she looked otherwise composed.

"Archivist Cillian," she greeted him, in what he'd learned to identify as her in-control, lady-of-the-high-house voice. "I'm told to ask you to go in now."

"Ah, thank you, Wizard Alise." He was enough of a dork that, in fumbling to stand up from the oversized chair, he dropped his book. Reaching for it, he nearly bumped heads with Alise, who'd crouched to retrieve it. She naturally peeked at the title. He really hoped he wasn't blushing. Even more strongly, he wished for a hole to open up in tower floor, drop him twenty stories, and kill him immediately.

"Not your usual reading fare," she commented, raising a brow. She'd know perfectly well that he hadn't brought the book on their journey, which meant she'd also deduce that he'd grabbed it specifically to read while waiting to be fired.

"Research for a special project," he said, immediately regretting the choice of words. *What project would that be, Cillian, you idiot?* "It's really quite awful, how Sylus behaves," he babbled on, kicking himself mentally for still talking. As usual around her, he couldn't seem to stop himself. Also, he didn't want Alise to think that *he* thought about women that way. "A terrible example, in truth."

Then he caught the slight wrinkle of her nose, a wince of discomfort at the corners of her eyes. "Have you read it?" he asked belatedly, with a very bad feeling.

A smile quirked her solemn mouth. Alise rarely smiled in full, always restraining herself. "I did. I believe I filched Nic's copy and read it at an age far too young for some of the content."

"I loved that book," Priyan said on a dreamy sigh. "I used to fantasize about being Lyndella, swept away by Sylus."

To Cillian's surprise, Alise's smile warmed, and she nodded at Priyan. "I think we all did."

"You?" Cillian blurted out—saying the wrong thing for the one-thousandth time in a row in Alise's disconcerting presence. "I mean, you don't seem like you would go for Sylus's brand of..." He didn't finish, decidedly uncomfortable choosing any of the several words that popped into mind. He regretted his outburst even further when Alise's smile froze, then shattered entirely as she averted her gaze.

She handed him the book without looking at him again, saying offhandedly. "I was young and naïve."

"Oh, to be that young and naïve again," Priyan said, clapping a hand over his heart.

"Familiar Priyan," the provost said from the doorway, sounding stern, but with amusement in her expression. "Can I ask you to leave off fluttering over romantic heroes and instead send in my next appointment?"

"Yes, Provost," Priyan answered, but with a cheeky flutter of his lashes.

"Wizard Alise," the provost said with much less amusement. "I believe I told you to be gone—and pursuing any number of more productive activities."

"Going, Provost Uriel," Alise replied, sounding chastened, but she gave Priyan a wink and left without acknowledging Cillian further.

He hadn't even thought to ask her how it had gone with the provost, he'd been so flustered. As he turned to follow Provost Uriel's preemptory gesture to enter her office, he reviewed Alise's set expression and the provost's parting comment. Alise had been upset, flushed and unhappy, but it sounded like she'd been given a reprieve and would remain at the academy—a relief for both of them.

Well, a relief for her, but not for him if he didn't remain at Convocation Academy. Given the provost's attitude, nothing boded well for that eventuality.

He was definitely getting fired.

~ 3 ~

ALISE HURRIED HER way out of the provost's office and plunged down the long, winding steps that led ever earthward. Offices ringed the tower at each floor, on both the inner and outer circles, open doors emitting the chatter of conversation and rustle of paperwork. Ratsiel couriers flew over her head in a steady stream of myriad directions, carrying the communications of the busy academy. Some of the office workers glanced at her as she went by, giving her nods of respect. She might be the subject of gossip from all and disdain from some, but she was still her father's daughter, when all was said and done, and a wizard.

No one wanted to cross an Elal wizard. Today's mud-covered, disgraced student could be tomorrow's Lady Elal, after all. Never mind that Alise wasn't interested in intimidating anyone. For that matter, she had no intention of improving her wizardry. She'd caused enough damage as it was. She would find a way to learn the bare minimum to graduate, then contrive never to use her abilities again, for any reason. Never again would she risk doing what had killed her mother.

She could add how she'd treated Cillian to her long list of transgressions of how she'd failed everyone around her. He'd looked so flustered, barely meeting her gaze, acting upset. He was probably worried about getting fired. And why had he had he been reading *The Saga of Sylus and Lyndella*? That was so out of character for him. Then teasing her about liking it. Yes, of course she recognized the unrealistic aspects of that torrid romance, but it was *fiction*. Well, mostly. No doubt Cillian would be able to tell her exactly how much of the tale was historically accurate. Had his getting the book—and ostentatiously reading it where she'd run into him—been a way of trying to get a rise out of her?

No. She shook that away. Cillian had said he was pursuing some project with the book and had no reason to lie about that. After all, he had a much bigger life than assisting her research, projects he'd likely had to put on hold to help her, plus being dragged into House Phel business. Probably he was pursuing a project like parsing the history versus the fiction of Sylus and Lyndella, or some such and she was being emotional and paranoid, which seemed to be the new normal for her.

She didn't know up from down these days, only that getting from one hour to the next felt like such an unbearable slog that she wanted to crawl under the covers and not come out until spring. Maybe longer.

This, however, was not an option.

Class. She was supposed to go to class. Alise racked her brain trying to remember where she was supposed to be on this day, at this particular time. It seemed like months instead of weeks since she'd been at the academy, and... Well, shit. Today was her senior practicum. The worst possible class to have to endure. Worse, the hands-on lasted all afternoon and required active participation. Even the delay of changing her clothes wouldn't save her from several hours of pretending to know what she was doing. What dreadful luck.

But delaying further would only make it worse. So, Alise strode down the quiet hall in the dorm reserved for upper level wizard students. Everybody was in class at this time of day, a minor stroke of good fortune. She didn't care to answer any probing questions disguised as friendly conversation. As she drew near to her own closed door, however, she spotted someone leaning against the wall next to it, wearing the garb of one of the academy proctors, which was... very odd. Proctors didn't spend time where students weren't. Their literal job was to monitor students.

Alise slowed to give herself time to think. She shouldn't be in any danger, even though the academy proctors were all Hanneil wizards and despite the fact that House Hanneil seemed to be a part of the conspiracy to destroy House Phel, for unknown reasons. Still, not everyone beholden to a house supported that house's politics—she should know, as she categorically hated everything House Elal did—nor would everyone in a house even know much about what the higher echelons were up to. Obviously on a few high-level wizards would know about conspiracy-level stuff, not wizards who ended up as academy proctors.

Only medium- to lower-level wizards settled for the grunt jobs that were basically being hall monitors for unruly students. The proctors scanned surface thoughts and attempted to nip infractions in the bud. They were generally effective at that, but the faculty handled any major trouble.

As she drew near, she found she didn't recognize the proctor who was very obviously blocking access to her room. Even odder. At this stage of her academic career, after all these years of boarding and schooling at Convocation Academy, she recognized most, if not all, of the staff and faculty, if only distantly. A steady gig at Convocation Academy, even a lowly one—salaried, along with room and board—was nothing to sneeze at. Turnover was low. A proctoring job might not be the plum of the psychic wizarding world, but most of the academy proctors were wizards she remembered from more than ten years before when she first arrived at the academy as a girl.

That this unfamiliar proctor behaved out of character and clearly waited for specifically her sent a chill of foreboding down her spine. But Alise pulled her poise together and lifted her chin, channeling her best Lady Elal manner. "Can I be of assistance, Proctor...?"

The man smiled and sketched a bow. He had golden hair, pale skin, and a square jaw, classically handsome if you cared for that sort of thing. His coloring was striking with his black eyes. His psychic magic had an unsavory look to it, however, a murky quality that canceled out any physical appeal he might have. "A moment of your time, Wizard Elal."

"Phel," she corrected sharply, and his smile only curved as he tipped his head in dubious acknowledgment.

"I am Proctor Gordon Hanneil," he said. "I must have a word with you."

"Must you?" she inquired coolly. She set down her overnight bag, and her bag of books, folded her arms and waited.

"Go ahead. I need to change clothes and attend my practicum, as I'm sure you're aware, being a proctor." She added that last pointedly, since she wasn't at all convinced that was true. Proctor's robes were easy to acquire.

"In private," he qualified with a flash of a grin that was likely supposed to be charming, as he gestured to her door.

Oh no, boyo, I don't think so. She made a show of looking around the empty hallway. "You can speak here. There's no one to overhear."

"Elal spies are everywhere."

"So I always hear. I don't have a say in what House Elal does—but I can promise you that, if Elal has sent spirits to spy on this hallway, then they're even more certainly in my room. Lord Elal and I haven't exactly seen eye to eye of late. Speak here or nowhere."

Gordon's jaw flexed. "I will only deliver this *very important* message in the confines of your private chamber, Wizard Phel."

She shrugged. "I suppose you won't be delivering your *very important* message then, as I have no intention of letting you into my room. It's your *very important* message. You keep it."

"You're awfully cheeky for a young thing."

Alise was getting a bit tired of people treating her like a child. Yes, she was slight and looked younger than her years. But she had reached actual, legal adulthood, not to mention being a full-fledged wizard with not inconsiderable abilities. And she would only grow stronger, whereas this mid-level—at best—Hanneil wizard had topped out. She outranked him in every way and he thought he could bully her? Anger coursed warm under her skin, far better than the previous chill of trepidation.

"What I am is late for my practicum, *Proctor*," she bit out, emphasizing his job title. "Move away from my door and cease delaying me—or I shall report you."

His face took on such ugly anger at her words that Alise wondered how she could've ever thought him handsome, even objectively and in passing. "You wouldn't dare," he hissed. Darting forward, he seized her arm in a crushing grip that felt like it went to the bone. Equally numbing, his psychic magic wormed into her through the contact, sending invasive tendrils through her throbbing nerves to her brain. This was no low- or mid-level wizard. In fact—she realized, far too late—he was more powerful than she knew how to defend against.

Alise didn't know what he intended to do. Influence or control her in some way, that was certain. Psychic manipulation was also hugely illegal, but unless she could get to help, piffling laws didn't matter. Belatedly, she tried summoning a warrior spirit to get the wizard off of her, but her magic went nowhere, feeling as if it had bounced off a glass wall. He was blocking her somehow. She should have taken defensive action sooner. Hard on the heels of that regret, came a frisson of real fear.

"Listen to me, and listen well, sweetheart," he said into her ear, his breath unpleasantly hot on her cheek, the message behind his words pounding through her brain from the inside of her skull, reinforcing it with irresistible insistence. "You will cease looking for the House Phel archives."

She tried to jerk away, to wall out the psychic magic pummeling her will, encasing her in an ugly wall of dissonance, but his grip, both mental and physical, only tightened. Tears blurred her vision.

"You may keep up the appearance of conducting a search," he continued relentlessly, "but you will not be effective. Any information you learn, you will immediately forget. Any information you discover, you will hide or destroy so no one else can access it. Finally, you will tell no one of this conversation. You will be unable to speak of me or what we just discussed. Do you understand?"

"I understand," she heard herself say in dull obedience.

"Glad to hear it." He sounded smug, self-satisfied, no doubt pleased to have so easily bested her. To her shocked horror, he licked her ear. "Mmm, tasty. You might look like a little girl, but I bet you're all woman in bed. Be grateful I didn't decide to instill a compulsion for you to come to mine. Mind yourself, or next time, I will." He drew back and caressed her cheek with a finger, smiling when she shuddered.

"I can make you want me," he murmured. "Or I can let you loathe me as I sense in you right now and compel you to give yourself to me anyway. I enjoy that, too. Perhaps more. Your call, baby wizard. Do as I say: don't even think about retaliating or speaking a word about me other than to sing my praises, and I'll leave you alone."

At last he released his vise-grip on her arm, and the equally agonizing hold on her will, and Alise gasped at the sheer relief, then began shaking uncontrollably. The warrior spirit she'd tried to summon before suddenly manifested, looking to her for instructions. Gordon Hanneil glanced at it, then raked her with a salacious stare that left her feeling filthy, and shook a warning finger at her. Hastily, she banished the spirit.

"Not completely stupid," the other wizard said. "Though I was kind of hoping you'd test me. Something tells me you'll end up in my bed eventually, panting and eager, spreading your legs willingly, while your mind shrieks in useless protest. Mmm. I can feel it already. Are you a virgin? Ah, yes. Delightful." He paused, not waiting for a reply so much as enjoying her terror. "There. Message delivered. Was that so difficult? Remember your instructions."

He strolled away, whistling a tune vaguely familiar, but that she couldn't identify. Alise flung herself at her chamber door, fumbling at the Iblis lock coded to her and her alone. The door gave and she hurled herself inside, slamming and locking it as if it could protect her from what had already occurred. Only then did she release the sob of utter and horrified despair, realizing as her stomach spasmed that tears weren't all she'd be spewing. She made it to the washbasin and vomited, hard and painfully. Continuing to dry heave for a while, she wept continuously. Surely either puking or sobbing, or both, would provide a cathartic release and she'd feel better.

But she only felt soiled and ill.

At last, she got herself together enough to summon an earth elemental to clean up her sick. For those creatures, getting to consume anything was reward enough, but she was so grateful to it for removing the smell and visible evidence of her shame that she fed it an extra boost of magic, too. Sitting wearily on her narrow bed, she gazed bleakly around her small room.

The tiny earth elementals employed by Convocation Academy didn't allow for dust to gather, but the room still seemed stale with disuse. She'd had a much grander room, back when she'd been Alise Elal, heir apparent to House Elal, petted and spoiled by her papa. Now that House Phel had taken over her expenses, the days of being one of the wealthiest students at the school were over. Her sister, Nic, and her husband Gabriel, had apologized that they couldn't give her more, but Alise had been quick to shush them, knowing very well the precarious state of the House Phel finances. She certainly didn't want to be more of a burden than necessary on her new family.

She didn't long to go back to those relatively carefree days of wealth, when all she thought about was herself and her wizardry. She didn't even wish to go back to the time before she'd impulsively gone to Meresin to rescue her family under siege at House Phel. No, all she really wanted, with every aching bone in her body, was to go back half an hour, to before that Hanneil magic fouled her mind. She fervently wished, as if wishing could make it so, that the encounter with Gordon Hanneil had never happened.

But it had. And she would never be the same.

A knock on her door set her heart lurching in the cavity of her chest, then to pounding frantically. Had he come back, perhaps to make good on his threats? Gazing at the inside of the door in stark terror, she distantly groped at the idea that she should muster a defense of some sort.

The knock came again. "Wizard Alise Phel?" a voice called.

Female. Not Gordon Hanneil.

"Wh—who is it?" she stammered, her throat tight and burning.

"Proctor Divya Hanneil. You're quite late for your practicum." A pause. "Is all well, Wizard Alise? I'm sensing agitation from you. Please open the door."

Alise made an effort to strengthen her mental shielding, the annoyance that her distress had leaked through to the psychic wizard beyond the door helping to bolster her will. She made herself get up, unlock and open the door. "I'm fine. I just needed time to change clothes."

Proctor Divya gave her a long searching look—along with an assessing probe that made Alise flinch, even though it was the oblique, non-invasive variety she'd experienced from the academy proctors her entire life. Nothing like Gordon's lancing power that had laid her mind open as easily as a knife through butter.

The proctor noted Alise's reaction. "Perhaps you should attend the healers."

"No, no." The last thing Alise wanted was for more people poking at her, even if the Refoel healers used their psychic healing magic in an entirely different way. She'd be fine. And she really, really, really didn't want to risk anyone finding a trace of Gordon Hanneil's presence on her—and then face the promised consequences. No one could protect her from that. "I'm fine," she said with determination, willing it to be so. "I'll go to the practicum immediately." Alise gestured to the hallway, fully expecting the proctor to escort her there.

Proctor Divya raised a brow, her warm brown face concerned. She had always been one of the nicer proctors. "Wizard Alise," she said gently, "I am no fashion guru, but even I can see that you haven't changed your clothes yet."

Alise mentally kicked herself. She wasn't thinking straight. Probably she looked like shit, too. "Right. I just need a moment, if you'll wait for me?"

"Perhaps you should take today to recover from your journey," Divya said, a faint line between her elegant brows. "You don't feel well, clearly. You're upset. Did something untoward occur?"

"No!" Alise said, much too quickly and defensively. Divya's wizard-black eyes widened in surprise at her vehemence and Alise made herself take a deep breath. "It's just been a day, what with being castigated by the provost and all."

Divya smiled in sympathy. "Provost Uriel is a force of nature, to be sure. Still, I'm concerned about your current state of emotional agitation. You know we proctors are here to be more than hall monitors." Her smile twisted sardonically, making it clear she was well aware of how the students reduced their job description. "We also keep a finger on your emotional wellbeing. And personal safety," she added, with a lift of one brow that stopped just short of being inquisitive.

"I can take care of my personal safety," Alise replied, thinking wistfully of how she'd fully believed that only a short time ago, but she made herself sound firm.

Not firm enough, apparently, as Proctor Divya didn't budge. "A large part of our responsibility," she continued, "is to ensure that the overt and covert conflicts between the Convocation houses aren't played out in these halls. We don't imagine that we can prevent all power plays, but we can and *will* ensure our students' safety. The academy is neutral ground. You have a right to pursue your education without harassment. If something untoward has occurred, you may confide in me. I will handle the situation discreetly."

Alise suppressed a hysterical giggle at the prospect of informing on Proctor Divya's fellow House Hanneil wizard. That would go well. Divya might fully believe in the ethics of her profession, but house loyalty ran deep. Confronted with a conflict between the two, most wizards would choose house loyalty over a job. One could find new employment more easily than a new house, especially a high house.

Alise couldn't afford for Proctor Divya to go to Gordon, even with vague inquiries. So, she forced a smile, saying, "And we all so appreciate the proctors for your protection. Where would we be if the many house conflicts seeped into these hallowed halls?" Upon reflection, that phrasing might have been a little too sarcastic. "Nothing happened," she assured the proctor, willing her thoughts and emotions to support her words. "That is, a lot has happened recently," she amended. "Very difficult times."

That had the additional benefit of being actually true. Even without the unpleasantness with Gordon—she heard that word in her maman's voice, delicately alluding to the unspeakable, *unpleasantness*—she would still be emotionally reeling. The siege. Maman's passing. All Alise's fault.

"Is it exhaustion then?" Divya asked kindly.

"Tiredness, yes," Alise answered, seizing on the excuse. She couldn't possibly sleep now, however, and there was no way she wanted to sit in her room alone and think about what had happened. "But I'd prefer to get to class and start catching up. I'm already so far behind."

Proctor Divya nodded slowly, unconvinced. "Fine. I'll wait while you change clothes and escort you to your practicum. But I'm also putting in a ticket for you to see the healers at some point this week for an evaluation. I see in your records that you haven't had a full physical in nearly twelve months. It's been an eventful year for you, and I'm aware that Provost Uriel deliberately gave you an intense courseload, but surely it is not her intention for you to work yourself to collapsing. You will see the healers by the end of week. Are we agreed?"

Alise agreed with eager relief and a bone-watering sense of having escaped a terrible fate. She would recover her equilibrium and no one would ever know what had happened with Gordon Hanneil. She would never face that horrible fate he'd whispered so greasily into her ear, worms of psychic power crawling through her brain like maggots. Feeling her confidence falter, Alise promised to change with all speed, and just barely managed to close the door softly instead of slamming it in Divya's kind, intrusive face.

$$\sim 4 \sim$$

M IRACULOUSLY, CILLIAN HAD not been fired.

And so he returned to his cozy faculty apartment with a sense of happy homecoming. Nothing like returning to his own cozy nest. The piles of books everywhere, the scattering of papers and writing instruments, his mementos from role-playing games, all of it formed a cheerful chaos to the uninformed eye. For him, though, absolutely everything had its place. His scholarly brand of wizardry crawled over every object, great and small, every tiny bit of font and printed word, cataloguing, assessing, reassuring him that nothing had been moved and everything was as it should be.

More precisely: everything was *where* it should be. Still, something felt not quite right. The place seemed oddly empty, ever so slightly off, missing something—even though his wizardry assured him that wasn't the case. Everything was there.

Except Alise, he realized. She didn't belong in his chambers, obviously, but some part of him had half-expected her to be there, her Elal spirit magic filtering through the rooms like summer sunshine, leaving behind the vague scent of roses. A longing for her washed through him, bittersweet and intense.

Irrational. Alise would never again grace these rooms and he needed to get a grip on that reality. He could be friends with her and nothing more. Provost Uriel had been most emphatic on the point.

But he could at least enjoy being friends. To salve some of his longing, and as an alternative to wishing her there, he scribbled a note to Alise, asking if she wanted to meet that evening. He explained his perfectly rational (he hoped) reasoning: that they would need to discuss how to proceed with their original project, to discover the timeline of the disappearance of the House Phel archives and, hopefully, recover what information they could.

It definitely wasn't a date. Provost Uriel had been most pointed about Cillian maintaining a professional relationship with Alise Phel, even as she'd exhorted him to assist Alise in her independent study. He'd, of course, protested that nothing untoward had ever occurred between the two of them, all while the copy of Sylus and Lyndella's epic and vaguely disturbing love affair burned like a live coal in his hands. What had possessed him to grab *that* book right before going to the provost's office to face the consequences of his actions?

None of it made sense, least of all his own thought processes.

Provost Tandiya Uriel had naturally not disclosed her personal investment in discovering whether House Hanneil had tampered with the archives and the memories of the Convocation regarding House Phel. She'd cloaked her insistence on Alise continuing her independent study as being good for Alise. Still, he knew his history. House Uriel and House Hanneil had once been a single high house, one that split into two over the ethics of using psychic magic on others. Given their ancient enmity, Cillian could easily follow the logical path of internecine house politics.

Provost Uriel, probably at the behest of her house, wanted Alise to uncover this mystery from the past, and she wanted it enough that, instead of firing him, she'd appointed Cillian Alise's interim advisor on the project—provided that he keep the relationship strictly professional.

Naturally, and with as much sincerity as he could muster, he'd protested that his conduct with Alise had never been anything but professional, which was the absolute truth. Still, Tandiya had fixed him with her knowing black gaze, stopping just short of reading his thoughts. No one of House Uriel would commit that kind of invasion of mental privacy, not without a court mandate.

Still, she had the ability to evaluate his mental temperature. House Uriel had refined the ability to assess motivation and intention to a fine degree. That art allowed them to determine the honesty of an interview subject at a core level. It didn't matter what glib assurances or prevarications a person offered, a high-level Uriel wizard—and Tandiya was as high-level as it got, short of being head of the house—could sense the mindset behind the words.

Thus, the provost had no doubt sussed out the true state of Cillian's heart and mind: both that his relationship with Alise had always been strictly aboveboard, and that he longed to change that sad fact. Hopefully she also discovered his earnest desire to do right by Alise, regardless of his own yearnings. The provost had tipped her head, allowing a small sigh to escape.

"I know you'll conduct yourself with utmost integrity," she said, confirming that much. "You possess excellent self-discipline and the resolve to carry out your best intentions. Those are the *only* reasons I'm allowing you to continue to work with our young student. But, Wizard Harahel, I will caution you strongly: you must govern your passions."

"With all due respect, Provost," he'd replied with dignity, and deciding to discuss the cards, since she'd already laid them on the table, "I am a scholar, a devotee of the rational mind. Have I ever given any indication of being the sort of person to capitulate to wild and inadvisable feelings?"

"No," she said musingly. "Your intentions are pure—admirably so—but you would not be the first to find their better judgment and convictions eroding beneath the constant twin pressures of proximity and unrequited yearning. Don't underestimate the pressure you will be under."

He flushed, embarrassed by her too-accurate assessment of his mental and emotional state. "I will govern myself impeccably."

"See that you do," she replied, not unkindly, but with an authoritative mental tap of reinforcement. "None of us needs another Szarina incident," she added meaningfully. "Least of all you."

The flush burned. "I am well aware of the mistakes I made there."

"I would hope so. Therefore I shall not caution you further. Alise Phel's independent study is of great personal interest to me. You will do everything in your power to assist her and protect the project from… interference."

The way she said "interference" had him frowning. "Is there something I should know, Provost?"

"Nothing you don't already know, Wizard Harahel, if you've been paying attention to the politics of the last several centuries. If you haven't, then you don't deserve to be employed at *my* academy."

He absorbed that with a nod of acknowledgment. "If I may, Provost—I do believe the aborted excursion to House Harahel will still be necessary to successfully complete this project. I'll need Alise to accompany me for an official petition."

"I do wish," the provost replied acerbically, "that you would have considered that prioritization *before* you allowed your student charge to hare off on a dangerous jaunt instead of continuing on that approved mission. Had you remained firm, we might already be in possession of the information we need."

Cillian had nothing to say to that. Nothing relevant, anyway. He *could* explain that Alise—a far more powerful wizard than he—had threatened to use a warrior spirit to remove him from the carriage while she reprogrammed the air elemental driving it to take her to her new destination. The choice for him had been to go with her or be left by the side of the road.

"I understand," the provost said on a sigh, reading into him more than he liked, "that it can be difficult to handle our young wizards when their abilities so outstrip our own. But that is the sacred charge of the staff and faculty at Convocation Academy. We are here not only to educate our students in their magical abilities, but also to teach them restraint, to guide them away from their worst impulses during these formative years."

Cillian bit back two replies—an annoyed one that this teaching of restraint clearly didn't have a lasting effect, given the behavior of most wizards in the Convocation, and a somewhat desperate explanation that he was only a librarian who wasn't supposed to be guiding students anywhere except to the appropriate shelves for the books they sought. Provost Uriel fixed her black gaze on him, as if daring him to speak his thoughts. If he did, he knew she would assign someone else to assist Alise. And that he wouldn't be able to bear.

"I understand, Provost."

"You are her friend, Cillian," Tandiya said, dropping some of her stern formality. "I don't expect you to out-magic a wizard of Alise's nascent ability. I don't expect you to govern her, as we both know that probably nobody can. There are few wizards in the entire Convocation with the ability to contain her should she truly wield her magic to its fullest potential. What I do expect is that you will be there for her and show her the way. She respects you and has affection for you, however you managed that. I don't know of anyone else at Convocation Academy that she trusts like she trusts you."

That was news to him. "Did she say that?" he blurted in his flattered surprise.

Fully Provost Uriel again, she frowned at him sternly and tapped her temple. "Of course not. She is reticent and wary of confidences, our young and reluctant wizard. But she does trust that you will not betray her, as she rather expects everyone else to do. It's a powerful tool, that regard for you."

"I won't abuse that trust," he replied stiffly, horrified at the thought of that implicit betrayal.

"Exactly," the provost answered with a smile. "Therefore, yes, you may arrange a second expedition to House Harahel as soon as Alise's coursework allows. Need I specify that you will journey *only* to House Harahel and nowhere else?"

"No, Provost. Thank you. I won't let you down this time."

"See that you don't. I leave our young wizard in your hands. Don't make me sorry."

The provost's words echoed in Cillian's head as he studied the note he'd written to Alise. He needed to strike the right balance, to be her mentor as in the tales, not the romantic lead. That wasn't a new thought for him. Cillian had never been leading man material. He was the secondary character, at best, there to point the way, to open the right book, perhaps be the best friend. Well then, he would accept his fate and be the best friend and mentor for Alise that he could. And, when the time came for her to move along, he'd let her go with a smile.

Perhaps there could be a place for him in her life, in that minor role. He imagined a future where he'd visit her at the famously spectacular House Elal, where she would receive him as Lady Elal, enthusiastically squeezing his hands, perhaps exclaiming in delight over some rare tome he'd discovered and brought to her. They would sit in the library by the fire, or outdoors on a warm summer evening, and discuss philosophy and Convocation politics. She would ask his advice and he would give her thoughtful answers. People would take note and nod knowingly, commenting on their longstanding friendship. There could be a joy in that.

Reviewing the note he'd penned a third time, he decided it sounded appropriately professional. He added what should be welcome news that the provost had approved a new excursion to House Harahel. Smiling to himself, he anticipated seeing Alise in the library that evening to discuss their strategy. She'd been concerned about the coursework she'd missed, fretting about the backlog on their journey back to Convocation Academy. He could play mentor there, too, helping her prioritize her workload, perhaps even assisting with some of the more academic assignments. He could be her tutor on some subjects. Lay the groundwork for that lifelong friendship and advisory position he envisioned.

Satisfied that he could sublimate his feelings for Alise into that role, Cillian finished the note and gave it to a small Ratsiel courier to deliver to her when she emerged from her practicum.

Taking the copy of *The Saga of Sylus and Lyndella*, Cillian removed his bookmark and set it on the small table in the hall by the front door. He'd return it to the shelves when he reported for his shift in the archives that evening. And he'd concentrate on being his best self. No more dreaming about romance for him.

With that resolve, Cillian explored his kitchen stores, wondering what he could bake to bring to Alise that evening, to tempt her sweet tooth. Nothing untoward about that. He liked to bake, which Alise knew, and friends shared such things with one another. Perhaps in that future visit, he would bring Lady Alise Elal something he'd baked, as well, and they'd laugh and reminisce over her days at academy when he kept her fed.

~ 5 ~

Alise's Advanced Practicum in Manipulation and Control of Noncorporeal Entities, more commonly known by the students as Bossing the Bodiless, went terribly.

Because Alise was so late for the five-hour practicum, the other students had long since warmed up, completed the initial exercises, and were tackling the advanced application. And, of course, just to continue the trend of her horrendous luck, the day's assignment involved binding and releasing more complex spirits.

Spirit magic, like all forms of magic, functioned at escalating levels of difficulty. Anyone, even mundanes, could benefit from using the simplest and smallest spirits called elementals. Once bound and trained to a task, the elementals operated indefinitely on the instructions given to them by the binding wizard. Thus, most everyone in the Convocation, unless they lived in crushing poverty, had dust-eating earth elementals in their homes or fire-elemental heated floors.

On the next level up, anyone with some amount of magic, even familiars, could influence tamed spirits. With potent Elal magic thick in her blood, Nic had a knack for coaxing elementals and even more complex spirits into doing her bidding, despite the fact that, as a familiar, she couldn't actually wield magic. Nic was an exception to many rules, however. Alise had been surprised to see how Nic had refined her technique over the last year to use her ability to sense magic to create a kind of passive field to influence the "mood" of spirits, for want of a better word.

Similarly, even low-level wizards of any variety could give elementals new instructions. Thus, with the air-elemental powered carriages, for example, any wizard could program in a new speed or destination, but one absolutely needed a wizard for that. Anyone could ride in the carriage, so long as you had a wizard to set it up for you.

Low- to mid-level wizards capable of wielding spirit magic could call and bind spirits of ascending complexity according to their own magical potentials, their training, the type of spirit, and their access to magic, either from their natural reserves or via magic taken from a familiar. The universe contained many kinds of spirits, in branching echelons, from the mindless elementals that were the equivalent of single-celled organisms to sentient spirits too wily and powerful to be controlled by mere humans. The old tales contained stories of immensely powerful wizards who tamed djinn or daemons and harnessed them to assist in their plans, usually to rule the world.

Those tales were always cautionary. Those wizards who essayed such ambitious workings sometimes managed to carry off such monumental feats but, while their imaginations knew no bounds, magic did. A limited resource, magic always ran out eventually. Even with a bonded familiar or even multiple bonded familiars, as had been sometimes the practice in the past but was strictly illegal in contemporary Convocation society, a wizard could drain them dry and come up empty.

Controlling a being as powerful as a djinn or daemon required constant effort. They didn't take kindly to being captured by mere mortals. As soon as the magic ran out, they broke free. And took revenge.

Still, there were many, many kinds of spirits in the universe—many more than had been catalogued, so said her professor in History and Taxonomy of Non-Corporeal Beings. House Elal wizards all scoffed at the concept that there could be any entities they had not encountered, expressing their professional disdain, but Alise believed her professor. There was a great deal not known in the world.

At any rate, in Bossing the Bodiless that day, the advanced students all worked at the furthest extent of their individual abilities, both in magical potential and learned skills. That was the point of the advanced practicums: to push the boundaries of what the student wizards could do in their specializations.

The process of locating, summoning, and then binding a more complex spirit to a task was a threefold process. Unlike the numerous and ubiquitous elementals, the more complex the spirit, the fewer in number and the more difficult they were to find. As a wizard long practiced in Elal magic—one of Alise's earliest memories was of watching household imps dance to make her giggle while she clapped her hands for more—she possessed a stable of bound spirits for various tasks. Like the sword-bearing spirit she'd summoned too late to defend her against Gordon Hanneil.

Don't think about him.

The compulsion flexed painfully.

Forcing herself to concentrate on the warm-up exercises, which should be simple, Alise cleared her mind to locate a mid-level spirit. Professor Cixin would know if she tapped any of the entities currently bound to her. That would be cheating and grounds for a failing grade. If she were in the mood to push herself, as she decidedly was not, she'd locate and attempt to harness an entity along the lines of another warrior to add to her roster. She could certainly use more of them. But the one that looked to her now had been captured by her father and handed over to her after she manifested as a wizard, once she had enough skill to give it instructions and keep it bound. Locating and binding another from scratch would be a challenge, and she was not up for anything that might test her nerve.

Especially since this particular exercise skirted very close to how she'd murdered her mother.

When Nic had first suggested that Alise might be able to sever the wizard–familiar bond, she'd been intrigued. And young and arrogant enough to embrace the challenge without considering the potential consequences. So far as she and Nic knew, no one had ever *thought* of doing such a thing. Certainly none of the records even hinted at the possibility, and Alise had looked. Well, she'd performed a cursory search as time allowed, but her teachers had always been emphatic that the bond was unbreakable, severed only by death, and perhaps not even then. It wasn't as if anyone had data on that. Even Elal wizardry didn't reach the spirits of the once-living. Cillian might be able to uncover more, but he didn't know what Alise had done, so had no reason to look.

It hurt to think about how excited she'd been initially, to *see* the possibility of the bond-severing and know that she could execute a trick every single person in the Convocation believed to be impossible. Even before she attempted it, she'd known she could pull it off with a bone-deep certainty such as she'd never before experienced. And it had been exhilarating, a triumph of skill and power that left her exultant, filled with giddy delight in herself. She'd actually been *proud*.

Foolish, foolish girl.

Only later did she realize the horrible consequences of her impulsive power flex, as the two familiars she'd separated from their wizards—Maman and Laryn, a traitor offered the option as an alternative to execution—both began wasting away until only empty, mindless husks remained. And then died.

Alise could never, ever risk committing such a terrible crime against humanity again.

Trying to keep her mind on her practicum, she smoothly finished the requisite warmup exercise of locating a number of likely, mid-level spirits. For someone of her heritage, often the challenge was getting the spirits to leave her alone, especially the mischievous and curious ones. Spirits of all sorts had always been attracted to her. That was part of having a high MP score in spirit magic. When she'd manifested as a wizard, that had become exponentially worse. Spirits pounced on her, demanding to be noticed, and fed with magic.

Fortunately, the academy, for all its faults, truly shone in instances like that. Her professors had been prepared for that exact eventuality, taking her under their collective wing in those early days, shielding her from the more voracious entities intent on manipulating or forcing her into doing *their* bidding. It had been a rough few days, receiving an intensive course in recognizing the more malicious spirits, regardless of how they attempted to trick her, and then protecting herself from them.

Spirits of all kinds still came readily to her call whenever she chose to admit them through her shielding, so assembling a variety from Professor Cixin's list on the board took little effort. They bustled there at the edge of her wizard senses, gathered in her mental grip like a bouquet of eager, sentient flowers. She only needed to choose one to bring through the veil and into their world to add to the complement of spirits bustling around the workroom.

The various entities the other students had summoned obediently swirled through obstacle courses, ringing bells, floating objects, and shining lights as directed. Except for a few cases where the student-wizard had lost control, or never fully had it. Professor Cixin was assisting with one of those at the moment, standing behind Grey Ananiel, hands folded behind his back as if reminding himself not to take action, calmly coaching Grey to control the gremlin currently perched on a high shelf, shrieking with fury.

Alise should pull one of her eager guests and get it over with, but found herself balking at pulling through even the least of them. If she did, she'd have to bind it, lest she end up like her unfortunate classmate, chasing a rogue entity, to the disdain of all, in order to run it through the exercises laid out by Professor Cixin. He wanted the students to test the strength of the bonds, using the lightest possible touch, then severing the bond as the spirit executed its task and reestablishing the bond again.

The exercise was meant to teach them how to regain control of an entity they'd summoned, in the event they lost it for some reason. Such as in a lapse in available magic, inattention, improper establishment of the initial bond, or because an enemy wizard severed it in an attempt to take your defenders away. Alise had learned all of this early on, along with intensive education on the nature of bonding, the information rolling through her mind in the voices of her various teachers. The advanced practicum, naturally, brought that intellectual understanding into real-world application.

Rattled, beyond tired, and unnerved by the possibility of going anywhere near any kind of bond-severing again, Alise just couldn't make herself do it. So, she fudged it.

She was clever and good enough at her skills to make it seem like she'd made a strong effort to complete the task and just hadn't quite been able to manage it. She summoned a relatively docile spirit, bound it, and half-assed her way through the most difficult exercises, working as slowly as possible and drawing it out. That should be believable, given how behind and out of practice she was at the objectively arcane techniques. A lot of the more complex skills the academy taught were famously impractical. The wizard students often complained that they'd never use most of them in real life—how many of them, really, would find themselves in a pitched duel against another wizard?—and that these more complex tricks were simply hoops to jump through.

Finally, the El-Adrel clock high on the wall relented and pinged out the time signaling the end of the practicum. And Alise congratulated herself for getting through the practicum without collapsing or drawing undue attention. Mentally she thanked Grey Ananiel for being such a screwup that he'd lost control of a fairly minor gremlin, absorbing Professor Cixin's attention until, with a sigh of exasperation, the professor finally seized control of the obnoxious creature and banished it. He'd then sternly lectured Grey, assigning him to remedial work on elementals until he could bind them in his sleep.

Alise headed for the door with the flood of other student wizards, burying herself in the midst of their flow while keenly aware that she had no one to chatter companionably with as everyone else did. At least she wasn't in Grey's position, the young wizard having flung himself furiously out the door first and even now complained bitterly to a circle of sympathetic friends.

"Wizard Alise," Professor Cixin called. "A moment please."

Alise nearly groaned aloud, her steps slowing as she gazed at the open doorway, escape so close and yet now out of reach. Reluctantly, she turned back, hoping she wasn't literally dragging her feet as she returned to the professor's desk. Professor Cixin had turned his attention to some notes in Grey Ananiel's file and he held up a finger for her to wait.

So, for the second time that day, Alise found herself shuffling her feet, waiting like a child to be called on the carpet. The seeping dread was ridiculous. She'd faced down vicious hunters, malevolent automatons, and other monsters. She'd nearly died, for dark arts' sake, so a dressing down from a professor should hardly feel threatening. Somehow though, even with Gordon Hanneil's vile threats still curdling her stomach, his compulsion worming in her brain and undermining her will, this felt like the last straw that might bring her down.

At last, Professor Cixin looked up, scrutinizing her, but thankfully without any psychic magic. He'd been a House Elal wizard for some time, though he'd moved to teaching at Convocation Academy long before Alise had been born, apparently as a form of semi-retirement. He taught only the Advanced Practicum in Manipulation and Control of Noncorporeal Entities and Alise had been his prize pupil at one point, enough so that she'd been referred to as teacher's pet. Not so much anymore.

"What happened today?" he asked without preamble.

"I apologize for my tardiness, Professor. I only just returned to academy a few hours ago and had to meet with Provost Uriel before I could return to class. It won't happen again." She hoped that was all he referred to.

He waved that off. "Proctor Divya explained. I mean, what happened with today's exercise?"

So much for that hope. "I know I'm lagging behind on the material. I promise I'll catch up. It's a priority for me."

Giving her a long look, he sat back. "Let's shortcut this conversation, Wizard Alise. I know what you are capable of. I probably understand the full scope of your abilities and potential better than any other living person in the Convocation, including your illustrious father. That assignment should have been a mere stretching of the legs for you, the equivalent of an extra lap around the track for a long-distance runner. Had you actually *tried*."

Stung, Alise glared at him. "With all due respect, Professor, I did try."

He dashed a hand sideways. "Had you actually attempted the task, you would have succeeded. No more prevarication. We're both well aware that you are on probation here. Shall I tell Provost Uriel that you are not putting full effort into your advanced practicum, arguably the single most important course for you to complete for graduation?"

Alise struggled to contain her immediate argument. Every professor always thought *their* class was the most important, so that wasn't worth debate. But for him to threaten her with this when he knew exactly how precarious her position was at Convocation Academy felt like an exceptionally low blow. And she was in no state of mind to take any more blows. "No, Professor," she answered tightly.

"Then explain the problem." He gave her a long stare from sharp wizard-black eyes under bristling white eyebrows.

She took a breath, hoping the words would spring to her lips. Blew it out again when nothing came to her. No way could she explain her real problem, but then what *could* she say?

"I am a master-level wizard of spirit magic, young Alise," Professor Cixin said. "However, my MP scores in psychic magic are woefully low. I cannot read your mind, even should I wish to, which I do not. Therefore I require that you answer my question, explicitly and honestly."

Alise stared back, feeling fully alone and helpless, the sensation overwhelming enough to make tears prick her eyes, which was even worse than all the other emotions.

"Come now, child," the professor said, not unkindly. With a twitch of magic, he established a silencing shield around them. "If you cannot confide in me, the teacher you must rely upon to guide you to your fullest potential, then who can you?"

No one. The easy and obvious answer came to her. She could never share with anyone the potentially earth-shattering news that she could break the wizard–familiar bond. That wasn't just paranoia, either. That information could upend the entire power structure of the Convocation on a massive scale and, on a personal scale, doom herself to execution, imprisonment, or a long tenure of curtailed liberty and being experimented upon, followed by execution.

But she clearly was going to have to say something to Professor Cixin—unless she wanted to let everyone down by being expelled for a third and final time, the first in her family to fail to graduate—and say it soon, as Professor's impressive brows were drawing together in a thunderous expression promising imminent explosion.

"I'm afraid of becoming like my father," she blurted, surprised to discover as she said it, that it was true.

Unfortunately, Professor Cixin didn't seem to buy it. He sat back and steepled his fingers. "Piers Elal is one of the most powerful wizards in the Convocation and head of one of the largest high houses," he said. "Why wouldn't you want to follow in the footsteps of your sire? Despite recent kerfuffles, he will almost certainly reinstall you as his heir-apparent.

Regardless of what your brother tells everyone who will listen, Elal has yet to name him as heir—or to formally disinherit you."

Was this a test? If so, was it a test of her loyalty to House Elal or of something else? It suddenly seemed that a great deal rode on her response and she was playing blind.

She attempted to assemble her scattered thoughts, tried to think what Nic would say and do. One of the fallouts of Nic being the elder sister, with such magnificent MP scores across all categories, and with everyone's expectation that she would manifest as a wizard and become the next head of House Elal, was that their father had devoted his considerable attention and training to Nic, not Alise. Nic had been the one to learn the finer points of house politics and navigating conversations like this. Even their maman had given extra attention to Nic on matters of etiquette, arcane details of Convocation society, and how to be a high-house lady. Probably Maman had believed she had time to teach Alise such things when she was older. But they'd all run out of time.

Alise had only her own instincts to go on. Here went nothing. "Tell me, Wizard Cixin," she said, deliberately dropping the honorific demanded by his current station, "why did you leave House Elal? By all accounts you had a high position there, well paid, and with considerable influence."

He tapped his steepled fingertips together, not angry or offended as Alise had expected, but quietly thoughtful. Perhaps, unless she missed her guess, even intrigued. "I was not happy with the... expectations placed upon me in my position there," he said slowly. "Now, I answered your question. You answer mine."

"I am afraid of the effect on me of having too much power," she said, bluntly enough, a nice ball of truth to obscure what she couldn't afford to confide. "I've seen too much in these last weeks, of huge amounts of power, both magical and worldly, used in terrible ways."

To her surprise, he smiled slightly. "Ah, now we are coming to the heart of the matter. Thank you for your trust, young Alise. In return, I shall offer you this advice: you wield enormous magic whether you wish to or not. That ship has sailed. In truth, it was never up to you whether you would be a wizard, no more than it was mine, no more than it was your sister's choice to be a familiar."

"Nic would've handled being a wizard better," Alise muttered ungraciously.

"I agree." Professor Cixin nodded at her shock. "Do you know why Nic would have made a better wizard?"

"Because she's smarter and more capable?" Alise offered sardonically.

"Not in the least. Because *she* was never afraid of it."

That was true. Nothing frightened Nic. Whereas Alise felt like a slowly unraveling ball of terror.

"The thing is," Professor Cixin continued, "fear or not, you must learn to control your magic to the finest degree possible. Only then can you make a considered decision on how to employ your immense power—and only then can you have any hope of following through on any resolutions you might make regarding the ethical use of it."

Alise stared at him, disconcerted. "Maybe," she finally said, "there are some abilities no person should ever have."

"That could well be. However, whether you *have* them is not up to you. Whether you use your abilities, what you use them for, that is all you can control. And for that, you must study and apply yourself. You must engage in diligent practice. Only by knowing exactly *how* to do something can you make a choice *not* to do it, and also exert the control required of you to stick with that resolve. Otherwise you will become a danger to yourself and to the Convocation. Am I understood?"

She didn't love that answer, but she had to admit the sense of his argument. "I understand," she acknowledged, her voice sounding as glum and, well, spiritless as she felt.

Cixin regarded her somberly. "Despite my lack of psychic potential, I can nevertheless intuit that there is much you haven't confided still." He held up a hand when she opened her mouth to protest. "No, I shall not press you for further answers. You are at the center of a brewing storm, young Alise, and I do not envy you what you have thus far endured, nor the role you'll play in what is yet to come. I am telling you now, however, that you may trust me. I do not expect you to do so immediately or easily, but I will teach you everything I know and guide you into the uncertain realm of what I do not know when you surpass me, which you inevitably will. Remember that and come to me when you need to."

Even more taken aback, Alise nodded.

"In the meanwhile, you will return during your next free period to make up today's exercise," he said crisply, banishing the silencing spell.

Alise nearly groaned aloud, biting back the question, *what free period?* "Yes, Professor."

"As soon as you demonstrate your competency with it, you will be free to go," he added. "I do not imagine it will take long, if you actually apply yourself."

No, that was true. "Thank you, Professor Cixin," she said, with considerably more enthusiasm.

"You can thank me by learning your assignment," he replied, more brusquely, stacking his notes together. "Remember: diligent practice will serve you well. Now, off with you to the dining hall. You look hungry."

She *was* hungry, but also still queasy, so she didn't know if she'd be able to eat. Probably she should try, so that everyone would stop trying to feed her. Exiting the classroom at last, she flinched when a tiny Ratsiel courier flew at her. *Just a messenger,* she told herself scornfully. *Stop jumping at the least little thing.*

Taking the folded paper, she read Cillian's message and sagged against the wall of the busy hall, students parting around her as if she were a piece of furniture, ignoring her easily. Good news was, he hadn't been fired. Bad news? Cillian had been appointed to supervise her independent study and expected her in the archives later.

What in the dark arts was she going to tell him? Gordon Hanneil's nasty compulsion flexed, reminding her she could say nothing.

Whatever she did manage to say, it would have to be firm. And final.

~ 6 ~

CILLIAN TUCKED THE fresh kolaches into a basket, fussing a little with the cloth napkin as he tucked a tiny fire elemental into the folds to keep them warm. He'd fed Alise enough cinnamon rolls, he'd decided, and while sweets always had a place in the world, he worried about Alise getting sufficient protein. Ever since the battle at House Phel, she'd looked thin to the point of fragility, too pale, and strained to breaking. Knowing her, she'd skipped the evening meal in the dining hall to catch up on her schoolwork. The meat-stuffed pastries smelled hot, fragrant and delicious. Alise wouldn't be able to resist.

She hadn't replied to his earlier message, but he hadn't really expected her to. As a general rule, students didn't have access to Ratsiel couriers. Even those students with families who could afford personal couriers were allowed to use them only for external communication with their sponsoring houses, not within the academy. That was reserved for staff and faculty. No teacher wanted a swarm of Ratsiel couriers interrupting their lectures. So, he wasn't surprised not to hear from her, but he was bothered, and then concerned, when she didn't show.

He kept an eye on the antique El-Adrel clock as it ticked away the evening hours and the library gradually emptied out. Cillian always liked taking the night shift—which was fortunate, as him being the newest hire meant he didn't have a choice—because of the quiet that allowed him to read and pursue his own modest research projects. Now the lack of busy work felt crushing as he fretted, continually checking that the elemental had kept the pastries warm in the drawer he'd stowed the basket in. It hadn't taken him long to catch up on the small backlog of work and correspondence from his absence. He wasn't all that important, far from irreplaceable, which was usually fine by him. But time moved slowly, dragging by as the few queries from students and faculty needing assistance had dwindled to nothing as the witching hour approached.

And still no Alise.

He went back and forth any number of times on sending her another message, but that would be weird and needy. She'd received his note. The courier he'd sent had confirmed delivery, as had the small enchantment he'd embedded to alert him when it had been read. Besides, he told himself, Alise had often not made it to the library until this late or later, with the insane hours she kept. No doubt her schedule was even worse than before, with her additional absence. And *her* backlog of work would not have been light. Or, she could have turned in early, getting rest and taking care of herself for once. He could hardly be irritated about that.

Though she could have told him.

No, he reminded himself of that, too—she owed him nothing. They didn't have the kind of relationship where she would let him know what she was up to or what she was doing or even how she felt about anything. Alise was a closed book, nearly impossible to read, and not for him to pry open anyway.

Still, he was her supervisor on this independent study now and she could have given him at least the courtesy of—

He lost the irate thought when Alise walked into the library, looking like the ghost of some ancient princess. His heart gave a helpless, hopeless lurch at her exquisite, ethereal beauty, and he knew himself to be a lost man. Her gaze fastened on him with unerring precision—no surprise there, as he was always in the same spot—her wizard-black eyes luminous with some pain that hadn't been there the last time he saw her.

Mundanes thought that all wizard eyes were equally black, and there was some truth to that. Aside from the early days post-manifestation, when a wizard's eyes gradually darkened with magic use, at faster or slower rates, depending on how much they practiced and how powerful their native magic, all wizards had black eyes. And black was black, more or less. But Cillian had made a study of it—and had done a bit of research into the phenomenon, out of curiosity—and he'd decided he could discern a great deal about a wizard by the depth, shine, and, for want of a better descriptor, sharpness of the iris coloration.

Alise had beautiful eyes, not only because of their large size in her piquant face, the lavish fringe of her lashes, and elegant framing of her arched brows. No, it had to be because her black shimmered like a starless night, profound and full of the secrets of the universe. Alise complained that her slight stature made people treat her as younger than she was. Those people were fools. They needed only look into her soulful gaze to see someone far older occupied that delicately shaped skull. Privately, Cillian thought people saw the inherent wistfulness in Alise's resting expression, something she was unaware of. That wistfulness made him want to cuddle her on his lap and feed her bites of melting sweet pastry until she smiled with true warmth.

Alise cocked her head at him, her blue-black hair sliding in glossy feathers around her perfect face. "Are you quite yourself, Wizard Harahel?" she prompted, making it clear she'd addressed him once already.

"Erm, ah, yes," he stuttered, sounding like the fully bedazzled and brainless idiot he was. "Ah, hi. How have you been doing?" There was so much he wanted to know, needed to ask.

"I'm fine. How are you?" she returned politely, with the vaguest hint of impatience.

Yes, right. This was not the appropriate moment for less than formal conversation. "I was beginning to be concerned," he offered, waving a hand at the ticking clock, as if that explained anything. "It's quite late. I'd expected you much earlier." He didn't exactly trail off, but his voice faded with uncertainty at the end of his sentence, in the face of her chilly expression. He very nearly asked if something was wrong.

"I apologize, Wizard Harahel," she said coldly, not sounding in the least apologetic. "I received your missive regarding my independent study, but I was unaware that you expected me at a set hour."

"Oh, well, no," he babbled on, clearly unable to stop or rescue himself. "I didn't set a time, it's true. It's only that, in the past, you know, you were usually, um, here… earlier." Cillian briefly considered using the tiny fire elemental in the pastry basket to set his hair on fire. He might have, if fire wasn't such anathema to an archivist like himself. Even bringing the tiny creature into the library had been a violation of several rules, personal and professional.

Alise continued to watch him blather on, head still slightly tilted, her full lips pressed tightly together, lines of strain bracketing her mouth. She always seemed to be locking words behind compressed lips with ruthless determination.

"Still," he said finally. *Think about work, not kissing those lips until they softened and opened,* he sternly instructed himself. *She is not for you.* "You're here now. Shall we discuss our research strategy?"

She gave him an odd look, one he couldn't quite interpret. Well, even more so than usual. "About that…" she began, then slid her eyes to the side.

Oh! He was such an idiot. The library was mostly deserted, but not entirely. "Allow me," he said. He couldn't match Alise for wizardly ability, but what he could do, he did very well. With a flick of magic, he installed a silencing shield around them. He performed that exercise tens, sometimes hundreds of times every day, primarily to ensure the requisite silence for study and to set a good example. The reference desk needed to be able to hear and answer questions, so the silencing shields came in handy. "We're private now," he told her, though she would obviously sense that. "How are you really? I brought you something."

"I'm *fine*, Wizard Harahel," she said frostily, arresting him as he brought out the basket from his lower desk drawer. "But I have a great deal of work to do and very little time to do it in. That's what I came to tell you. I'm going to have to temporarily table the independent study."

"What?" His mind had gone blank. As void as the expression she turned on him, one that said she barely knew him. Or, worse, was somewhat familiar with him and didn't think much of him. "Alise. You can't back-burner that project. We need to—"

"*I* need to focus on my primary coursework if I have any hope of graduating," she interrupted. "I can't afford to be *distracted* by side projects." Her night-dark gaze lingered on the basket of pastries he foolishly still held aloft, halfway between here and there, accusation in her eyes, the distaste with which she pronounced the word "distracted" lingering in the air like a bad odor.

"Provost Uriel assigned you that independent study," he said, grasping for sense. "She appointed me your supervisor and—"

"Yes," she said, cutting him off again. "I received your missive," she added, pointedly reminding him that she'd said so already. "I'll devote what attention I can, when I can, and will speak with the provost, if necessary, but I don't think I'll need much supervision. Or assistance. Much as I appreciate the offer," she added, a light flush on her high cheekbones, as if she only then became aware of her rudeness. "I won't take up more of your time than I already have."

"What about our excursion to House Harahel?" he asked, disappointment already settling into his stomach. "I have good news there, you see. The provost approved the trip again and—"

"I can't possibly afford the time away," she interrupted dismissively.

"But…" Realizing he *still* held the basket of kolaches, Cillian set it down midway between them, as a barrier or an offering, he wasn't sure. He'd been so looking forward to showing Alise the house of his birth—the endless archives and shelves and reading nooks. The lake, which would be frozen this time of year, but where he'd thought they might go ice-skating. He'd planned to teach her to skate, if she didn't know how already, and imagined her surprise and delight at seeing his skill at the spins and leaps. And his parents… he'd imagined introducing her to them, how they'd take to her sweet reserve and dazzling intelligence. How he'd talk to them privately and say how he knew she wasn't for him, but they'd say, well, stranger matches had been made and—

"It simply won't be possible," Alise said firmly, putting paid to all of his admittedly foolish romantic imaginings.

"But, the petition…" he said weakly into her stony resolve.

"House Phel can handle that. If they even decide to pursue it. Likely they won't. Who has any use for musty old records anyway?"

Her scorn seemed directly aimed at his heart and it thudded home with painful accuracy. *Who has any use for musty old you?* she might have said.

"Alise, have I… done something?" She had always placed a

certain distance between them, always so careful of herself, maintaining a cloak of protection like an enchantment to ward off the slings and arrows of the world. Always so deliberately alone. But she'd never treated him with this chilly disdain. "Did I say or do something to offend you? To hurt you in some way?"

She laughed, softly, without humor, cutting mockery in it. "Don't be absurd, Wizard Harahel," she answered, making it clear a low-level nonentity like himself could hardly harm someone as lofty as she. "I realize our recent… adventures may have invited a certain level of familiarity, but I'm simply a student and you are faculty. It's not as if we are friends."

The remark sliced across his heart, deftly delivered to wound. "No," he replied faintly, feeling the blood loss from his face, a chill contraction of skin tightening over his cheekbones. "I suppose we are not friends, and never were."

"I do, ah, appreciate all of your help," she offered, her cold poise thawing for the first time and looking away, as if unable to meet his gaze any longer. "In the past. You were… kind to me, when you didn't have to be. I won't forget that." Her voice wavered, just a tiny bit.

That small crack in her composure told him everything. Alise was deeply upset and trying to hide it. Trying to push him away. He'd seen her do it to others, isolating herself in a pillar of solitary independence. And she was crumbling under the pressure of whatever was going on. He refused to abandon her to it.

"I take it back. I was and *am* your friend, Alise," he said with firm intensity, hoping to reach her in whatever cave of self-reliance she'd retreated into. Something had happened, he was sure of it, and whatever it was, she shouldn't have to face it alone. "I will always be your friend, no matter what you say or do to try to push me away."

Her startled gaze flew up to his and, for a brief moment, a hint of vulnerability flickered there. Then she caught and composed herself, shifting her gaze to stare a thousand leagues into the distance past his ear. "A very kind offer," she said, as if he'd invited her to tea some day. "If you should ever need a favor, I owe you one."

He nearly spat that he didn't need her favors. Fortunately, his better judgement took over before he could open his foolish mouth. She'd offered him a more than gracious gift. If Alise did end up as the head of House Elal someday, having Lady Elal owe him a favor could be priceless. He'd be a fool to refuse. Besides which, a favor owed left a door open between them through which he could still be attached to her, if only in the smallest way. He might need that leverage.

"I am grateful," he said, pinning a square of Calliope paper with his index finger and sliding it to her, nodding at a cup of styluses. "If you would be so kind as to write that down?"

He'd startled her with that, enough so that she met his eyes, hers full of honest emotion for the first time since she'd walked into his library, and she flushed—in anger at his effrontery or embarrassment at her heartless treatment of him, he wasn't sure. But Alise was a class act and she barely hesitated before plucking up a stylus and scribbling the promise. He claimed the square of paper before she could change her mind, sealed it indelibly with his archivist magic, then tucked it into his shirt pocket where it felt as if it would burn through the thin material.

"Are you sure you wouldn't care for a kolache?" he asked, making sure he sounded cheerfully solicitous, dipping his chin at the basket. "They're still warm and you look as if you haven't eaten, quite thin and pale." He added that last with the smallest bit of malicious pleasure, knowing how it annoyed her when people commented on her frail appearance. He was only human, after all.

A direct hit for him and she flushed deeper, definitely in anger this time. "Thank you, no," she replied harshly. "And I'm surprised at you, Librarian Harahel, bringing a fire elemental into the archives. I understood that was against the rules. Let me take care of that for you."

With a scalpel-precise whip of her magic, she squelched the elemental. Then turned her back on him and left.

~ 7 ~

S HAKING INSIDE, AS sick and full of turmoil and as a foul and muddy Meresin bog, Alise scurried like a fugitive through the midnight corridors of Convocation Academy. She'd followed this route so many times, traversing the familiar path from the library to the dorms practically in her sleep, some-times even more exhausted than she was at the moment, but never before feeling quite this terrible.

Never before so gut-wateringly ashamed of herself.

Hurrying for no good reason, other than the guilt chasing her, she nearly ran through the shifting shadows of the moonlit halls. As always, the shadows seemed to curl and twine like living beings, independent of the objects casting them. The academy was so steeped in magic from centuries of research, supervised practice, and the occasional accident from a fledgling wizard, that it infiltrated the very stones of the hallowed halls. Regular cleansing by House Zomen bled off the residual magic and defused anything becoming *too* animated, but they must be about due for a sweep, by the feel of it. Nothing repressed the ambient magic for long and it always burgeoned just before the next cleansing.

Alise only wished she could enlist a Zomen wizard to

cleanse her interior self of the foul residue of her actions. She'd been awful to Cillian. She could tell herself it was for the best, which it was. She'd had no choice but to create distance between them. She couldn't risk him ever finding out the threats Gordon Hanneil had made. Cillian couldn't be involved in what came next, because this would only get worse and more dangerous. Possibly not just for her.

Yes, House Hanneil had frightened her as intended. But this wasn't over. Alise had spent the hours since Bossing the Bodiless organizing her task list and prioritizing her efforts, something she always found soothing. She'd skipped dinner—as Cillian had perhaps not so astutely surmised—since her stomach hadn't recovered enough for her to risk putting anything else in there. Then she'd buried herself in reading for exams in the morning, taking refuge in thinking only of what she needed to memorize and nothing else.

The time alone with her thoughts had helped. With a few hours distance, Alise could see what Gordon's attempt at intimidation truly meant: House Hanneil was afraid of what she'd find if she kept looking.

Which meant there *was* something to find.

Alise hadn't yet decided how to handle things from here. House Phel needed this information and she couldn't allow Hanneil to stop her research—even if that cursed compulsion flexed painfully every time she thought about it, convulsing like a will-eating worm embedded in her brain.

Maybe Nic and Gabriel really could and would file the petition to open the sealed archives at House Harahel. In the aftermath of the battle for House Phel—not to mention

Maman's death—there hadn't been a lot of opportunity to discuss the fact that every bit of information regarding House Phel seemed to have been scrubbed from Convocation Archives. Alise had explained her and Cillian's fortuitous appearance at the siege in the nick of time by telling everyone about the excursion to check the House Harahel archives. But they'd all been exchanging stories and, with Jadren's dramatic rise to Lord El-Adrel, and truly astonishing and unprecedented newfound magical abilities, plus Seliah's discovery of her glamourous alternate form as a big, black marsh cat, a trip to the library hadn't garnered a lot of attention.

Then Nic and Gabriel had sent Alise back to Convocation Academy, their attention split in a dozen different directions— which Alise absolutely understood—and they hadn't given her much in the way of instructions except to keep up the good work and graduate.

Really, there wasn't much Alise could do here at Convocation Academy if every important bit of information regarding the precipitous fall of House Phel had been removed—or destroyed—as it seemed. And yet… would Hanneil have taken such an extreme step to stop her if there wasn't something to find right here?

Regardless, definitely the first step had to have been cutting Cillian out of the loop and she'd at least done that, if not cleanly, then quickly. Without him looking over her shoulder, Alise could manage the appearance of pretending to be compliant with Hanneil's threats. She could continue her search while seeming to be working on other things. But Cillian was far too perceptive for her to deceive him that way.

And, though the compulsion prevented her from speaking of Gordon Hanneil's more loathsome threats, she couldn't run the risk that the astute librarian-wizard would detect her upset and dive into solving the riddle. He wouldn't be able to resist the puzzle and, with his brilliance, he'd probably figure out everything, which would be a disaster. She and Cillian in no way had any kind of romantic relationship, but she felt in her bones that he would take the way Gordon had spoken to her very badly. Cillian had a bit of a white knight tendency, usually a charming trait, but he couldn't save her from this. Not with cinnamon rolls and whatever a kolache was.

No, she'd absolutely done the right thing, for Cillian's sake, for House Phel's, and for her own. She only regretted that last bit of showing off, squelching his fire elemental. That had maybe been too petty.

But he needed to *stop* baking for her. She'd really wanted whatever was in that basket. Whatever a kolache was, it smelled savory and delicious. The enticing aroma had made her mouth water and too-empty stomach clench. It annoyed her no end that Cillian had somehow kept track of the fact that she hadn't eaten dinner, and that overwhelming irritation had prompted her impulsive bit of minor vengeance, putting his fire elemental to sleep. She felt bad about it now, though that drop of guilt barely pinged in the bucket of the rest of it.

Like that look on his face when he'd asked if he'd hurt or offended her. So stricken, so genuinely concerned for her, even in the midst of her deliberate cruelty, as she stood over him and did everything in her power to ice him out, to thoroughly and irrevocably destroy any friendship between them. She shouldn't have offered him that favor. In truth, she hadn't meant to, but she'd felt so guilty, like such a monster, when he'd said he'd always be her friend. The favor had occurred to her in the moment, as a way to formalize the distance between them.

What she really, *really* shouldn't have done was write down that she owed him a favor. That was truly irresponsible. If her father didn't hate her already, he'd want to kill her for that alone. An Elal scion owing a member of another high house an open-ended, unnamed favor? Unthinkable.

And yet, when pressed, she hadn't been able to refuse. Cillian hadn't requested she write down that promise out of calculation, she reassured herself. He didn't have a manipulative bone in his body. No, that was the archivist in him, where he simply had to have a record of every little thing, let alone a potentially major transaction like that. Good thing she wasn't fated to become a high-house power or a favor like that out in the wild could be a major problem.

Knowing Cillian, he'd pick something small and innocuous anyway, like meeting for a cup of coffee. That would be fine. She would pretend to be friendly and gracefully duck any intrusive questions, and then her obligations to him would be dispensed with. Everything would work out for the best.

A murk condensed across the hallway. Alise slowed her steps.

That was odd. Then things got even odder, very quickly.

The shadows coiled into a shape like a person. Alise altered her course to go around the mirage. Whatever direction or diffuse consciousness drove the behavior of the ambient magic that sometimes manifested as these swirling shadows, it had a sense of whimsy that bent toward mischievous. It liked to scare people, or at least startle them.

Therefore, it wasn't a surprise, exactly, when the "person" tracked her trajectory, gliding into Alise's path. With a sigh of exasperation—she was tired, and hungry, and full of guilt and unaccustomed shame, roiling with impotent angst over Gordon Hanneil, and *so* not in the mood for prankster shadows—Alise erected a woven wall of air elementals to ward off the nebulous magic.

Most of it was illusion, a variety of psychic magic that to her senses colored the space with prismatic shimmering. She wasn't terribly concerned, as the ambient magic never accumulated to levels potent enough to cause real problems, but it had kind of trapped her near the corridor wall and she'd had more than enough of *that* for one day. She also prepped her basic self-defense, just in case, ready for anything, learning from her past mistakes.

So, when the shadows parted and a young woman stepped out, Alise launched her spirit warrior to behead the person out of sheer, panicked reflex. A tiger instantly melted around the woman, appearing from nothing, reared up, and batted the warrior's sword away like a play toy.

A *real* freaking tiger and not illusion.

Alise goggled, shocked into inaction, the worst possible reaction. Freezing in stunned surprise was never the correct response, either magically or not.

"Before you counter," the woman said quickly, wizard-black eyes dark in her brown face, "please stay your hand. I mean you no harm."

"Do the people who *do* mean you harm announce it up front?" Alise retorted sardonically, but she also pulled back her magic. She could kill the tiger. She also didn't want to, it was so beautiful. "Is that an actual tiger?" she inquired as a cover while she inventoried her options—and reserve of magic. Without a familiar, she was limited to only what she had stored within, which was more than most wizards, though she hadn't yet fully regenerated what she'd used up in Bossing the Bodiless. It certainly wasn't enough for a pitched battle, especially against what appeared to be a high-level House Ariel wizard.

Spirit warriors were all well and good for intimidation purposes and they *could* cause real life damage, but mostly excelled at being intimidating, which didn't work well against animals. Non-corporeal entities in general tended not to affect animals that much. Oh, animals could perceive spirits very well, far better than mundane humans could, or even wizards without spirit magic. They just didn't bother about them for the most part. Animals had an enviable ability to live in the moment and spirits fell into the realm of non-immediacy. Even if the spirit could inflict real-world damage, no animal worried about that until it happened.

"You're asking me if the tiger is real?" The woman, chestnut hair cut so it fringed around her face and just brushed her shoulders, cocked her head slightly. Her emerald green necklace stirred, looping of its own accord, and sleek snake's head poked through the hair beside her ear, forked tongue flicking in Alise's direction. "You think I'd spend that much magic to make an illusion of a tiger with no ability to defend me?"

Alise very nearly retorted that she had zero idea of what this wizard would or wouldn't do, but held her tongue. It had been an admittedly foolish question. A falcon flew out of the shadows and landed on the wizard-woman's shoulder, on the opposite side from the snake. "I'm going to guess House Ariel," Alise commented drily.

The woman dipped her chin in an affirmative. "Please forgive the somewhat dramatic entrance, but I needed to speak to you without witnesses."

You and everyone else in the Convocation apparently. Alise stopped herself from saying that aloud, too. Still, what was up with wizards jumping her in the hallways lately? "I can't imagine why a clearly high-level House Ariel wizard would want a clandestine conversation with a Convocation Academy student in a darkened hallway in the wee hours of the morning."

"Can't you?" The wizard sounded amused. The snake flicked its tongue as if taunting Alise for her foolishness. The tiger wrapped a tight circle around the wizard, trailing her tail along the woman's waist in apparent affection, then lay down before her, panting lightly. The falcon flexed its talons but otherwise didn't move. Was one of the three the wizard's familiar in alternate form? Probably. Not that it mattered, as the Ariel woman couldn't access her familiar's magic while they were in animal form. She wouldn't necessarily need an extra boost of magic, however, since she would be able to compel her companions to attack Alise. And Alise didn't know what she'd do then.

"As you surmised," the wizard said with a hint of impatience, making Alise realize she hadn't yet replied, "I represent House Ariel's interests. I am the Wizard Courtney Ariel and I bear a message for you."

"You know," Alise replied, not relaxing her guard in the least, keeping a keen eye on those animals while gathering a few spirits to aid her, "there are these convenient things called Ratsiel couriers. You can task them to carry messages for you. Very handy. No need to ambush people in dark hallways."

Courtney smiled thinly. "Your sarcasm betrays your discomfort and fear, but again, I reassure you that I mean no harm. I come to you this way to say what cannot be entrusted to Ratsiel courier."

Despite herself, Alise's curiosity stirred. Another high house lining up to take sides? But why they were talking to her instead of someone with actual power, she had no idea. *You are at the center of a brewing storm, young Alise.* Professor Cixin's words floated through her mind, leaving unease behind. "All right, I'm listening."

"Would you establish a silencing shield, please? I'm rather taxed maintaining control of the animals and the illusion that conceals my presence here."

So Alise hadn't been wrong when she sensed some kind of illusion magic at work, which made her feel a little better. Wizard Courtney clearly intended to appear as if she'd emerged from a portal, though that kind of magic occurred only in old stories and no modern wizard thought it was even possible. If it ever had been. Many opined that the tales were based entirely on myth. Lots of wizards, however, used various parlor tricks to make it seem as if they'd manifested from nowhere. In House Elal, for example, wizards loved to employ shrouding spirits to create that exact effect. It only worked on non-wizards, though, so most people rolled their eyes at such magic-wasting efforts.

Technically, illusions were not in the purview of House Ariel. Their trademarks were limited to psychic magic in relation to animals, including control and breeding. And yet Courtney had taken the risk of using illusions, which had to be for more than trying to look fancy, especially with Alise who would know better. More curious than ever, Alise circled a finger in the air to indicate she'd established the requested soundproofing, realizing belatedly that she'd picked up the gesture from Cillian. It shouldn't hurt to think about that.

"Speak," she told Courtney. "I'd really love to get some sleep tonight."

"I wish you easy rest then," Courtney replied, making it sound like she found the probability of that very unlikely. "I'll be brief. My message is this: beware House Hanneil."

Alise nearly rolled her eyes, which at least felt better than the bone-watering terror Gordon Hanneil had instilled in her. "Got it. If that's all then—"

"That's *not* all," Courtney interrupted with sharp impatience. "Dark arts save me from disrespectful teenagers."

"Hey, you came to me," Alise pointed out, not at all bothered and, in truth, a bit maliciously pleased to be annoying someone *else* for a change.

"I came to you out of duty and necessity, not my own

inclinations. I am sent to warn you that House Hanneil may attempt to halt your research into the tampered archives."

Alise bit back the words *too late*, and focused with interest on the implications. First, House Ariel knew about the vanished House Phel archives. Second, Ariel knew enough to predict Hanneil's interference. Third, Ariel *didn't* know enough to be aware that Wizard Gordon had already threatened Alise. Fourth and finally, why in the dark arts did House Ariel have a stake in this festival of power-grabbing?

Alise, naturally, didn't verbalize any of these speculations. Instead she just said, "Oh?"

Courtney pressed her lips together, not at all pleased by the lackluster response to her dramatic declaration. "Have they contacted you in any fashion?"

"Wizard Courtney," Alise said, exhaustion and exasperation making her abrupt, "with all due respect, why does House Ariel care about any of this?"

Courtney narrowed her wizard-black eyes. "For a mere student, you have a great deal of attitude, young Elal."

"Young *Phel*," Alise corrected pleasantly. "And I feel compelled to point out, yet again, that you came to me. I didn't ask for this clandestine interview. I refuse to be placed in the position of supplicant."

More unamused than ever, Courtney spat, "I'm here to help your ungrateful ass."

"No," Alise corrected calmly, "you're here to serve the interests of House Ariel. You even said so. How about you share what those interests are and maybe we can have a conversation that goes somewhere."

The wizard gathered her poise. "My house is no ally of Hanneil's. That's all you need to know."

No, it wasn't. Not by a long shot, especially as it was hardly news. Hanneil had very few allies, particularly since the wars after which House Hanneil was sanctioned and stripped of many of their most lucrative trademarks and placed under extreme restrictions to prevent them from exercising psychic control on unwitting Convocation citizens of any stripe. Not only did Hanneil have almost no allies:furr they had almost all enemies.

"All right," Alise said. "Message delivered. Can I go now?"

"That's not all," Courtney snapped.

Alise tried to look politely interested, though she had to stifle a yawn. Then she reconsidered. Why should she? Unleashing the jaw-cracking yawn, she waited.

Wizard Courtney really hated that Alise didn't beg for her precious messages, which gave Alise a bit more petty satisfaction. Finally the Ariel wizard bit out an exasperated huff. "House Ariel has received word of... tampering with the wizard–familiar bond."

Alise forced herself not to show any indication of her suddenly alert interest, and precipitously dropping stomach. Instead she feigned confusion, even as her heart rate accelerated. The snake flicked a forking tongue at her—possibly detecting her tension and informing its wizard.

"Tampering..." Alise shook her head in what she hoped was a convincing show of puzzlement. "Is that even possible? The wizard–familiar bond is eternal, unbreakable except via death."

Courtney scrutinized her closely. "What if I told you we had evidence it had been done?"

"I'd wonder how House Ariel had come by such evidence and why the entire Convocation doesn't know about such an alarming development. I am only a humble student of Convocation Academy, but I'd have to wonder what stake Ariel has in the matter. I don't know of any connection between House Ariel trademarks and the magic that creates the wizard–familiar bond."

That last wasn't entirely true. The origins of the enchantment that created that bond remained shrouded in mystery and obscure history. Even the oldest texts referred to the wizard–familiar bond being a well-established phenomenon. However, from what her family at House Phel very carefully *hadn't* said, Alise had gathered that when wizards learned to invoke the magic upon graduation from Convocation Academy, it was accompanied by a geas of some sort. Even the wizards who seemed to want to discuss it couldn't and didn't.

Further, it made sense that binding animals to a wizard would be much the same as binding a human familiar to one. Especially knowing House Ariel was so vitally interested.

Courtney remained unmoved by Alise's implicit and accusatory question, watching Alise intently. "I'm sure you're aware that there is a great deal of overlap between Elal and Ariel areas of expertise. Though our trademarks and areas of business vary extensively, both houses select for wizards with strong MP scores in psychic magic."

"Though with very different subgroup strengths," Alise pointed out. She refused to be baited. "For example, I can't wrest away control of your animals any more than you could take over my warrior spirit. And neither of us can read or control minds."

Courtney smiled grimly. "*You* might not have the ability, young Elal," she said, ignoring Alise's previous correction, "but another wizard of your house very well might. There is something fishy going on and you are hip-deep in it."

"As I indicated previously," Alise said with dignity, "I no longer have a connection with House Elal. Whatever the house of my birth may or may not be doing, it has nothing to do with me."

"Doesn't it?" Courtney smiled grimly. "Your own mother, Lady Elal, a familiar, was somehow separated from her wizard master, your father, Lord Elal. It seems you are *intimately* connected to the question."

Alise covered her alarm—and the wave of grief—by snorting. "Wizard Ariel," she said in a tone of excessive patience, "I know everyone's stations and titles in my immediate family. You needn't reiterate them."

Her face darkened with an angry flush. "What do you know about the situation? Where is Lady Elal?"

Was her father behind this in some way? And odd that the news of her mother's passing hadn't reached House Ariel. Though she supposed no one at House Phel had reason to advertise it. "Maman passed away," she informed the Ariel wizard with quiet dignity, allowing her grief to show. "I'll thank you to mention her with due respect."

Definitely shocked her there. "I'm sorry for your loss," Courtney murmured, the snake's tongue flicking rapidly and the tiger's tail tip tapping. Clearly the wizard couldn't wait to report that news.

"Thank you." Alise waited, glancing toward her destination pointedly.

"We are aware that Iliana Ariel has been hiding out at House Phel," Courtney said, which might have sounded like a non-sequitur to most people, but made perfect sense to Alise. Iliana had been one of the familiars Alise had helped to escape Convocation Academy with her familiar-lover, Han.

Alise only raised her brows. What Courtney expected her to say to that, she didn't know. Except that it had sounded like a threat and Alise had stomached enough of *those* for one day, also.

"Keep your head down and your fingers out of dangerous pies, student wizard," Courtney advised, shaking her head. "You are being closely watched." Abruptly, she brought her cloak up in a sweeping motion to cover her face. Smoke and shadows billowed up in a wave and, when the haze cleared, she and her animals were gone.

At last, Alise allowed herself to roll her eyes for the theatrics, then continued on her lonesome way. No longer full of self-recrimination, she brewed up her own personal strategy. Try to intimidate her, would they? Warn her off by threatening her peace of mind, her friends?

Well, she might no longer claim Elal as her house affiliation, but Alise had been born an Elal and the blood of the most powerful wizards in the Convocation ran hot in her veins. No one tangled with an Elal and came out the better for it.

Alise had plans to make.

$$\sim 8 \sim$$

DESPITE HER EXHAUSTION, the late hour, and the siren call of her bed, Alise didn't succumb to the temptation of sleep. Locking the door and adding her own privacy seal of earth elementals to hold it securely shut, she surveyed her little room. The first step in taking control of her fate was to eliminate the possibility of being spied upon in her own place. Fortunately, that could be taken care of, if not easily, then with a bit of focused effort.

In the past she hadn't bothered. Now, the stakes had ratcheted to the highest level. Wizard Ariel had hinted that House Elal was working with House Ariel, and certainly Alise's father was no friend of House Phel, so removing any Elal spirit spies made eminent sense.

"All right, let's see," she said to herself thoughtfully. The most obvious spies would be spirits, both the canned variety that could be purchased and used by any reasonably powered wizard and more sophisticated ones specifically tasked by an Elal wizard. There were even some available on the general market that a mundane could use via an embedded enchantment that could be triggered by the unmagical also. Although "only" a student, Alise had enough skill and native Elal magic in her little finger to detect the canned spells of either variety. Ones specifically bound and tasked by a wizard of her house would be more difficult, though not impossible to locate and neutralize. For the most part.

She'd always assumed her father had spies on her and her siblings. That had been true all their lives, though as children they'd learned ways of ducking their unseen—but not unsensed—observers. That had been relatively easy because they'd been safely ensconced in House Elal, inside the heavily guarded territory of Elal, with little to threaten them. No, their beloved papa had mainly tasked elementals and other non-intelligent spirits to keep track of them in case they got into mischief. Which meant that any plans to be disobedient had included provisions to escape detection.

In retrospect, Alise could see that Lord Elal had likely known everything his children got up to and allowed it, to an extent. They'd only gotten called onto the carpet for truly egregious violations—usually Nander, as Nic and Alise had been dutiful daughters—and they'd assumed their father had found out via other means. Now it was clear he'd always monitored them closely. For the first time Alise wondered how Nic had not only escaped House Elal, but how she'd evaded the spirit spies. She wanted to be able to ask her older sister the question with a desperation completely out of proportion to the moment.

More, she longed to confide in Nic and get her advice on how to handle this dreadful situation. She and her sister hadn't been close in years, especially when Alise manifested as a wizard at young age at about the same time Nic, substantially older, turned out to be a familiar, to her profound and devastating disappointment. That had driven a wedge between them deep enough—and due to circumstances so far outside of their control—that neither had tried to mend the rift. Not until Alise turned up on the doorstep of House Phel with fugitive familiars, Han and Iliana, in tow and bearing an absurd notion that Nic needed rescuing.

That seemed to be the story of Alise's life: always trying to do the right thing for wrong-headed reasons. Well, that was going to change. She had no one to rely on but herself in this current situation. She did have a clear task and goals. Her enemies had conveniently made themselves manifest. She could figure out how to avoid them and—as necessary—handle them.

But in the meanwhile, she needed privacy and discretion most of all.

Wishing she could kick up her magic stores with a familiar's help, she set that aside as a futile hope. Cillian had advised her to use the familiars hired by the academy to top off her reserves and once even hired one for her. Ever since Nic turned out to be a familiar, though, and since all Iliana and Han went through, Alise had felt wrong about taking magic from familiars. Wizards weren't supposed to think twice about using familiars for this purpose. In truth, most wizards, with a few singular exceptions, regarded familiars as existing solely to provide magic for them.

As an additional rationalization, since familiars couldn't express magic on their own, they needed a wizard's assistance to bleed off the magic they generated before it built up to such toxic levels that it drove them insane. Viewed through that lens, wizards provided familiars with a desperately needed service. Or, at least, so they had convinced themselves.

But having access to a familiar's magic—especially a familiar bonded to you for life, creating in them a near-desperate adoration that meant they'd give anything to their wizard—was critically important to the wizards. They weren't selflessly assisting familiars; wizards exploited them to increase their own power and influence. Any wizard could release a familiar's magic; a familiar didn't need to be bonded to a wizard for that.

Sure, everyone acknowledged that familiars were also people, but when it came down to the laws governing the Convocation, wizards had the most rights and familiars almost none.

Somewhere along the way, Alise had developed squeamishness around the whole unseemly enterprise. Or a conscience. She supposed how one described it lay in the eye of the beholder. Alise didn't know what her future held, but being head of House Elal wasn't in it. And, while she understood the need to master her own magical skills, she had no desire for power. She stopped short of mentally vowing to never bind a familiar of her own, but she rather felt she never would. If she had to imagine her future, it looked like some sort of monastic sojourn. Maybe she'd travel to the lands without magic. No one would expect her to have a familiar there.

No one would know expect anything from her at all. The thought was both comforting and lonely. On the heels of that idea, it occurred to Alise that she'd be following in Nic's footsteps. Pregnant Nic, who'd fled to magicless Wartson to escape Gabriel Phel, with the idea of raising their child alone. If the Convocation hadn't sent hunters after Nic—and if Gabriel had been a bit less in love with her—she might have succeeded in disappearing. As a wizard, Alise would have an easier time of it. No one would pursue her.

Another thought both comforting and lonely.

Setting aside her morose ruminations, Alise concentrated on her task. She should have enough magic left to do what she needed to, and in the morning, she'd be refreshed and replete again. Mostly, anyway.

Summoning her reserves and ignoring the twinge of discomfort of pulling magic from what felt like the hollows of her bones—*thin and brittle enough to punch a fist through,* Nic's concerned and irritated voice sounded in her head—Alise cleared her mind and focused all of her magic on sensing the unseen. Fortunately, she had drilled all her life in meditative techniques to still her emotions and separate them from her thinking. True, her teachers were thinking primarily about their students being able to control their fear during an attack, but this pretty much counted as an ongoing battle.

She channeled her tumult of keen emotions into a blade's edge of wizardry, searching all levels of spirit manifestation within the walls of her room. There was no sense in scanning all of Convocation Academy. She knew what she'd find if she did that and it would be overwhelming. From tame fire elementals heating the floors to meticulously bound and warded demons serving the dark arts professors, the hallowed halls of the academy teemed with spirits of all kinds.

But Alise didn't need to find every incorporeal entity in reach of her wizardry: just the ones tasked to watch her. Breathing so slowly an observer might worry she'd died, she drew her attention over every pore of the stone walls, of the rough grout between, in the fibers of the throw rugs on the floor, and the furry space between. She combed through the weave of her blankets and the vanes of the smallest bit of down in her pillows and mattress. With deft skill, she eased her awareness through the Byssan glass of her small window that overlooked an enclosed courtyard and the tiny gaps between the fitted frame and the much older stone of the wall.

By the time she'd finished, hours had passed and she'd located and isolated forty-seven spirits of all echelons. The ones that weren't supposed to be there, anyhow. She, naturally, left unmolested the heating elementals and the dust-eating ones. She also disregarded the more sophisticated spirits installed to raise an alarm should there be a surge in magic, as happened occasionally with newly manifested wizards with shitty control.

Not that there was any danger from Alise—no, she was at her most dangerous at her deliberate best—but they posed no danger to her. The ones she did tether to her will, however, those could have caused trouble if she hadn't captured them. She didn't sever their bonds to the wizards that had tamed them, as that would alert those wizards, but she also couldn't allow them to continue to report back. She counted the signatures of nine different Elal wizards in her little herd of spies, including Lord Elal himself. Never content to leave anything entirely to his lackeys, her father had assigned three spirits of varying sophistication to watch his wizard-daughter.

Very tempted to snap their leashes so their master would feel it and know her power, Alise restrained herself—along with the flare of vicious hatred for her father. Wouldn't he be surprised to know how far her skills and ability had grown? She could break any spirit-bond he could make. Maybe, eventually, she could do so without him feeling it. That would be a valuable skill to pursue. But she couldn't risk that yet. He thought disinheriting her, real or threatened, had her cowed, whipped and beaten. It would serve her purposes for him to continue to believe that.

For the time being, Alise confined the forty-seven spirits to a bottle she'd quickly emptied of its commercially bound grooming imp, temporarily attaching the creature to her mirror instead. The task felt a bit like balancing a stack of plates in one hand while pouring sparkling wine into a delicate goblet with the other, and trying not to defizz it in the process, but she managed. The spirits she'd gathered up twisted and struggled in her mental grip. They didn't take up physical space, so wedging them all into one small bottle wasn't impossible. Still, they didn't like overlapping so much, especially those with opposite natures, like earth and air or water and fire.

None of them could resist her wizardry, however, especially as they'd already been tamed by another wizard, and soon all were stuffed into the bottle, which she sealed with a cork and an indelible cap of magic. It wasn't a permanent solution, but it would suffice for the rest of the night. Which, she suddenly realized, along with her scratchy eyes, dry mouth, and aching head, was nearly over.

Considering the El-Adrel timepiece on the wall, Alise contemplated through the dense fog of exhaustion whether it might be better to simply stay awake—get some coffee, perhaps study a bit—than go to sleep for such a short time that she'd wake up groggy. Somewhere in the midst of debating with herself over the pros and cons of each option, her body decided for her, and she conked out.

WHEN THE WAKE-UP bells rang, Alise came out of a dead sleep with a crooked neck from where she'd apparently crashed onto her side and possibly the worst headache of her life. Her magic had not only not replenished during the too-short nap, but it felt lower than ever. Belatedly she realized that, by tethering all those spirit spies to her will without breaking their bonds to the wizards that had tamed them, she'd engaged in an ongoing battle for control of them.

Not at all wise, but done was done. She couldn't release them now or they'd report back to their wizards what she'd attempted. Instead she staggered to her feet, weaving only a little on wobbly legs on her way to the wash basin, and invited the little water elemental to splash cold water on her face. Slightly more alert from the bracing effects of that, she dragged wet hands through her short hair, hoping to flatten the spikes sleep had pressed in the wrong direction, with only partial success. Good thing she'd never had cause for vanity. She'd long ago given up on extracting anything close to beauty from her oddly thin face, with her pointed chin and widely spaced eyes. At the moment, those eyes also sported purple bags big and puffy enough to stow her entire wardrobe in, an effect highlighted by the arrows of red lines creased into her cheek from the wrinkled bedding.

All in all, not her best look. Stripping off the stale, slept-in clothing from the day before, she then dragged on pants and a shirt from her closet, just as the bell for breakfast sounded, making her stomach clench in hunger. Food would go a long way toward helping her body replenish at least her native magic, and it sometimes worked as a substitute for sleep. More or less, anyway.

Knowing the vial of bottled spirits would drain her magic less in close proximity, she tucked it in a thigh pocket of her baggy pants, buttoning it closed again. The slight weight of it bumped against her leg. At least she'd been smart enough to pick a small vessel, which she could keep on her without drawing attention.

Unlocking her door and removing the other enchantments she'd added for security, Alise checked the corridor for any lurking enemy wizards, then plunged into the thin stream of wizard-students heading down the hallway. They didn't provide robust cover, but she was grateful for their presence as she'd never been before. The other students might sneer at and snub her, but they wouldn't attack her with tigers or employ illegal psychic pressure to subvert her will. She even found herself grateful for the by-now standard cold shoulders they presented to her and how they pretended she didn't exist. There was a comfort in that, in invisibility, a surcease the remorseless mirror had failed to give her.

Hurrying along to breakfast, Alise mentally reviewed her schedule for the day, as best she could recall it. In her haste, she'd left the document the provost gave her back in her room. She rather envied Cillian's ability to access records magically. That would be a handy trick to master, and theoretically one she could learn, so long as she never used it for profit. As if she had time to learn anything else. Probably Cillian wouldn't teach her the proprietary Harahel techniques anyway. Besides which, they weren't speaking to each other. She shouldn't even be thinking about him.

With her tray of the standard breakfast plate and an extra-large coffee, Alise looked for a place to sit. She hated this part and had since she'd become a pariah. Before that, she'd always had a place at a table with the wizard-students from the highest houses, to the point that people would shift around to make a place for her. Everyone had wanted Alise Elal to grace them with her presence. There had been a time when she'd held her tray and chosen from a half-dozen options, tables of different friend groups waving to her, beckoning her to join them.

Now no one even met her eyes. Invisibility cut both ways: both a comfort and a cold slice to the heart. She had a choice between equally unpleasant options: find an empty table, and good luck with that; quietly slip into a seat at the empty end of an occupied table and pretend along with everyone else that she didn't actually exist; or brazen her way into a group and shame them into publicly acknowledging her existence. That last absolutely wasn't going to happen, as Alise was so not up to anything requiring the least bit of fortitude, let alone brazen courage.

In fact… The thought of the other two options curdled her stomach sufficiently that the fragrant breakfast that had made her salivate only moments before now smelled nauseating. Oh well, she didn't have that much time anyway. She could skip eating and instead retrieve her class schedule and maybe figure out what to tackle next on the mountain of past-due coursework material. Taking her tray to the clean-up station, she set it down, retaining only the infinitely precious cup of coffee.

"I don't think so."

Alise nearly jumped out of her skin at the sound of Cillian's voice right beside her. Giving her a dark look, he picked up her tray before it slid into the chute where earth elementals eagerly waited to devour anything organic, and started walking. Then he paused and glanced back at her. "Come. Sit. Eat."

"Woof," Alise replied sourly and the reproving look he gave her wasn't amused either.

"I waved," he said pointedly. "You looked right at me."

And clearly thought she'd ignored him on purpose, as opposed to being willfully blind to everyone in that room because she was too fragile to withstand the shunning. Not at all wanting to explain that, she muttered something about being tired and blurry vision.

He *thunked* her tray down on the end of a partially occupied table, his own mostly empty tray there. The people at the other end of the table appeared to be lower-level faculty like Cillian, younger and no one Alise knew well. A couple of them nodded at her absently before returning to their conversation. Cillian had a pile of his things on the chair beside him, which he moved and dumped under his seat with his typical disregard for any of his possessions that weren't books, and pointed at her to sit.

He'd clearly been saving the seat for her—completely disregarding their conversation of the night before—and Alise plopped herself down, though careful of the precious coffee she still clutched, agitated and uncertain. It annoyed her no end that he acted like nothing had changed between them and expected to have breakfast with her, and at the same time it moved her immeasurably that at least one person wanted her to sit with them. Sure, Cillian was faculty and not a student, but he also had good reason to never want to talk to her again.

Abruptly weepy and dreadfully embarrassed that Cillian might see, Alise stared fiercely at her eggs. They'd looked so delicious when she heaped them on her plate, along with the buttered toast with honey and stewed grains. Now she worried she wouldn't be able to swallow them through a throat vising with emotion. What a mess she was. *You're just tired,* she told herself.

"Staring at your food won't get it inside where it will do you good, Alise," Cillian said gently, far more so than she deserved after she'd been so unkind to him.

You were mean to him for good reasons, she reminded herself. *He can't be involved, so buck up and deal.*

Firming her resolve and not looking at him, knowing that

looking into his warm black eyes would undo her, she forked up some eggs and made herself chew and swallow. She barely got them past the knot in her throat. Her achingly empty stomach lurched when the food hit it, acid rising up like steam when water hits hot oil. But she held it down and, feeling defiant, shot Cillian a triumphant glare.

He didn't see, however, instead paying attention to digging something out of the worn satchel he'd tossed under the chair only moments before. "I found something interesting for your independent study," he was saying, speaking loudly enough for the other faculty at the table to hear, rather pointedly reminding her they had an audience and that Alise, at least on record, still reported to him as her study supervisor.

Since she didn't trust herself to answer, Alise shoved another fork-load of eggs into her mouth, following up with a bite of the honeyed toast. Her stomach seemed to be getting on board with the concept of food and settling down to get to the business of digesting, sending up enthusiastic invitations for more. She took a deep swallow of coffee, sighing at the warmth hitting her belly and resulting tingles of energy prodding her tired mind.

"Better?" Cillian inquired too quietly for anyone to overhear.

"Fine, thank you, Archivist," she answered with formal neutrality. "You said you had something for me?"

"I do, yes," he replied with some of his usual enthusiasm, brandishing what looked like an index. "It occurred to me that, while some records might be entirely missing, seamlessly enough that their disappearance went undetected, that a tangential search, while it would consume more time, might reveal a forgotten cross-reference that…Alise? Are you listening? What's wrong?"

What was wrong was Gordon Hanneil standing across from her, wizard-black eyes sharp as daggers.

~ 9 ~

C ILLIAN WATCHED AS what little healthy color Alise had in her pale face drained away entirely. Her lovely black eyes that had already been shadowed in a way that made Cillian want to wrap her up in a soft blanket and hold her until she fell into much-needed sleep—never mind how inappropriate that would be—went haunted and bottomless in her taut face. He put a hand on her arm to catch her as she swayed in her seat, in case she actually fell.

"Alise?" he prompted, and followed her gaze to where she stared across the crowded dining hall. She looked as if she gazed into the abyss, like a monster lurked there, poised to devour her. But Cillian saw nothing. He even tried stretching his limited archivist-wizard's senses to determine if something magical lurked there. Still nothing. But Alise was a far more powerful wizard and, more to the point, exceptionally talented in spirit magic, capable of detecting entities most wizards could not. "Is something there?" he asked in a lowered voice, squeezing her arm lightly to penetrate her stupor. "Something malevolent?"

She jumped in his loose grip, startling him with the violence of her reaction, her wide-eyed, panicked gaze flying to his. "No! Nothing. I'm fine."

"Don't you lie to me," he bit out. "Tell me or I'm going over there."

She swallowed hard, clearly frantic. "Please don't. Please, Cillian."

"Then tell me."

"Don't look though. The proctor," she whispered. "Directly ahead. Staring right at us. At the end of the table."

Confused, Cillian surreptitiously searched for who she meant. Several proctors monitored the dining hall, as usual, keeping tabs on the minds and emotions of the magic-bearing adolescents of varying ages, some powerful enough to level the building and a few quite capable of doing so in a fit of temper. He didn't see anyone of note—and definitely no one standing where Alise's gaze had been fixed. "The closest proctor I see is Wizard Divya, near the coffee pots." And Alise wasn't looking at her.

"Then you can't see him," she whispered, her expression crumpling in despair.

"Do you know his name? Or can you describe him for me?"

Pressing her lips together, she shook her head, steadfastly not looking in the direction she'd indicated. Refusing to answer, he thought, not that she didn't know.

"I'm not crazy," she said, her harsh whisper beseeching.

"Of course you're not," he agreed easily, though the pitch of her emotions seemed off the scale. Alise had no reason to fear one of the academy proctors. Still, something had frightened the usually unflappable Alise and he believed her fear was real. "I believe you."

The look she turned on him, the immense gratitude in her expression, was nearly as good as if she'd said she longed for him like he did for her. "Let's try this. I count nine proctors," he said, very quietly, just loud enough for her to hear him, "all of whom I know."

She swallowed hard. "There are ten."

Alise wasn't one to make mistakes, especially careless ones. Acting nonchalant, Cillian sat back and counted again, backing up the visual scan with his wizardly ability to assess quantities. "I still get nine."

Making a choking sound, she abruptly pushed back and stood, using enough force that her chair clattered to the floor. "I'm sorry, Archivist," she said, not sounding sorry at all. She also punched the words loudly enough to silence the debate underway at the other end of the table. Alise flicked a glance at the place where her invisible proctor stood, then fastened a pleading gaze on him. "I appreciate the effort you've put into organizing my independent study, but I simply have no time. I cannot work on it. Period." With that, she seized her coffee and her book bag and scuttled away before he realized her intent.

"Student wizards," one of his colleagues commented, shaking her head in disgust. "No respect for faculty anymore."

"Report her to the provost," her companion advised. "Particularly that one. This isn't her first transgression, as I'm sure you know."

"Or even the second," another said.

"Or the worst! Those Elals think they can get away with

anything," another added.

But Cillian was no longer listening, having barely listened to begin with. The lower-level faculty tended to resent the more powerfully talented and highly placed wizard students. It stuck in the craw of some people that these "ignorant kids" already enjoyed more wealth and influence than they would. Employment at Convocation Academy in the lower ranks would never lead to full professorships and endowed chairs, so the positions weren't exactly highly sought. Cillian didn't mind because he basically got paid to hang out in one of the best libraries in the known world.

Most of his peers resented their dead-end jobs, however, and the only thing those petty minds enjoyed more than seeing one of the student wizards suffer some kind of failure was witnessing the stumbling or toe-stubbing of one of the high-house scions. The same thing had happened when Alise's sister, Nic, so widely believed to be the next head of House Elal, manifested as a familiar instead of a wizard. The unholy glee at her loss of prestige, power, and even basic citizenship had been frankly awful to witness.

Cillian fully understood Alise's insistence on being called by her House Phel affiliation instead of Elal. Even if her father wasn't a monster who'd committed his worst deeds against his own intimate family, being an Elal wasn't doing Alise any favors these days. The gossiping faculty proved that, falling into an exchange of lurid tidbits about the Elal progeny and the house itself. Cillian ignored his colleagues and their callous remarks, taking his empty tray and Alise's barely touched one to the discard station, which led him past the spot where she'd seen a proctor he hadn't.

Though the hairs stood up on the back of his neck, Cillian otherwise sensed nothing unusual. And that reaction could be attributed to Alise's markedly odd behavior. He'd watched her face down hunters and automatons wielding wheels of blades. And the sight of a proctor terrified her to speechlessness? No, something very strange was going on and he wouldn't lose this opportunity to gather any information he could.

So he waved to Proctor Raya Hanneil, a friend from student days. She gave him an absent smile, brushing her brown hair out of her eyes before glowering at a group of young, uncategorized students in a rising shouting match. "Hey, uncats," she called, "inside voices or I mute you for the rest of breakfast."

They subsided sullenly, continuing the argument at lower levels. "Can you really do that?" Cillian asked, electing to take a moment for friendly chatting before grilling her.

She winked. "I can make them think I can do that."

Laughing, he gave her a little salute. "Clever. I'm curious, Raya, are there always ten of you working the breakfast shift?"

Wrinkling her nose, she laughed. "Cillian, I know your curiosity knows no limits, but how could you possibly care about that?"

"I've been reading up on crowd control," he answered on impulse. "Of course, students aren't rioting mundanes, but..."

"They're that not far different either," she finished drily.

"Angry adults without magic are less dangerous than children with it," he agreed amiably, "but I'm interested in the commonalities. I know House Hanneil has a contract with the

Convocation to provide crowd control in certain circumstances."

She slid him a sideways glance, clearly refraining from comment. Yeah, it wasn't common knowledge, but not exactly a secret either. Still, high houses tended to guard proprietary information zealously, whether or not the secrecy mattered.

Cillian held up his hands in a peacemaking gesture, hoping his sideways approach hadn't taken so long that it cost him his quarry. "That's not something I need to know. What I'm wondering is, how it's decided how many proctors should be assigned per expected student? For example, are there nine or ten of you here this morning? I think I counted nine, but…"

"Ten," she answered with confidence.

"Are you sure? I only count nine."

She rolled her eyes, confident in her authority now. "Ten, Cillian. Where's your archivist's ability to count?"

"I see you, Divya…" He pointed and recited the names, counting them off on his other hand. "That's nine."

"And Gordon Hanneil, right there." She shook her head at him, grinning. "Maybe you need a Refoel healer to check your eyes."

"Oh!" he looked that direction and still detected no one. But a Hanneil wizard could see through a psychic manipulation that he could not. "Silly me. I don't remember seeing him around before."

She shrugged. "New hire. Replaced Beck, who retired."

"Striking," Cillian commented, fishing for any physical details she might give.

"Want me to introduce you? He's handsome with all that

golden hair and those bulging pecs, but I'd have to warn you that he's got a rep for being unkind to his lovers."

"Thanks, but no," Cillian answered with a dry laugh. "Not at all my type."

"That's what I thought. Though you might seriously consider going with beefy, arrogant, and male. Better than going doe-eyed over a student," she said with significantly arched brows. "You should know there's gossip about you and Alise Elal."

"Phel," he corrected. "Wizard Alise is House Phel now," he explained in the face of Raya's bafflement. "And I'm surprised you listen to gossip. I've simply been assisting Alise with an independent study requiring deep research in the archives, at Provost Uriel's behest, I might add."

"I didn't say I was listening," she replied with a shrug.

"Just repeating."

"Warning a friend," she corrected. "I know all about your white knight tendencies, Cillian, remember?"

He flushed, in irritation and embarrassment. Old friends knew too much about you at times. "Szarina was a different story."

"Was she?" Raya nodded in the direction Alise had gone. "Pretty, waifish wizardlings have always been your weakness. But you can't save this one any more than you could save Szarina. And Alise Elal—Phel," she corrected with a sigh when he started to interrupt. "Even if you could somehow rescue her from the pit she's dug for herself, she wouldn't thank you for it. She's not going to reward you for your service to her. Or, if it occurred to her, she might make you House Elal archivist, where you'd probably get paid even less than you are now—but she's never going to make a low-level Harahel wizard her consort." She snickered. "Imagine you as Lord Elal, even in name only."

Cillian was remembering why his friendship with Raya had tapered off. "As I said," he replied with stiff formality, "I have no designs on Alise. She is my advisee only."

"Yes, well, a word to the wise—let her go her own way. She's meddling in dangerous waters and this 'research project' of hers is not looked upon favorably by any number of powerful entities."

Cillian's neck prickled. He looked again in the direction of the invisible Gordon Hanneil. "Entities like House Hanneil?" he inquired mildly.

"Any number of powerful entities," Raya repeated with slow emphasis. Then she softened, smiling. "We've been friends a long time, so know that I'm only thinking of your best interests. This is not an arena for a wizard like you. Stick to the books and the baking. That's where you shine and you'll be the happier for it."

"So noted," he said.

"Aww, don't be like that." Her smile turned inviting. "You know I always appreciated your baking. Especially breakfast in bed. That was the upside of your dalliance with Szarina—she taught you well."

He made himself laugh, as if pleased. "I'll keep that in mind."

"Do. You know where to find me. We always had a good time together."

He thought that was highly debatable, but he might need Raya for more information, so he kissed her cheek. "Nice to catch up."

"Yes, and—Hey!" She fastened her attention on a pair of wizards with their heads together. "I hear what you're thinking and not in my cafeteria."

Grateful for the reprieve, Cillian ducked away while Raya was preoccupied, gathered his things, and headed for the library. The archives might be mysteriously missing reams of information on House Phel, but they contained certain information without a doubt. That included the personal profiles of every Convocation citizen.

This Gordon Hanneil would have to appear on the rolls to have been hired as a Convocation Academy proctor. He might be using his psychic magic to obscure his presence from some eyes and not others, but other Hanneil wizards like Raya knew of him and so he must exist on paper.

Cillian would use all his considerable skills and wizardry to find out everything there was to know about Gordon Hanneil who was unkind to his lovers. Cillian might not be white knight material, and he'd never be the hero of anyone's story, but he could do this for Alise. Gordon Hanneil had terrified Alise and Cillian would find out why.

And put a stop to it.

~ 10 ~

A LISE PRACTICALLY FLED to her first class of the day, slamming through the doors with an urgent sense of reprieve that was especially ironic given that the class was her least favorite one of all: Alchemical Mathematics. Ugh.

She also quickly realized her error in judgment in fleeing the dining hall so abruptly, besides the spectacle she'd made of herself, acting like a crazy person upset by a wizard no one else could see, and leaving her breakfast uneaten. She'd left the dining hall far too early and arrived in her classroom well ahead of anyone else. She was alone.

She spun around to correct the situation and wait in the relative safety of the corridor. But she was trapped.

Gordon Hanneil slithered into the classroom with a stark smile and shut the door behind him, putting his back against it and making it clear Alise would have to go through him to escape. Soon, however, other students and the professor would arrive, she reminded herself, rather desperately. He couldn't trap her in there forever. And surely he couldn't make good on his threats, with witnesses imminent.

But Cillian had looked right at Gordon and hadn't seen him. What could Gordon force her to do while others looked on, smiling blandly and chatting, noticing nothing?

"I didn't break your rules," she blurted at Gordon, feeling like a small, panicked bird cornered by a cat.

"You certainly shouldn't be able to," he said agreeably, but with iron beneath. "Not after our previous conversation. I'm wondering what failed to stick to your addled brain." A lance of psychic magic stabbed at Alise's mind, painfully slicing her thoughts into helpless disarray and piercing her will.

And yet… She wasn't taken as unawares as the day before. Now that she'd experienced this sort of psychic attack once, she could better observe the parameters of what he could and could not do. One very important discovery: he'd thought the compulsion he'd implanted in her would prevent her from more than it had. That was promising. After all, she might not want to own her Elal origins, but they were known as one of the most powerful families of wizards in the Convocation for a reason.

House Elal had been one of the leaders in the war that defeated House Hanneil and imposed the sanctions on them. She might be a baby wizard, but she was from a tough and ancient bloodline. In that self-knowledge, she found that not all of her mind and will lay vulnerable to the unscrupulous man. Part of the psychic manipulation, it seemed, was making her believe that he controlled her.

"I… I haven't worked on the project *at all*," she stammered, trying to sound pleading, giving herself time to think. And for people to arrive. She couldn't see the El-Adrel clock on the wall from where she stood, but surely it couldn't be that long until first bell.

"Ah, but you were discussing the project with that Harahel archivist, your independent study lead. *He* certainly seemed to believe you were continuing the work."

"I have to tell him *something*," she whined. "The provost herself assigned the study. If I fail, I won't graduate."

"That's your problem. Tell me what he discussed with you."

So, Gordon didn't know everything. Alise shoved the intense relief at that realization down deep, far below the surface thoughts, so the proctor wouldn't read it in her. A non-wizardly trick she'd known how to do for years.

That was a perhaps unintended consequence of Convocation Academy's pervasive use of Hanneil wizards as proctors to monitor student behavior. Even as young uncats, the students learned to mentally duck the proctors and find ways to conduct illicit activities under their noses without detection. One didn't need brilliant psychic defenses to pull it off, just a level of mental agility and strong motivation.

Getting away with shit in school had incentivized many a clever student to find ways to fool the proctors. Alise recalled those early lessons now, something she'd been too rattled to do on her first encounter with Gordon. She didn't need major psychic shields or battle magic, just a bit of student cleverness. To amplify the feeling of whiny, put-upon student, she said, "I don't even know what that boring librarian was maundering on about. Blah blah blah with cross-referencing I don't know what."

The Hanneil wizard narrowed his snake-black eyes, his magic rudely probing her mind. She wanted to vomit from the violation, but she held her pose of pitiful vulnerability, pretending to be unaware of his invasion.

"I've heard that you and that low-level wizard-archivist have a *special* relationship," he crooned, curling his voice lasciviously around the words. "Is he your boyfriend, Alise? You can confide in me."

"No," she breathed. "He's old and boring. A low-level wizard with no future except the same as what he's got right now."

Gordon didn't move, but his magic wrapped around her with slimy familiarity. "That's not what I heard."

"From where?" she scoffed. "My so-called friends in the student population? They'll say anything to make me look bad, to kick the underdog while she's down. I'm sure the provost would be thrilled to hear some rumor that I'm diddling a faculty member instead of doing my best to graduate. That kind of thing might get me finally expelled."

Gordon *tsked* at her. "Silly little Elal. You forget who you're dealing with. I can read minds and that Harahel boy is head over heels in love with you. Even if you don't return the feelings," he added with less certainty, his magic picking away at the layers of thought her stunned surprise had liberated from hiding.

She scrambled to squelch them again, throwing her very real shock and confusion to obscure what he could read in her. Cillian... *in love with her?* No, it wasn't possible.

In fact, it was so impossible that Alise realized Gordon had said it only to manipulate her. Effective approach. But still, she didn't want the Hanneil wizard's attention on Cillian, who couldn't defend himself, magically or politically.

"You didn't know," Gordon murmured, a pleased smile crawling across his loathsome face. "But what is this I sense? You're protective of him."

Dark arts take her. She needed to fix this fast. So, she curled a lip and shrugged. "You think he's lusting after me, a student? Maybe he's more of a social climber than I gave him credit for."

"Everyone is a social climber, baby Elal. Some just hide it better than others."

She'd argue, but in Convocation society, status and power were everything, so Gordon had a point. Except that she knew Cillian and he only cared about books and baking. Maybe those game figures he collected. But all as harmless as it got. He deserved to enjoy that kind of life, far away from the kind of power-struggles she'd been born into and likely would never escape, not even in far Wartson.

"You will stay away from the librarian," Gordon informed her, apparently coming to a decision. "The next time I detect *any* communication between you, I will take action."

"I can't refuse to communicate with my independent study advisor," she contested hotly.

"Figure it out," he shot back. "You're so clever."

"Cutting off contact would look suspicious. It would attract *more* attention, and you don't want that, do you?"

"I can handle that part," he sneered, waving off her argument. "Don't forget who I am."

"Even against Provost Uriel?" she persisted. "That seems like an extreme move, risking House Uriel becoming aware of

House Hanneil interference."

That, at least, gave him pause, and Alise allowed herself to enjoy the brief flush of triumph. A minor victory, but every tiny triumph chipped away at his control over her.

"Don't let it come to that," he advised, adding a bit of psychic pressure. "Speak to the Harahel boy if you must, but only to put him off. I'll be watching your every thought and if I detect the least hint of rebellion…" He grinned, gaze lingering on her bosom, which was so slight and so concealed under her baggy shirt that she knew he couldn't possibly see anything. Still, the hint served to turn her stomach. "Well, I will make you regret any disobedience."

"House Phel won't take an attack against me lightly," she warned him. "Even House Elal will take it amiss if you harm me."

"Oh, I'm not going to harm *you*," he returned. "Though my promise to make you eagerly squirm in my bed stands. Who knows? You might find you enjoy it after I release the compulsion that made you crawl to me in the first place."

She regarded him impassively, refusing to give him the pleasure of revealing her profound revulsion. The Hanneil wizard—the stereotypical version of the worst of that house—clearly got off on frightening her and on his own prurient fantasies of rape, mental, emotional, and physical. Someone rapped sharply on the door, shouting a question. Finally.

Gordon's smile went thin. "No, baby wizard. If you can't follow instructions, the person who will be hurt is the librarian."

CILLIAN SETTLED AT his favorite study desk, the one in the quiet corner near the windows, surrounded on the other two sides by shelves of obscure treatises on early Convocation experiments on soil amendments. The very stale information possessed the infinitely magical quality of repelling all comers. Nobody ever visited those materials. In fact, of all the shelves in the vast archives, this corner of obsolete academia was the least visited. Cillian had determined that quite some time ago and quietly moved a battered desk and comfy chair into it. With the addition of an old lamp with an aging fire elemental that produced light so grudging no one would miss it, Cillian had the perfect refuge, the polar opposite of his station at the reference desk where anyone could interrupt him and regularly did.

With a sigh—not exactly happy, as the circumstances were far from pleasant—he arranged the piles of bound records. The situation was beyond terrible, but he couldn't help that he did love a bit of a research project. This one might end quickly, with the standard information easily located and presented as expected, but...

As he'd suspected, however, neither Convocation Academy graduation records nor the citizenship rolls turned up a wizard Gordon Hanneil. Almost certainly that was the name he'd given when he was hired as an academy proctor, but with a little psychic push on the correct low-level, data-entry personnel, a false name could be applied to his hiring dossier. The underlying records would be more difficult to falsify and could lead to trouble if a person needed to prove their citizenship. Why take that risk when a new name for a new job was much easier?

No, Gordon Hanneil existed, Cillian was certain of that—and was equally certain that wasn't his name. Sent by Hanneil, almost certainly, but not Gordon and maybe not entitled to use the house name as his own. Cillian would find him.

He began by going through the House Hanneil roster, which Cillian fully expected would yield nothing. The pages were arranged chronologically in reverse order, with the youngest members listed first in the binder, each given their own page as the Convocation proctors confirmed possession of magical talent. Usually in-house proctors made the first assessments of children under the aegis of the house, if the house in question could afford to keep a specially trained Hanneil wizard with an oracle head to make the determination. Naturally, House Hanneil had no such issues, able to assess all children born to their denizens frequently and in-depth.

Thus, the House Hanneil pages for each individual showed a relentless amount of testing, usually starting at birth. However, the Convocation relied upon their own rounds of examinations to make the official determinations, which generally started when the child was around five years old. Though magically gifted children were admitted to Convocation Academy around the ages of eight or nine, depending on their MP scores and relative maturity, they didn't manifest as either a wizard or familiar until well after adolescence, when the brain finished its final maturation. In some rare cases—Han came to mind—late bloomers didn't manifest until their early to mid twenties.

Thus, every individual's page held rows of testing dates and the results as spoken by the oracle head, including an identification number indicating which oracle head had delivered that particular verdict. The oracle heads were never wrong, but a great deal of Convocation law and practice depended upon that fact, so identifying details were meticulously documented. The official Convocation testing entries stood out in bold lettering at intervals—when the child in question had been officially registered as magically gifted, along with their MP scores at the time of testing; their scores at the time of admission to Convocation Academy, and at regular intervals following that.

The newest entries, of course, belonged to infants, and Cillian paged through those rapidly, Hanneil children seeming to grow before his eyes as their charts lengthened into multiple pages, their portraits gazing up from the archival-quality House Salis paper, the kids seeming to age as he flipped through, faces losing the softness of childhood, sharpening with understanding and, in many cases, cynicism. Eventually the array of eye colors lessened, the variety of greens, blues, hazels, grays, and browns giving over to a predominance of wizard-black. Oh, the familiars retained their native eye color, but they faded into the background compared to that intensely magical black of their wizard fellows.

He supposed that could be a reflection of his own ingrained Convocation-instilled biases. Only wizards mattered in the world of Convocation Society, with familiars retaining more of their humanity, perhaps, along with their natural eye color, but falling into their support roles to the only people with actual power: wizards.

Cillian snorted softly to himself at his own thoughts, mentally amending the observation to specify "high-level wizards." As a librarian without spectacular skills of any kind, he lacked power worth mentioning. But then, at least weak wizards and familiars made it to citizen status. None of the house binders included the countless mundanes who inhabited Convocation lands, living their lives unrecorded and largely unnoticed, except that their labors produced coin that filled the coffers of the Convocation houses in return for the goods that improved their otherwise magicless existence.

Dark arts, he was in a morose mood. Though, with all that had happened since he and Alise had returned to Convocation Academy, who could blame him? Certainly he couldn't be suffering heartbreak over losing someone he'd never had to begin with.

In truth, though he hastened this research with his native wizardry, paging through, reading, and sorting the information faster than anyone without his abilities could, a great deal of what he brought to the task involved simple intelligence. The same ability to parse and interpret data that any mundane could bring to bear. Though he could have used magic to index the House Hanneil binder—and then cross-referenced with House Hanneil hires, as Wizard Gordon wasn't necessarily born to that house and could have been hired on at any point—Cillian wanted to add that extra layer of quality control by examining the information physically also.

Another stack on his desk comprised the Convocation Academy graduates for each year for the last century. This Gordon Hanneil had to be in there somewhere. Cillian would probably start two decades previous and work backwards and forwards, alternating a year before and a year after, to find the wizard. Whatever name he'd used then, he'd show up in some fashion.

Cillian didn't exactly know how he'd recognize the wizard. Even if he had seen the man's face, Gordon might not look the same now as in the records. If he had the wizard's MP scorecard, Cillian could use his archivist magic to index for that and cut this whole search short. Every wizard's and familiar's MP scores were as unique as their fingerprints. Yes, the scores fluctuated until manifestation, but once an oracle head was able to give the final determination of wizard or familiar, those MP scores remained fixed for the remainder of their lives. The only variable after that point was how the person in question used their magic. The MP scores tested potential only. Execution was something entirely else.

But, whoever he was, this wizard possessed Hanneil magic sufficient to be hired as an academy proctor. Cillian began assembling a mental list, using his magic to remember the profiles perfectly and bookmark their locations, of possible candidates. He would find this person and then he would discover why the wizard was tormenting Alise.

What Cillian would do at that point, he wasn't certain. But he had to do *something*. Alise needed his help, which mattered more than anything to him. Also, though, if House Hanneil was working to interfere with Alise's investigation into the missing House Phel archives, then someone had to ferret out their plans.

And who better to compile that data than a librarian?

~ II ~

ALISE MADE IT through her classes somehow, the bottle of restless spirits bumping against her thigh, draining her magic like a slow leak as they continued to fight her hold on them. The day passed in a blur of fatigue, worry, and occasional frissons of panic. Fortunately, the crushing pressure of catching up with her already freakishly difficult courseload provided sufficient distraction every time her thoughts began to spiral into a loop of wondering how to solve any of her current problems, including how she could speak to Cillian without jeopardizing him.

He was so obdurate, so determined to solve the riddle she'd presented him with, even nobly inspired by some ideal of saving House Phel, that nothing she could think of seemed likely to dissuade him. Certainly she'd failed to put him off with cutting and cruel behavior. That had rolled right off him and he'd been as kind and solicitous toward her as ever. The man was a study in forging his own, quiet path, implacably strolling along to the strains of a distant music only he could hear. She doubted anything she could say or do would change his mind, now that he'd made it up, even if she could bring herself to be sufficiently unkind.

And she just didn't have it in her. Apparently she wasn't Elal enough for that.

Letting out a soundless bark of laughter at the profound irony of that, Alise trudged back through the main halls, hoping for an hour in the quiet privacy of her room to sit and *think* before the dinner bells rang. She couldn't skip dinner. Even she could recognize that missing so many meals—there had been no time for lunch—was taking a toll on her. "You should have taken the kolaches," she muttered to herself.

"Wizard Alise?" A dark-skinned girl Alise vaguely recognized hopped off the deep windowsill where she'd been sitting and waved awkwardly. "Brinda Chur," she added, her brown eyes full of earnest appeal as she chewed her bottom lip.

"Ah, hi." It had been so long since another student had approached her that Alise almost didn't know what to do with herself.

"I know this is untoward at best and rude at worst," Brinda hurried on to say, waving her hands to encompass a wide circle before clasping them again, "a familiar addressing a wizard without permission and all."

"There's no rule against it," Alise pointed out, still taken aback and a bit wary. Was House Chur sending a warning now, too? If so, at least they'd chosen an innocuous messenger and a nicely public venue, streams of students parting around them in the busy hallway.

"Yes, well." Brinda blew out a demonstrative breath and smiled weakly. "House Chur is big on formality and etiquette. If my mother knew, I'd be sat down for a long lecture on how high-house scions ought and ought not to behave. You know how the old high houses are and House Chur is one of the oldest," she added, as if that explained anything, which maybe it did. "Almost as old as House Elal, which I'm sure you know. I don't know why I told you that. I'm really nervous and I'm babbling."

"How can I help you, Familiar Brinda?" Alise asked, not unkindly and trying to be patient. Brinda looked to be about the same age as her, but Alise felt infinitely older than this sweet-eyed daughter of a high house.

Alise did understand—for the most part—what Brinda was attempting to explain about etiquette and the house of her birth. House Chur, indeed one of the founding high houses of the Convocation, governed the powerful magics of sun and fire, rather the polar opposite of House Phel's moon and water magic, come to think of it. Their trademarks had survived centuries of challenges by upstart houses and, while they brought few direct products to market, their monopoly on the powerful magics that fueled so many other manufacturing processes provided a solid income to bolster their already massive, old-money coffers.

Brinda slid her eyes from side to side, as if anyone paid them any attention, which none of them did, and twisted her long, slender fingers together. "Could we—that is, would you condescend to, ah, speak with me, um, privately?"

Condescend. Alise nearly demanded to know who Brinda thought she was, some sort of wizard-princess too good to converse with commoners? But she bit back the harsh reply. The word reflected House Chur archaic manners and Brinda's clear sincerity about imposing on Alise's time and goodwill. *It's not her fault you're in a horrible mood,* she reminded herself firmly.

At the same time—call her paranoid, but—she was leery of all these high-house driven requests for "private meetings." Not that a familiar could hope to harm her, but Alise was taking no chances. "Can you tell me what it's regarding?"

Brinda flushed, looking down at her twisting fingers. Seeming to notice that she'd been busily picking at one of her undecorated nails and had it half torn off, she clenched her hands together. "It's...ah, personal," she whispered.

How curious. Alise gestured to the window alcove where Brinda had been sitting—and clearly waiting for her. "Let's sit there and I'll put up a silencing shield."

Brinda's crestfallen expression brightened with relief and gratitude. "Perfect! I always forget that you wizards can do things like that." She hopped onto the cushioned sill and crossed her legs, hands folded neatly in her lap, beaming at Alise expectantly.

Alise followed her, hoisting herself up, the bottle of spirits banging against her leg and clanking against the wooden ledge. Brinda glanced that way, startled, but politely averted her gaze. The window overlooked the same courtyard that Cillian's did, from the opposite side. From where she sat, Alise could easily see the faculty wing that housed his rooms, but stopped herself from counting over to figure which were his. He could be there even now, reading, or perhaps gazing out the window, and... And what in the dark arts was *wrong* with her?

She focused on Brinda who waited quietly. "What's going on?" Alise asked. "The shield is up," she added when Brinda looked around. Alise had forgotten to make it clear she'd done so.

"Oh!" Brinda smiled and tapped the side of her head. "Silly me." She sobered. "So, I wanted to ask you something and I know it's asking a lot, but you're the only person I can think of who might be able to help me. Well, not the only one able to, but the only one willing to, maybe."

Alise began to get a bad feeling about this. "Help with what?" she prompted anyway, feeling the longed for hour of quiet in her room ticking away like sand through her fingers.

"I graduate soon. We're in the same class. I don't expect you to remember that, or care or anything," she hastened to assure Alise, who was chagrined to acknowledge, if only to herself, that she hadn't remembered that. "I manifested early, but some of the coursework took a while," she confided. "Especially Convocation History. I just can't seem to remember all those dates and names and—" She clapped a hand over her mouth. "And I'm wasting your time! My apologies, Wizard Alise. Maman always says I'd talk the dead to sleep."

"It's all right," Alise said, trying to be patient and holding on by her mental fingernails. "But I will have to head to the dining hall soon or risk missing my dinner."

"Yes! Yes, me too. All of us." Brinda laughed nervously, twisting her fingers in her pretty flowered skirt. At least she was leaving her poor nails alone. "See, the thing is, when I graduate, I'll return home, to House Chur," she clarified unnecessarily. "And then I'll start the Betrothal Trials." Brinda flushed and stared out the window.

Ah. Alise understood now. The Betrothal Trials were exactly the sort of archaic tradition House Chur would insist upon, just like House Elal. Nic had endured several months of the Betrothal Trials—Alise had to admit to herself that she wasn't sure how long it had been, she was that awful of a sister—before meeting Gabriel Phel. Some called the practice barbaric, and surely it was, and inflicted only on female familiars. Effectively locked away from all male contact, the women received wizard "suitors" once a month, a different one each month, until they turned up pregnant. With their fertile compatibility confirmed, the wizard bonded the familiar and they became a permanent pair.

The oldest houses swore by the tradition, saying the practice ensured the vitality of their bloodlines. Male familiars sometimes endured similar testing, but—due to the happy difference in biology—didn't have to be sequestered. Their female wizard partners kept track of ensuring parentage. The Betrothal Trials didn't offer familiars much of a choice in their wizard partner, but familiars rarely had the autonomy to make that choice anyway. At least the Betrothal Trials rules allowed the familiar to veto any suitors she didn't care for. Alise imagined some houses made the choices for their daughters, but she knew that their maman had coached Nic and they'd gone through the applicants exhaustively. The process had given Nic a small bit of control over her fate, allowing her to choose the houses where she'd be likely to become the lady of the house, if only via her wizard. It was far better than many of the alternatives.

But it worried Alise that Brinda was asking *her*, in particular, given this looming future. There could be only one reason why. "I can't help you escape," Alise said, lowering her voice furtively even though no one could overhear. "I understand why you're asking, but I'm on probation here and if I step out of line, even the smallest amount, I'll be expelled and never graduate."

Brinda's increasingly puzzled frown cleared. "Oh! You think because of Han and Iliana? That I want to run away, too?" She laughed with bizarre heartiness, given the topic.

Alise's head spun and she resisted putting fingers on her throbbing temples. "You don't?" she asked. It was obviously a rhetorical question at this point, but she needed Brinda to get to the point.

"Why in the name of House Chur would I want *that?*" Brinda asked with earnest scorn. "Han and Iliana… They were *bad* familiars. Disobedient. Thinking they'd fallen in love with each other, defying their families. Breaking the *law.*" She shook her head, the picture of disappointment. "And now they'll miss out on *real* love, a true, deeply bonded partnership with a wizard. It's sad, really. Someday, they will come to their senses, but no wizard will have them then. They'll live out their lives alone and miserable, begging for someone, anyone to bleed off their magic." She nodded at Alise, inviting her to agree.

Dumbly, Alise nodded, figuring that would be the most likely path to her escape from this excruciating conversation. Jadren El-Adrel loved to make withering remarks about the group insanity at House Phel, the wrong-headed idealism that communicated itself like a disease, infecting everyone it touched. He'd even cheerfully agree that he'd caught it, too, with no hope of cure.

In that moment, Alise realized that she'd been so thoroughly inoculated with Phel thinking that she'd forgotten how completely most Convocation citizens believed in the current system. Brinda displayed all the glowing fervor of the faithful— and of someone who had no idea what the reality would be like. Given that, however, Alise didn't at all understand why Brinda wasn't heaping some of that scorn on her, as well, the person without whom Han and Iliana could never have escaped. There was no way she wanted to hear that answer though.

"I *can't wait* to meet my wizard master," Brinda went on, losing her nervousness in her enthusiastic gushing and saving Alise from having to think up a response. "My parents have selected twelve suitors for me, all from the *best* families and houses. I have excellent MP scores and my physical health is perfect, along with my *fertility*." She confided that last in a whisper.

"I still don't understand what you want from me," Alise said, some of her revulsion leaking into her tone, dimming a bit of Brinda's glow. "Forgive me," she added. "I'm tired and hungry."

"No, no, Wizard Alise," Brinda rushed to say. "I should apologize! Here I am taking up your precious time with my stupid nonsense." She laughed self-consciously, flushing, and Alise abruptly itched to slap the family that had taught their daughter to think so little of herself.

"It's fine," Alise said gently, trying to be encouraging. "*You're* fine. How can I help you?"

Brinda brightened again. "Your sister, Nic. She conceived in just the fourth month of her Betrothal Trials. How did she do it?"

Alise found herself blinking as she attempted to assimilate the question. Surely Brinda knew the mechanics involved. The academy strongly discouraged romances and sex among students. Iliana and Han's love affair perfectly illustrated why such student liaisons disrupted everyone and everything. Even though wizards had considerably more latitude in choosing their fates, very few academy graduates ended up in love matches. The Convocation perpetuated itself by breeding magic to magic and partnering the most powerful with each other. Sentimentality didn't enter into the picture. But none of them were ignorant of the realities of life.

"Ah," Alise stammered, stalling. "I'm not sure what you mean. The usual way?"

Brinda giggled, high-pitched, full of nerves again. "I know *that*! I mean, would you ask her for me? I don't want to spend a year or more waiting to click with the right wizard. The Betrothal Trials chamber at House Chur is underground and *ugh*." She wrinkled her nose prettily. "I've heard talk that Nic tipped the balance to land Lord Phel, if you know what I mean." She laid her finger alongside her nose and winked.

"How could she have done that?" Alise asked, fully bewildered.

"There are ways," Brinda said, nodding earnestly. "I've heard there are."

"I don't know what." Alise truly didn't. Also, Nic had run from Gabriel when she found out that he would be the one.

She hadn't wanted him to begin with.

"The Fascination," Brinda breathed. "I've heard Nic felt it right away with Lord Phel. Is it true?"

Reluctantly, Alise nodded. Nic openly talked about how the Fascination had hit her hard and fast as soon as Gabriel walked into her tower chamber. Though the academy professors were divided on the topic—and Nic herself hadn't believed in it—the Fascination persisted as a subject of great interest among students. The familiar Lyndella supposedly felt the Fascination for the wizard Sylus, making her ultimately unable to resist his allure, much as she and her family fought the match. Familiars supposedly Fascinated by their wizards gave themselves to the bonding with utter surrender. Come to think of it, Alise had heard speculation that Fascination and fertility were intertwined. Which sounded like more romantic nonsense to her.

At Alise's confirming nod, Brinda squealed and clapped her hands together. "How did she do it?"

"I don't think she did?" Alise answered, her confusion tipping it into a question.

"Would you ask? I've heard the Fascination can be induced."

Brinda seemed to have "heard" a great deal. "Where could you have heard that? It doesn't sound likely at all."

"People talk." Brinda shrugged. "I'm prepared to siphon my magic to you. As much as you want, until graduation, if you'll just ask her for me."

Alise dearly wanted to suggest that Brinda ask Nic herself, but of course the young woman would feel she couldn't do that. She'd been terrified to approach Alise, a fellow student. No way would she write to the lady of a high house—however probationary the status of House Phel—to ask such impertinent and potentially dangerous questions.

"I'll ask," Alise conceded, mostly because she figured agreeing would end the conversation sooner. Brinda rewarded her with a squeal of joy, lurching as if she wanted to hug Alise, but fortunately remembering herself. "But I don't need your magic."

Brinda frowned. "With all due respect, Wizard Alise, you're very low on magic. And something is draining you. Instead of regenerating your native magic, you've lost more just as we've sat here."

Alise felt her jaw slacken in surprise, though she managed to keep her mouth from falling open.

"I'm very good at my job," Brinda assured her, with rare confidence. "I've paid very close attention in my Care and Feeding of Wizards classes, plus my professors say I have a natural talent for assessing magic reserves. I plan to be the very best Familiar I can be for my wizard master, so giving you magic will be excellent practice for me. And you must know, Wizard Alise, that fire and sun magic is the universal donor. You can use it for anything!"

"All the same, that's not necessary. I'm simply heavily involved in a few intensive projects. And I need to eat," Alise said meaningfully. Then, given Brinda's reference to her classes in the Care and Feeding of Wizards, which were not their official names any more than Bossing the Bodiless was, she added, "at the dining hall."

"I don't presume to know the arcane business of wizards," Brinda replied, almost primly, "but I'm certain your projects are vitally important. You need magic for that. And at House Chur we are not ingrates. I cannot accept your help without giving in return. Please allow me to siphon my magic to you. And then you can eat a hearty meal and rest."

Feeling neatly cornered into doing two things she didn't want to do, Alise surrendered to the inevitable. Besides, her magic reserves had fallen low enough that a headache threatened to split her skull and she felt lightheaded. If she ran into Cillian—and he'd no doubt look for her at dinner—he'd cart her off to the infirmary and she wouldn't be able to fight him on it.

"Fine," she said on a sigh, then realized how ungracious she sounded. "That is, thank you, Familiar Brinda. I would be grateful."

Brinda gave her a funny look, because apparently wizards didn't thank Familiars like that, but proffered a hand, taking a deep breath and closing her eyes. "I'm concentrating on opening a channel to you, Wizard," she said in a quiet voice, "but do let me know if it needs adjusting. I'm committed to excellence in my practice."

Alise wrapped her fingers around Brinda's narrow wrist, feeling awkward and somewhat soiled, no matter how many times she'd done exactly this in class with a Familiar who wasn't friend or family. As promised, Brinda's magic positively gushed into her, bright as sunlight and scorching hot, filling the achingly empty spaces within Alise. She immediately felt so much better that she nearly gasped aloud in relief, her headache vanishing and the sense of wellbeing so profound she nearly laughed with the pure joy of it.

Replete in next to no time, she opened her eyes to find Brinda beaming at her. "You look much better," Brinda proclaimed. "I mean, you're always so beautiful, but now even more so. Did you get enough?"

"More than enough," Alise answered, letting go of Brinda's wrist. "You're absolutely right. I feel ten-thousand times better and your magic is wonderfully pure."

"Thank you, Wizard Alise." Brinda visibly preened at the praise. "It's the one thing I do well. That's why I know my wizard master will cherish me and care for me always."

The hallway suddenly teemed with students, a sure sign that the bell for students to eat had rung. Brinda hopped off the window ledge and said something more, which Alise couldn't hear since Brinda had stepped outside of the silencing shield. By the time Alise had banished the spell, Brinda had disappeared into the mass stampede of students heading for the dining hall.

$$\sim 12 \sim$$

C ILLIAN SAT ALONE at dinner with a book open, pretending to read, but surreptitiously scanning the incoming students for Alise's arrival. Faculty and staff ate first, and most of them had already supped and gone, preferring to avoid the cacophony of student diners. It wouldn't do for him to be obviously watching for Alise, given the apparent gossip. Still, as he had the evening before, Cillian lingered over his meal, ostensibly absorbed in his reading, waiting to make sure she ate.

She hadn't shown yet, however, and if she skipped one more meal… Well, he'd make good on his threat and inform the healers. He understood her pride and stubbornness, but he couldn't stand by and let her drive herself into the ground. With a bit of time before he started the night shift in the archives, Cillian kept an eye on the clock, resolved to go directly to the Refoel healers on the way.

But then she walked in.

So absolutely gorgeous that she stopped his heart in his chest and he stared at her, riveted, completely forgetting that he'd meant to be discreet.

Alise glowed, shining with magic, as replete as he'd ever

witnessed—making him realize that he'd never actually seen her with her reservoirs filled. Even when she'd accepted magic from others, she must not have taken as much as she could have, which just figured. Whatever she'd done this time, she'd finally gotten plenty. Her skin, smooth and radiant, beckoned to be caressed, her black eyes snapping with fiery sparks, and Cillian fancied he could scent her magic even from across the room, sun-warmed roses on a hot summer afternoon, redolent and sensual. He caught himself inhaling, perilously close to falling into an erotic reverie. Quickly getting a grip, he glanced self-consciously about to see if he'd been observed—and found Proctor Raya's knowing gaze on him.

Wiping the guilt from his face, he nodded at her, then kept sweeping his gaze around the room, attempting to look thoughtful, as if simply taking a break from his reading before returning his attention to the book without looking at Raya again. After a moment, he slid a peek at Raya from the corner of his eye. She had turned her attention to a group of students, scowling at them, and allowing Cillian to quickly check on Alise.

To his immense relief, she'd piled food on a tray with a semblance of enthusiasm, though she did not need to be drinking that huge mug of coffee this late in the day. Head down, she moved deliberately to an empty table, not bothering to look for spots with any of her friends. Former friends, he mentally corrected, noting that everyone carefully avoided noticing Alise, the social ostracism very near total. Cillian mentally kicked himself for not realizing how isolated Alise had become at Convocation Academy. Granted, he tended to be a loner himself, happy to be ensconced with his books and projects, but he also knew not everyone was like that.

Before she'd helped Han and Iliana escape, Alise had been a social butterfly, one of the reigning royalty of student-wizards with high MP scores, excellent grades, and a high-house pedigree. It was good to see her regain some of her previous radiance and he wondered who'd given her magic. He squelched a niggle of envy that perhaps Alise had a nascent romance with some familiar. He should be happy for her in that case, that she'd be getting both deeply-needed affection and companionship, along with boosting her magic. Still, he wanted it to be him. Not at all reasonable, and yet…

He shook himself out of the reverie and quickly finished his meal. Now that he'd verified Alise's wellbeing, he could move on. He certainly couldn't sit with her anymore, not with Raya and apparently half the academy—or more—watching and speculating. Cillian had never been a figure of interest to anyone before, so it hadn't occurred to him that anyone would pay attention. He also wasn't naturally inclined to gossip about others. He had, however, occasionally envied—that emotion again—the laughing groups of friends, the social elite. He'd been the guy with a few good friends, but never the center of anything. Mostly he'd been fine with that, though in a down moment a wistful, maybe bitter part of him had wished it otherwise.

So, for the first time, he perceived the ugly side of that kind of social admiration. Those bright and shining students worked well as a pack, impervious to all who thought to attack them. But they turned on each other with equal fervor, banishing the wounded and imperfect with ruthless ease.

Alise never saw him, never looked up as he passed out of the dining hall. At least she was eating, he told himself. And she'd gotten magic. So, no need to turn her in to the healers.

Also, he had information for her, plenty sufficient as a peace offering and enticement to visit the archives, and him. He hoped.

ALISE GLARED AT the Ratsiel courier perched on the lintel over the door to her room. An innocuous owl-like creature in Convocation Academy colors, it was exactly the sort of messenger used by faculty to communicate with students. It could have come from any of her professors, but she didn't have to guess who'd sent it: Cillian. How in the dark arts was she supposed to protect him if the man couldn't take a freaking hint?

Resigned to the inevitable—the courier would simply follow her around until she accepted the message—she held up a hand for the ethereal owl to land. It did, making contact with her skin with a tiny buzz of magic. House Ratsiel also wielded spirit magic, summoning and taming entities, shaping them to specifications for their Convocation customers, from tiny to enormous. The wealthier houses and iconic institutions loved to have their branding reflected by the couriers they used. The academy owl deposited a small scroll into her palm and, objective achieved, flitted away.

Unlocking her door, Alise stepped inside, the scroll folded in her palm. She could decline to open it, but that delaying tactic would go only so far. First, however, she scanned the room for any spies that might have arrived since her scouring efforts. Happily, the measures she'd taken to seal the room against further intrusion seemed to have worked. Using a measure of her newly acquired reserves, she strengthened the wards she'd placed to keep any new spies away, then triggered the seal on the courier's missive. It would register that she'd received it, but oh well.

As expected, Cillian had sent it, asking her to meet him in the archives that night to discuss her project.

Crumpling the parchment into a ball, she hurled it across the room, where it bounced harmlessly off the wall and fluttered to the floor. Dark arts take that wizard! A complex emotion balled up within her, comprised of equal parts frustration, desperation, affection, and hatred. She didn't hate Cillian—she knew that—but she hated for him to be involved, hated his stubborn refusal to be put off. And she hated herself for being unable to do anything about it. She would not go running to his beck and call, however. Definitely not right away. She had more important things to do, after all. Like figure out how to stabilize her bottle of teeming spirits so they wouldn't drain her to the nubbins while she slept, like the night before. And she needed to keep her promise to Brinda Chur and write a letter to Nic, which would take a while, figuring out how to subtly elicit the necessary information. Fortunately Nic had gifted her with a few pre-packaged Ratsiel couriers that would convey a letter home, just as soon as she composed it.

Then there was the mountain of schoolwork, which she had yet to prioritize. She really needed to triage all of that. "I have no time for your games, Cillian," she muttered to herself.

Much as she'd love to avoid him altogether, she couldn't refuse the summons any more than she could have declined receiving it in the first place. Like a Ratsiel courier, Cillian would metaphorically follow her about, hovering over her shoulder, pinging her attention—and drawing notice. If Cillian thought Alise hadn't noticed him in the dining hall, he was sorely mistaken. Lingering over his meal while pretending to read. He was about as subtle as a violet rhinoceros.

The more she fumed about it, the hotter her annoyance boiled, until it became abundantly clear that she would have no attention for anything else until she dispensed with the problem of Cillian. This time, however, she'd be smarter about not flaunting her conversation with Cillian for Gordon Hanneil to take note.

Taking a page from Courtney Ariel's playbook, Alise opted for disguising her movements. Yes, she'd always viewed the way some Elal wizards used spirits to hide themselves from sight as a vain party trick, but it could work to her advantage. She could also learn from the enemies of House Phel—which probably included House Elal—and how they'd hidden the encroaching army from detection until Phel was surrounded. That bit of subterfuge had very nearly won the war before it even began.

Grateful for the infusion of Brinda's magic, which was as

bright and potent as advertised, Alise prepared to summon an entity of sufficient nature to cloak herself with. Then thought again. Feeling particularly clever, instead of summoning a new spirit, Alise repurposed one of her throng of bottled entities. If they were going to be draining her magic, they might as well be useful while doing it. It took a bit of finagling to extract a couple of the types she wanted from the tangle of seething spirits demanding release, but she managed without too much difficulty. In fact, she performed the intricate balancing act more easily than the night before. Nothing like having a sufficient reserve of magic to get the job done.

Also, she observed wryly to herself, there could be something to Professor Cixin's concept of diligent practice. Go figure. Not that she'd ever been a lax student—certainly nothing like Nander-level slacking—but she'd also always had enough talent to skate by. Only now, forced to dig deep in order to catch up and due to enemies popping threats out of the woodwork, did she discover that she could improve, and quite rapidly, when she cared enough.

In the back of her mind, a cautionary voice warned her about getting *too* proficient. *Remember what you did,* the insidious whisper echoed in the dark places. *You murdered your own maman. Look at your papa. He started the destruction that eroded her mental and physical health, but you finished it. You're even worse than he is.*

The harsh truth of that upset her enough that Alise nearly bobbled the job of extracting the spirits she wanted from the bottle—which would release them all and she'd have to start over with tethering and trapping them again, all the more difficult because they knew what lay in store for them. The entities didn't exactly think, but they weren't stupid either. They learned from experience, especially unpleasant ones. Avoidance of bad situations didn't take a lot of intelligence.

In fact, Alise felt a little bad sealing the bottle against the trapped spirits, all trying so hard to escape. She had to find a real solution to her temporary storage bottle. There had to be something between having the bound entities free to spy on her and keeping them in a miserable purgatory.

For the moment, however, with her captives safely constrained again, Alise focused on the two entities she'd extracted. They'd report back on her excursion to the archives, but that would come as no surprise to their handlers. Alise had spent weeks already going to the archives nightly. Tonight's subterfuge was entirely to keep Gordon Hanneil from knowing her movements. If she played this correctly, this would be her last time having anything but the most distant interactions with Cillian.

Ignoring the pang that prospect gave her, Alise shrouded herself in the obscuring cloak of the large, diffuse spirits. Checking her reflection in the mirror, she confirmed that she'd vanished from ordinary eyesight. Her wizard senses easily penetrated the deception, but perceiving incorporeal entities obviously fell squarely in her greatest expertise. Other wizards might sense something unusual, but only if she drew their attention.

Alise had no intention of doing anything to attract scrutiny. Unlocking her door, she stretched her senses to confirm that the hall was empty. The academy didn't have a lights out rule for the older students, but they did strictly enforce quiet hours, which meant no lingering in public spaces. If you were going to be up late, you'd best be somewhere quiet doing legitimate work. The night proctors saw to that.

As she skimmed down the hall, making sure to walk softly and silently—the spirits muffled sound, but didn't silence and it took a lot of concentration to maintain a silencing shield on the move—she passed a proctor staring into space, stationed at the entrance to the wing to keep non-wizard students out. *Too bad they don't keep malevolent proctors out,* Alise thought acidly. The good news was that the bored proctor never even blinked as Alise passed.

So far, so good. She passed students, proctors, and the occasional faculty member on her way to the archives, all of them blissfully unaware of her presence. It was incredibly restful. Why didn't she think of this a long time ago? *Because you never before existed at this level of crushing paranoia,* she reminded herself. *Oh, right.*

She made it to the archives without incident, feeling quite pleased with herself, all things given. Approaching the reference desk where Cillian worked the night shift, she realized the major flaw in her plan. How to notify him of her presence? Alise pondered the problem as she watched him assist a young, blonde uncat. Cillian had erected a courtesy silencing shield, but Alise could guess at the conversation from the visuals. He seriously explained something to the girl, probably about sixteen years old, who giggled and nervously twirled her hair around her finger. Suspicious, Alise noted two of the student's friends hovering a short distance away, avidly observing. Ah, so that was the way of it.

Alise rolled her eyes, since no one could see her, and settled in to observe the amateur flirtation underway. Cillian, naturally, remained utterly oblivious to the blonde's posturing, even when she bent over his shoulder, frowning prettily, to read whatever he pointed to. She turned her head to ask him a question, her face much too close to his and Cillian replied without looking at her. Typical Cillian. If the girl lived in a book, he might notice her, but no chance otherwise. Why was she interested anyway? He was much too old for her.

Not so much intrigued as bored with waiting, Alise sidled closer to the spectating friends, shamelessly eavesdropping on their conversation. They whispered to each other quite audibly.

"Dark arts, he is *so cute!*" the first quietly squealed.

"I can't believe Treena won the draw," the other pouted. "Wizard Harahel has barely looked at her."

"He's so serious, so thoughtful. I would love to be his familiar."

"Yes, he'd be a lovely wizard-master. Such a cinnamon roll."

That raised Alise's brows. Cillian baked cinnamon rolls for these students? Not that he wasn't free to distribute his baked goods to all and sundry, and probably did, but she'd somehow thought she was special.

"What do you mean?"

"You know, all sweet and soft and warm on the inside. The perfect man."

The two sighed in dreamy unison.

Sweet? Thought Alise. *The guy was bossy and annoyingly stubborn.*

"He has the best mouth," one of the pair said in a reverent hush. "So pretty."

"Like an angel. I bet he kisses like one. Or like a demon!"

"And those black curls. What wouldn't I give to run my fingers through them?"

"They're not black—they're more like dark chocolate. Those ringlets are just long enough to for you to get a good grip and hold him down while he devours you like one of his pastries," the other agreed, both breaking into a spate of giggles.

Alise blushed furiously, face hot as she belatedly got their meaning. She knew about sex, naturally, even the… ah, variations, the girls giggled over. But Maman had raised her to be a lady. Alise had never been so *ribald* with friends in discussing potential bed partners. Although, the more she thought about it, the more Alise could see that she'd never really had that many friends, at least not to giggle over romance with, even before she became a social pariah. And how pitiful was that?

She grew impatient with Treena's extended flirtation attempt, and with listening to Treena's friends extoll Cillian's many virtues—observable and fantasized. Cillian showed no sign of flagging, clearly re-explaining the same concepts to Treena. Alise nearly threw up her hands in frustration when another two students queued up, waiting their turns. At this rate, she would be there all night.

At least the new arrivals made Treena give up her personal

siege. With a batting of eyes and a last, longing glance that was utterly lost on the oblivious Cillian, she dragged herself away, then fell into a gleeful analysis with her friends. Alise continued to wait, shifting from foot to foot, unable to stop thinking about the many admiring and frequently salacious comments the students had made about the quiet archivist.

He did have soulful eyes, full of compassionate intelligence, with a fringe of black lashes that softened the sharper lines of his face. "Cheekbones to cut glass," the girls had said, and a "bow of a mouth" in a "heart-shaped face." Alise couldn't help considering their descriptors. She supposed all that was true, though never how she would have described him. It was his kindness that shone through for her, that innate ability to look for the best in people. Even in her, she who least deserved it.

Cillian finished with the final student and looked directly at Alise. "That's a long time to lurk," he commented, startling her. Before she could think up a reply—she really hadn't thought this part out—he added. "I've got a private place for us to talk."

Setting out a sign next to a spelled Ratsiel courier, encouraging patrons to send it to fetch him if they needed immediate assistance, Cillian came around the desk and began walking briskly to some remote corner. With no other recourse, Alise followed, firming her resolve. No matter where he led her, they would finish this and be done.

They ended up in an obscure nook of the library Alise had never seen. Judging by the stale feeling of the corner, neither had anyone else. A desk piled high with binders sat to one side and Cillian confidently moved to them. "You can drop the spirit cloak," he told her. "No one will see us here."

Feeling a bit foolish, she let the entities float up to hover near the ceiling. "How did you know I was there?" she demanded.

"I smelled your magic," he said, tapping the side of his nose with a wry, half-smile. "I know it's not really a scent, but that, of course, is the synesthesia via which most of us experience the magic of others."

"Synesthesia?" she echoed.

"Essentially a kind of sensory crossover, though that doesn't apply perfectly when one is sensing the presence of magic." He sorted the binders, continuing in a professorial tone. "Our physical senses didn't evolve to detect and interpret magic, but our sensitivity to magic still alerts us to its presence and our brains decode it as something that is standard sensory information. Olfaction, being the oldest sense, is the most common synesthesia, but a significant portion of wizards and familiars experience the presence of magic as a visual field, or even somatosensory. Auditory is the rarest, for unknown reasons. Anyway…" He cleared his throat. "I smelled your magic the moment you walked into the library." He inhaled deeply, smile fully blooming. "Roses and hot sunshine."

So freaking charming. Alise glared at him in impotent annoyance. "Brinda Chur gave me some magic. That's the hot part you sense. Or smell." Immediately she regretted telling him that. She'd wanted to combat his sentimentality, not confide sensitive information.

"Ah, I wondered who did that. Very nice of her." His

pleased expression faded as he searched her face. "Or was it?"

Alise waved that off, not at all about to explain. She couldn't quite predict what he'd make of the bargain, but she didn't want to hear his opinion, either way. "Irrelevant."

He nodded slowly, unconvinced, studying her—then pointed to the hovering entities. "Impressive trick, with the cloaking. I didn't know you could do that."

"Not terribly effective if any wizard can smell or see my magic anyway," she noted. How did the others handle that aspect?

"Probably not just any wizard," he reassured her, leaning a hip on the corner of the desk and crossing his arms, gentle black eyes earnest. "I'm attuned to you. That is..." He uncrossed his arms and rubbed his palms on his thighs, gaze shifting away. "From being around you. Nothing untoward. And Nic!" He clapped his hands together and joined them. "Your magic feels the same. I just, ah, happened to notice it at House Phel. Interesting phenomenon, really, that Elal magic is so distinctive. Lord Phel's is too, for that matter. And House Chur—you may have noticed, with Brinda—they have a distinctive scent/feel to their magic. Not every house does. That would be an interesting study. Of course, many houses are built around a particular business area that requires wizards and familiars of a variety of magic specialties, so they wouldn't have a homogenous feel to the magic. Still, most houses also have a central familial line, sometimes maintained by very tight inbreeding, so they might be more likely to have a distinctive magical vibration that translates as a consistent scent or visual via synesthesia. Not to say that House Elal is inbred! I'm simply observing that—" He broke off with a wince. "I'm simply babbling, is what I'm doing. I apologize."

Alise, bemused, found herself relaxing, her unfounded irritation with him dispersing like an unbound spirit. "It is an interesting question," she allowed. "I didn't know about the synesthesia, but for me it's visual and sometimes tactile, depending."

His smile bloomed. "Fascinating stuff. But that's all beside the point. How *are* you?"

His assessing, penetrating stare stirred her annoyance again. "I'm fine. You don't need to worry about me, Cillian."

"And yet you travel under a cloaking illusion. We're alone here. No one ever bothers me in this little corner, so you're safe—but don't try to tell me you're not afraid."

"I'm not *trying* to tell you anything," she snapped, abruptly over the edge again. "I have no reason to be afraid, of anyone. I'm only being discreet. There are rumors about us, if you aren't aware." She hadn't really meant to say anything about that, either. Cillian's tendency to blurt out every thought that crossed his mind was rubbing off on her.

"I'm surprised you care about idle speculation," he said quietly. Not contradicting her, she noticed. "People love to imagine things. No one with any sense believes there is anything going on between us, other than a collegial relationship. A mentor/mentee association. Totally aboveboard. You may send anyone who questions that to me and I will set them straight."

He looked so uncharacteristically stern, sounded so impassive, that Alise definitely doubted what Gordon Hanneil had said. Cillian was obviously *not* in love with her. She had offended his sense of order and academic compliance by trying to discontinue the project with him. She'd confused her own murky feelings about him with… Well, with whatever.

"Understood," she replied in an equally neutral tone. "And I don't. Care, that is. I just thought to be discreet."

"Ah," he said, clearly not believing her. "Well, I asked you to see me tonight because I have some information for you about Gordon Hanneil."

The spinning of the world came to halt so abrupt, Alise nearly staggered, the blood palpably draining from her face, making her cold all over. "Uh, ah…" she stammered, her tongue thick. "Who?"

The look he gave her was all disappointed supervisor. "Let's have honesty between us, please. I found out the name of the proctor who frightened you yesterday, the one who'd disguised himself from me. I discovered something else, too. Gordon Hanneil isn't his real name."

~ 13 ~

ALISE COULDN'T BREATHE. Her ribs closed in hard around her heart, sending it thumping frantically, and she couldn't seem to force them to expand to draw in air. Sparkling black stars shot in around the corners of her vision and the world lurched into spinning motion again. No that was the room, twirling like a top around her. Fast. Too fast. The black stars burst and dragged her under.

She blinked her eyes open right away.

Or was it right away?

Somehow she'd ended up on the floor, the cavernous ceiling of the archives looming above. The entities she'd harnessed had vanished. Well, fuck.

"Alise," Cillian said, squeezing her hands. "Can you hear me?"

"Of course I can hear you. I'm not deaf." She pushed to sit up.

"Don't move just yet. Are you dizzy still?"

"Why would I be dizzy?" Come to think of it, she was kind of muzzy headed. Probably the power of suggestion. But how had she ended up on the floor? She extracted her hands from his and levered up. She decided against standing just yet.

"Because you fainted."

"Don't be absurd." Her voice sounded just like her maman. "I've never fainted in my life."

"Well now you have," he informed her. "Did you hit your head? I couldn't catch you in time. I'll summon a healer."

"No!" She couldn't reel back the too-strident denial, but she could make an effort to be rational and stop any impetuous actions on Cillian's part. "It's not necessary," she added with a weak smile. "People faint, right? First time for everything."

Cillian, who'd been kneeling beside her, plopped his butt down and rubbed a hand across his forehead. "Alise, this has got to stop."

"What has to stop?" she demanded. "If you mean the independent study, I've been trying to stop it. You're the one who—"

"I don't mean the cursed independent study and you know it!" he fired back, with eyes blazing, no sign of the mild-mannered librarian about him. "You're running yourself into the ground. Exhausted, overworked, underfed, and so terrified of this Gordon Hanneil that you literally collapsed at my feet at the mere mention of his name."

The bones of her skull throbbed and she dropped her face into her hands, despair welling up to sting her eyes. She'd utterly failed to do a very simple thing. All she'd had to do was keep her head down and her mouth shut. Essentially avoid doing something wrong, and she'd screwed that up within only a couple of days. And now both of them would pay the price.

"Alise, Sweetheart." Cillian gently pried her hands from

her face. "I'm sorry. That was harsh of me. I didn't mean to make you cry."

"I'm not," she said, aware of the lie as she spoke it, the taste of salt tears on her dry lips.

"You're going to tell me what this Gordon Hanneil did to you," he said, holding her by the wrists, his expression fierce. "And then we're going to deal with this situation."

"Cillian, please," she begged. "You have to stay out of this. It's not safe for you. You're already in danger and you have to let me go."

He cocked his head, as if he hadn't quite heard her correctly. "You're terrified to the point of fainting because of whatever this creep said or did to you and you're worried about me?"

She bit her lip against saying anything more, pleading with her eyes for him to understand, to let this go. "You have to walk away," she whispered urgently. "This isn't your fight."

"You're a real piece of work," he said slowly. "You know that?"

Alise flinched, unable to meet his accusing stare. She knew it. And she didn't blame him for hating her. Though it gave her a pang to realize she'd dealt the killing blow to whatever friendship they'd begun. Still, he didn't release her wrists, tightening his grip when she feebly tugged away.

"Alise Phel," Cillian said with the deliberation of someone speaking a vow, "I'm not going anywhere. I'm certainly not abandoning you to this… situation, whatever it is. I might be only a librarian-wizard, but—"

Her gaze flew up to his. "I never meant it that way! I'm

only trying to protect you."

His tight face softened, along with his grip on her wrists, and he stroked his thumbs over the backs of her hands. "I appreciate that. It means a great deal to me that you feel that way. Is it then so difficult to understand that I have the same desire to protect you?"

She had no words, gazing at him helplessly, thinking she couldn't let him do this, but also how some agonized part of her deep inside leapt in aching need. If only he *could* protect her. "I don't know how you can," she whispered. "Not because you're a librarian," she added hastily, unwilling to hurt him again, "but because… You just don't know."

"With House Hanneil involved, I have an idea," he replied grimly. "But whatever it is, you're not handling this by yourself. That only makes things harder and worse. You're not alone in this, Alise. There is no way I'm walking away to leave you to deal with the problem on your own. I hope I've made myself clear."

This firm, determined Cillian was new. Or was he? He'd certainly pushed her into eating and refilling her magic the first time they met, like a velvet-covered elemental carriage rolling over her protests. "I just don't know what—"

He laid a finger over her lips to stop her words. "We'll figure it out," he insisted softly. "Just let me help. Let me prove I can take care of myself—and of you."

Mute, feeling dizzy again, for a different reason, she nodded. The movement dragged his finger along her lips, and his gaze dropped to her mouth. Feathering his fingers over her cheek, he leaned in, as if drawn by an invisible string, hovering there for an endless moment.

She should pull back.

She didn't want to.

His lips breathed over hers, a barely there caress that nevertheless tingled with bright sparks of delight. The cold, hungry, empty places inside her seemed to thaw, receiving the kiss, opening to him.

With an incoherent sound of profound need, she moved into the kiss, deepening it hungrily. Cillian met her more than halfway, running his hands into her hair and cupping her head, holding her while he returned the kiss, feeding and nibbling on her lips as if they tasted delicious. Hesitant at first, she lifted her hands to his black curls that the girls had so rhapsodized about, finding them as deliciously silky as they'd speculated. He hummed deep in his throat as she touched him, encouraging her, and she found they'd both risen to their knees, all the better to press together, clinging to each other, kisses almost frantic. Alise had never felt anything like this, a wildness rising in her demanding to be freed, craving more and more and more.

Cillian broke the kiss, holding onto her still, but staring at her, his expression distraught. "We can't do this," he whispered, sounding stunned. "*I* can't do this. I apologize. I shouldn't have. This can't have happened."

A giggle welled up in Alise, entirely inappropriate given his chagrined horror. "It did happen, though," she confided. And she was… happy?

"But I—I promised," he stammered. Seeming to realize he still clutched her close, he let her go suddenly enough that she nearly fell. Which, naturally, meant he reached out to steady her—and then yanked away his hands again, holding them out a short distance from her, like they might soil her if he got them too close. "What have I done?" he cried.

"Oh, Cillian," she said on a laugh. "It was a kiss. Nothing more."

"How can you laugh? This is a disaster."

No, the disaster had been everything else, one terrible event piled upon the next, until the accumulated pressure became crushing. This was the one good thing that had happened in… certainly longer than she could remember, maybe the best thing to ever happen to her. She patted his cheek and pressed a light kiss to his parted lips, a kiss he was still too stunned to return. "I liked the kiss," she told him, surprising herself by admitting it. And not above taking the distraction to extract a bit of reprieve from the uncomfortable interrogation. "Kiss me again," she invited.

CILLIAN'S HEAD WHIRLED, his body throbbing with unaccustomed desire. And there was Alise, acting like everything was fine. No, more than fine: her depthless, sharp black eyes sparkled with lively happiness, a very real smile curving her perfect lips, plump and shining from their kiss. Their kiss. He'd *kissed* Alise Phel. His younger self, the bookish, timid boy who'd regarded wizards like those of House Elal with considerable awe, fluttered in delighted surprise. His current self, the one who knew much better and should have been *thinking*, cringed in different, but equally strong disbelief.

What in the dark arts had come over him?

Groaning, he pulled at his hair, remembering how sweet her slim, delicate fingers had felt against his scalp, both soothing and stimulating. He wanted it again. And again. He'd uncorked a bottle that could never be sealed the same way. Speaking of bottles, though…

"Is that a bottle in your pants pocket?" he asked, gesturing vaguely in that direction and heroically attempting to banish the image of her slim thighs beneath the baggy material. As soon as he said it, he realized the question echoed a common bawdy joke. Alise's raised brows indicated she thought so, too. "I mean, I felt it when, we, ah—" He coughed into his fist, then deciding they were much too close, pushed to his feet and gazed beseechingly at the stack of information he'd prepared for her. That was the real and very pressing reason they were alone together.

"A bottle, yes." Alise stood up also, placing a proprietary hand on that pocket. "It's nothing."

That was a lie—and at least, it woke him to his senses. He rounded on her, planting fists on hips. He'd had flat enough. Yes, he'd made a massive mistake, but there was nothing to be done about it now. And it didn't change the bald truth that Alise had been hiding all sorts of unpleasantness—from him and from everyone else—and he'd resolved to put an end to it. For her own fucking good.

"No more lies," he told her. "No more prevarications, or

deliberate omissions, or deflections to conceal the truth."

She glared at him, cheeks flushed. "You don't tell me what—"

"Who else is there?" he demanded. "Who is taking care of you while you deal with *this*?" He stabbed a finger at the files he'd uncovered regarding the wizard masquerading as Gordon Hanneil.

Her gaze flicked to the stack of paper and away again, face tightening with such real fear that his heart broke for her. "Who else can you trust?" he asked, more gently. "Because you can trust me."

"I don't want you hurt." She shook her head as she spoke.

"Good, because I don't want to be hurt, and now you will understand how I feel."

"It's not that simple."

"Let's start with the bottle. If it's nothing, then you can tell me why you're carrying it in your pocket."

She sighed deeply, but complied, digging it out and handing it to him. "See? A basic grooming imp bottle."

"And you're carrying it around in case you have a grooming emergency?" Many students did, he knew, but they favored the smaller, portable ones. Not the heavy desktop variety.

Rolling her eyes at him, she reached for it, but he moved it away, giving her a pointed look. "I stuffed it with spirits," she said, as if that explained anything. "And it requires my attention to keep them in there, so its easier to have it on me. Proximity reduces the magic drain. May I have it back now?" She held out an imperious hand and he placed the bottle in it.

He wasn't done with this, though. Not by a league. Watching her tuck the bottle back in her pocket, he triaged his thoughts on the subject, deciding which to lead with. "Why," he inquired, as politely as he could manage, "did you stuff a grooming imp bottle with a collection of spirits?" Maybe she had a good reason. He seriously doubted it, but he definitely wanted to hear this one.

She flicked him a glance, buttoning the pocket. "I didn't want to be spied on, so I gathered all the spying entities in my room, then I had to put them somewhere."

He held onto his temper by a thin thread. "I know you're capable of banishing them."

"Yes, but then the wizards I stole them from would know I did it," she replied with impatience, as if that reasoning made any sense. "Though now I'm fucked because I used two of them for the cloaking on the way here and lost my hold on them when I… blanked out for a moment there."

Not admitting that she'd fainted, he noted. Stubborn woman. "What will the repercussions be?"

"I don't know," she admitted darkly. "I suppose I'll find out."

"Then let the rest go," he suggested. "The damage is done."

She put a possessive hand over the pocket holding the bottle. "I won't. I have my reasons."

"Even though it's harmful to you?"

"Even so." She stopped short of pouting, but the obstinate lift of her chin told him her pride was involved. Alise wasn't behaving rationally, that much was abundantly clear.

Cillian chose his words carefully. "I feel like this is not a long-term solution, if it's draining your magic."

"I know that." She held up a hand in tacit apology for snapping at him. "I need to figure out what to do. I just haven't had time. I thought about asking Professor Cixin, but how would I explain why this was necessary?"

He thought that question should be her first clue that she wasn't thinking clearly, but he restrained that observation. "Let me do the research for you," he offered instead. "I bet I can find something in the archives, in the records off-limits to students." He'd have to go carefully, to avoid questions from his supervisors, but he could always spin a tale about a personal research project tangential to the information he truly needed. He could pull that off. Nothing about it was illegal, so it wouldn't be anything like what had happened with Szarina.

The look of gratitude Alise gave him made it all worthwhile. "That would be amazing. Thank you."

Then she stepped up and kissed him lightly, cupping his cheek and giving him a radiant smile, and the conflicting emotions nearly wrenched him apart. He wanted nothing more than to pull her close and kiss her senseless. He also couldn't allow this to continue. Taking his willful romantic longing firmly in hand and shoving it behind a locked door, he pursued the most important course of conversation and dumped metaphorical ice water on the situation. "Now, tell me about Gordon Hanneil and what he did to hurt you."

~ 14 ~

A LISE HAD THOUGHT she'd dodged that arrow, but found it lodged firmly in her heart, piercing it through. "I can't," she told Cillian, aware she sounded more pleading than firm.

Cillian's face hardened and he smacked his hand down on his files as if she'd tried to peek and he wouldn't let her until she gave in. Well, he was wrong. She didn't *want* to know any more about Gordon Hanneil or whoever he really was. "Enough, Alise!" he nearly barked at her. "Don't be a fool. Let me help you."

She set her teeth. "Don't call me a fool," she warned him.

"Then don't be one," he fired back. "From what I've discovered, this is no game." He tapped the stack of documents meaningfully. "This guy is bad news. Not someone to take lightly."

She probably deserved a medal for not kicking Cillian for explaining the obvious to her.

"I know," she ground out, dancing around the margins of the mental compulsion, trying very hard not to think about Gordon, though a headache already throbbed around the periphery, like the oppressive feel of a storm about to break. She didn't know what would happen if she tried to actually speak of Gordon instead of just thinking about it. Would she just be unable to or would something worse happen. An even more distressing possibility—would Hanneil be somehow alerted and come find them?

She shuddered at that horrifying prospect. Unfortunately, the keen-eyed Cillian picked up on that.

"Are you cold?" He set hands on her arms, bared by her short-sleeved top and rubbed them briskly. Then stopped. "No. You're shaking from fear, not cold. What did he threaten you with?"

Gordon's vile threats rushed back in full force and Alise gazed into Cillian's lovely, concerned face, wishing she could speak past the lump in her throat. Maybe if she said it fast? The compulsion flexed, a headache spearing from temple to temple. Well, that answered that. She pressed her hands to the sides of her head, wildly trying to think of something, anything else. Focusing on Cillian, that kiss, how he was everything good and kind and all Gordon Hanneil was not. "Cillian…" she said, trailing off helplessly.

Understanding dawned across his face, such a brilliant transformation, she understood the metaphor with perfect clarity. "You *can't* say," he breathed, striking his forehead with the heel of his hand.

She released her own breath, not at all sure what this revelation would alter, but glad to have gotten that across to him. Hopefully, as clever as Cillian had shown himself to be, he'd figure out the rest without her needing to assist.

"Your head obviously hurts," Cillian mused, "so I'm going to guess he used psychic magic to lay a compulsion on you.

I'm also guessing you won't see a healer about this? Yeah, you're that predictable," he said to her frantic headshaking. "Don't look so panicked. I won't make you—not until we get to the bottom of this. But I am going to point out that a Refoel wizard with potent psychic magic and training in mental healing can likely remove this compulsion. Ah ha—see? You *didn't* think of that. This is why you need my help."

He tapped her on the nose with gentle affection, looking so pleased with himself that Alise didn't even mind that he'd treated her like a well-behaved puppy. "From what I know of these things," he continued, "which isn't reams, as much of it is ancient history, and obviously still should be as this sort of fuckery is extremely illegal—not that it would matter to *this* guy—it's best if you don't speak at all. Don't attempt to talk or to confirm or deny. I'll be able to read the truth in your expression." His gaze traveled briefly over her face, and he seemed to be about to say something more, then changed his mind.

"All right," he continued, "so, the rest is easy to put together, especially knowing this information." He laid a proprietary hand on the stack of documents. With the thawing sense of relief that Cillian would no longer try to make her speak—she would never tell him of Gordon's worst threats, no matter what—she at last found her curiosity stirring to know what he'd discovered about her tormentor.

Noticing her interest, Cillian nodded and pulled out the lone chair for her to sit. "I won't bore you with my methodology. No, no, don't give me that wide-eyed, innocent face. I know you tolerate my worst foibles in discussing library arcana. It's all right. Sometimes I bore myself." He laughed wryly. "Meet Tarin Tausa." With that declaration, he flipped open a binder emblazoned with the House Tausa crest, to a marked page with a portrait of a younger Gordon—no, Tarin—looking somehow both smug and dissatisfied. Cillian put a hand on her shoulder, squeezing it reassuringly, and Alise realized she'd flinched.

"He is of House Hanneil lineage, a by-blow of a side branch, one that typically hasn't produced high MP-scoring children. I can show you my research verifying that, but it's really not all that relevant except as background to young Tarin's early life. As you can see here, his psychic magic potential scored through the roof even as a toddler."

Cillian ran his finger down a list of repeated testing over the years and Alise marveled at the thoroughness of the records. Was there one in the archives with similar detail about her? There must be, as she'd been tested at House Elal by the in-house Hanneil wizard, and their oracle head, at regular intervals throughout her childhood. In fact, one of her earliest memories was of staring in fascinated horror at the mummi-fied, barely animated and gilded head resting in the decorated tabernacle whispering numbers through its carnelian-inlaid lips. She kind of wanted to see her file and also not.

"As you can imagine," Cillian continued, "the ruling family of House Hanneil plucked Tarin from his parents and raised him with a number of other children of similarly high scores, monitoring them closely. It's possible that Tarin and his cohort were subjected to various attempts to enhance and cultivate their magic."

At her inquiring glance, he grimaced. "I went down a bit of a research rabbit hole there, truth be told, but all knowledge is worth having and the information may come in useful before we're done. Also, it was fairly easy to correlate dates and find other individuals in this cohort who'd been tested at the same time. I can't hurl fireballs or summon spirits, but library magic is excellently useful for collating data and making connections between seemingly disparate sources of data. If you're wondering how I drew the conclusion that House Hanneil experimented with enhancing these children's magical potentials from the way scores fluctuated in predictable ways and how low-scoring children were removed from testing. None of that is really relevant."

"Except that all knowledge is worth having," she murmured.

"Exactly," he replied, clearly pleased. "Anyway, to sum up, Tarin was top of his class, basically the sole survivor of a rather ruthless pruning process that leads me to wonder what else he was taught. He completed the minimal coursework at Convocation Academy, graduated with remarkable haste after manifesting as a wizard—I do wonder what they'd have done with him had he turned out to be a familiar, but I imagine they had a plan to make him useful, regardless—and then disappeared from sight until recently. When he reappeared, he turned up with a falsified record, a new face, and the name Gordon Hanneil. Whereupon he was hired as a Proctor here."

"When?" Alise breathed the question, as if saying it quietly would evade the compulsion.

"The day you and I left for House Harahel," Cillian answered just as quietly, nodding when she glanced up at him, his expression sober. "Thus, the puzzle is easy enough to put together. He obviously does work for House Hanneil, but as a clandestine agent with considerable ability for psychic manipulation, to the point of being able to disguise his presence entirely, at least from a low-level wizard like me. Hanneil mobilized him to stop you from completing the petition to House Harahel and determining what became of the House Phel records. He waited for your return, threatened you to the point of terror—don't bother to argue, it's obvious to me—to stop your investigation and laid on compulsion on you to prevent you from speaking of it.

"Did he also threaten my safety if you didn't play nice? Ah, I see he did." Cillian sighed, then crouched before her where she sat, taking her hands in his, studying them as he stroked his thumbs over the backs of them. "I want to be able to tell you that you shouldn't worry about me, that I can take care of myself, but I'd feel the same way if our positions were reversed and you're a far more powerful wizard than I and much more capable of defending yourself."

She made a noise of protest, the compulsion flexing with painful strength before she even mentally formed the words. "It's true," he insisted, "and I'm at peace with that. I'm happy with who I am. I must apologize to you, however, that this… *person*," he spoke the word with profound distaste, "was able to use my feelings for you as a lever in such a terrible way."

Alise threaded her fingers through his hair, savoring the silky texture, her heart aching for him. *His feelings for her.* Was it true then?

Cillian rubbed his head against her touch, like a cat loving to be petted, then met her gaze with his gentle black one. "I didn't want you to know," he said softly. "I wasn't ever going to tell you. I know it's inappropriate in so many ways and you'll never return my feelings. No, don't try to speak because I can see how it pains you. As soon as we're done here, we go to the healers, no arguments or detours. I can deduce that the thoroughly unprincipled Tarin Hanneil—Actually, we should probably continue to call him 'Gordon,' lest we slip and reveal that we know his true identity. Anyway, he read my mind, didn't he? And then told you of my… strong feelings for you. I'm deeply sorry he burdened you with that and I want you to know—despite my unfortunate lapse in kissing you a bit ago, an incident I promise I shall never repeat—I won't bother you with my nonsense. I'm fully aware of the disparity in our social and magical echelons. I lost my head, it's true, but it won't happen again."

"Are you finished?" Alise asked drily when the river of explanation and declaration finally ran out. "Good," she said when he nodded. "I can speak regarding this, so stop trying to shut me up," she told him pointedly. "I already said I liked the kiss. I don't want your apologies." She didn't know what to make of the paradigm shift in how she regarded Cillian, but things had absolutely changed between them and she wasn't going to pretend otherwise. She'd failed to protect him by staying away. Therefore she'd do it by staying close. "I also don't want your assumptions about, well, any of the things you're assuming. We need to discuss this thing between us and what we're going to do about it."

He looked so shocked and chagrined that she squeezed his hands. "You're right that I didn't think of going to a healer. Let's do that now. Then we can have that conversation." Nudging him away, she stood and withdrew the bottle from her pocket.

"What are you doing?" Cillian looked like he wanted to snatch the bottle from her and smash it.

"I need another spirit to hide me. I can't be seen with you."

He put a hand over hers on the bottle. "Yes, you can. We're not bowing to this extortion any more. I'm calling in someone to cover my shift and going with you. Openly."

They were a pair, jostling to tell the other how it was going to be. It made her smile, which seemed to confuse Cillian. "All right," she said. "Openly it is."

THEY MADE IT to the infirmary without incident, not in small part because midnight had long since expired and the hallways empty of much of anyone. Though Alise kept a careful eye on the swirling shadows, especially the ones that coalesced in quasi-sentient observation of their passage, none produced any more harbingers from high houses.

Maybe that part of the program was over.

A single Refoel healer, wearing his signature deep green robe, greeted them upon arrival, a question on his pleasant, dark and freckled face. His wizard-black eyes, warm with compassion, matched the shade of the darker freckles, his skin a lighter brown. "Ah, some company for me," he said in a deep, melodious voice. He gestured to the empty infirmary. "In my line of work, it's always bad luck to wish for something to happen, and no patients is always a good thing, but the wee hours get lonely. I am Healer Jonathan Refoel. How can I be of service, Archivist Cillian Harahel and Wizard Alise Phel?"

For some reason, it came as no surprise to Alise that Healer Jonathan used her correct house affiliation. Though traditionally neutral, sometimes painfully so, House Refoel had unexpectedly come to the aid of House Phel during the recent attack. The new head of the house, Lord Chaim Refoel, quite obviously and painfully in love with Seliah, had been persuaded that standing back and doing nothing to prevent evil amounted to endorsing it.

Cillian invoked a silencing shield, raising Jonathan's brows. "We have a delicate situation. An unethical Hanneil wizard laid a compulsion on Alise."

Jonathan's brows rose even higher. "I want to say that's not done, but you already mentioned unethical. And it's clear even our discussion of it pains Wizard Alise here. Let me see if I can ease that first. Please sit here." He indicated a comfortable chair, the sort that beckoned one to curl up with a book, and much preferable to the nearby table for physical examinations.

Alise sat, the pain lancing from temple to temple making her vision blur. Cillian moved to her side, taking one of her hands in both of his and giving her an encouraging smile. If Healer Jonathan thought anything untoward about the gesture, he gave no evidence, instead laying soft fingertips unerringly on the exact locations where the compulsive pain anchored to her temples. Pursing his full lips, he hummed thoughtfully. "Yes, I perceive it now. Nasty bit of work this."

"Can you help her?" Cillian asked anxiously.

"Yes, fortunately I'm quite well-versed in healing wounds of psychic origin. That's why they have me on the night shift." He winked reassuringly at Alise. "We are creatures most at home in daylight and so the worst of the monsters and injuries that plague us emerge under cover of night, all the better to frighten us."

Unexpectedly, Alise gulped back a sob, one that had leapt into her chest at the healer's words. Though she hadn't thought she needed Cillian's solicitous hand-holding, she gripped tightly, trying not to writhe under Jonathan's mental probing.

"I know, darling, I know," Jonathan murmured in a soothing chant. "It's painful. But it can't actually hurt you. All bark and no bite in this one. Just hold on a bit longer for me. And... there!" With a sigh of satisfaction, he changed the press of his fingers on her temples to a glide of comfort and seeking. "What's this then?"

"What?" Cillian demanded, earning a quelling look from the Refoel wizard.

"I won't know unless I can concentrate," he answered pointedly.

Flushing, Cillian muttered an apology, squeezing Alise's hand even tighter. The worm of Gordon's initial compulsion slithered through her mind, totally unlike the precision clamp of the silencing-compulsion, the command to go willingly to the slimeball's bed slipped and turned around, giving not pain, but pleasure. She clamped her lips on a moan of need, swallowing it down with ruthless strength. *It's not real,* she told herself.

"No, it's not," Jonathan said softly, gaze locked to hers in sincere reassurance. "This one is more insidious, a concocted emotion tied to a physical need and woven into your true feelings. Thus more difficult to extract. This is not your shame. Allow me in. Trust me to take care of you. It helps if you focus on what you know *is* real."

Closing her eyes, she nodded slightly. She'd felt real desire in Cillian's arms earlier, true and burning need for his body against hers, the stirring delight of his ardent kiss. She wouldn't be fooled by the vile wizard's faked-up version of lust. Not only was it an empty shell with a corrupted core, but even the surface showed cracks.

Gordon Hanneil might understand something of lust, but he clearly knew nothing of real connection to another person. Nothing like she had with Cillian, even if she hadn't begun to fully explore that. Yet. Regardless of the propriety of their connection, the dubious wisdom of their feelings, what she and Cillian shared was potent and real and good.

"Yes, good," Healer Jonathan murmured in an echo of her thoughts. "Keep focusing on that. Perfect."

Probably she should worry that Jonathan likely saw everything about Cillian in her mind, but she couldn't care in that moment because the Refoel wizard also found those vile and webby strands that Gordon had interlaced through her thoughts, plucking them out and discarding them like blood-swollen leeches the people of Meresin pulled off each other after wading through murky bodies of water. The sheer release of each one gone made her keenly aware of how profoundly they'd impacted her even over a few short days.

By the time Healer Jonathan declared himself done, and her mind clean of influence, Alise felt as if she could burst into tears yet again, but from relief this time. Cillian watched her with concern, not having understood Jonathan's cryptic comments interspersing the long silences.

"Food and rest will have you back to rights," Jonathan said. "I've laid in some passive defenses against psychic intrusion that should last against any cursory attempts, but I'm also going to request that Professor Morghana Seraphiel give you emergency instruction to prevent another aggressive attack."

Alise knew of Morghana Seraphiel from all those late nights in the archives. The elderly professor passed most every night at the table unofficially reserved for her, the green-shaded elemental light focused on her rune-covered pages casting an eerie pool of emerald around her. She had the air of one of those people so singularly focused on her work that disturbing the professor's concentration didn't bear even considering. Not to mention the superstitious tales students whispered to one another about the terrible things the dark arts professor could unleash without blinking, simply out of mere irritation.

"Is Professor Seraphiel necessary?" Alise asked, more faint-ly than she'd have liked. "Professor Cixin is already teaching me to—"

"Consider this a prescription," Healer Jonathan interrupted. "I don't need to know details. In truth, it's better that I don't. What I glimpsed in your mind stays between us, protected by healer-patient confidentiality, but I saw enough to know you must take this attack *very* seriously."

He turned a somber look on Cillian, who was frowning at Alise like she'd done something wrong. "You'll address this problem with Provost Uriel?"

"Yes," Cillian answered immediately, saying it loudly and emphatically over Alise's protest. "She has to know about this, Alise. There could be other people affected," he added meaningfully. "We have a responsibility to protect everyone at Convocation Academy."

Glumly, Alise agreed, very much not looking forward to the provost's reaction to Alise being involved in yet another problem.

"You'll have to wait until the day after tomorrow, as it's a rest day," Healer Jonathan continued, jotting down some notes. "No work for you. I want you to actually rest."

"Oh, but I *can't*—" Alise began.

"You can and you will," he interrupted sternly. "I did deep work on you. You won't feel it yet, but what I did will exhaust you as much as a physical surgery would have. I want you to sleep in, sleep all day if you can. I'll give you a tea to make sure of it. You need to stay out of sight, away from everyone, until you can meet with Morghana, and you shouldn't be alone, for several reasons. Do you have someone you can stay with? Your brother, perhaps."

Her laugh came out bitter at the thought of asking Nander

to help her out. He'd be more likely to turn her over to her enemies, and dance a happy jig as he did so. "No."

"Then you'll stay here."

Alise gave the echoing, empty ward an appalled glance. "I'd really rather not."

"It's not exactly peaceful, especially when daylight comes," Healer Jonathan agreed ruefully. "However, you need someone to keep an eye on you in case there are any mental side-effects. And to keep you safe from further attempts at psychic manipulation. You can't be alone."

"She can stay with me in the faculty wing. Alise can have my bed and I'll take the couch," Cillian said, giving her an owlish and impatient glare when she opened her mouth to protest. "You know you're safe with me, right?"

She did know that, so she closed her mouth again. Still, staying in Cillian's small, junior-faculty apartments seemed unwise on an entirely different level. But avoiding this thing between them hadn't worked either so... "All right, thank you."

"Thank you for not arguing further," he returned wryly.

~ 15 ~

ALISE STOOD BACK, nerves in her belly, as Cillian thumbed open the Iblis lock on the outer door to his apartments, then popped the door open and invited Alise to precede him with a sweeping gesture. They hadn't spoken on the short walk from the infirmary. Alise had a very strong sense that Cillian was waiting until they were alone to pursue his many questions for her, now that she was free to answer them.

She probably should have opted for the infirmary.

Wandering to the center of the living area, Alise wrapped her arms around herself and surveyed the small, cluttered room. She'd only been there the one time and it felt like a lifetime ago. It also seemed like very little had changed since then. The teetering piles of books that looked haphazard still covered every surface. Notes, scrolls, pens, and other bits of writing things occupied the interstices. Several shelves contained not books, but numerous small figurines and collectibles.

"I'll brew your tea," Cillian said, setting a tiny fire elemental to heat the teapot. "And warm up something to eat. Then you can go to bed. Are you cold?"

"No?" she answered, puzzled, then realized she probably

looked like it, with her arms nervously wrapped around herself.

"There's a throw there if you do get cold."

Alise followed his pointing finger to the colorful quilt tossed over the back of what was clearly his favorite reading chair. Fingering the soft fabric, she knew it must be handmade, love in every stitch. For the first time she wondered about Cillian's family, probably totally unlike her own. The kind of people who sent him to Convocation Academy with a quilt made with hands, not magic.

Though she politely kept her gaze averted from the notes he'd scribed in a surprisingly stylish script, she couldn't help noticing the title of the book on the table next to the chair, bookmarked halfway through. *The Saga of Sylus and Lyndella.* "You're still reading it," she said aloud in her surprise.

"Yes. I apologize for my careless remarks about it. I still have issues with some of the content, but I believe I better understand why it's so beloved. Why *you* love it, in particular."

That arrested her. Also, this conversation was far better than the much-dreaded demand that she explain what Gordon Hanneil had said to frighten her so. "Interesting. *Why* do you think I love it?"

Cillian glanced at her from behind the high counter, meticulously measuring the herbal tea Healer Jonathan had given her. "It's a study in loyalty, isn't it? Beyond the intensity of the love affair, it's a tale of a magical partnership where Sylus and Lyndella are loyal to each other until death—and beyond. They'd both rather die than allow the other to come to harm. They become a true, unbreakable unit, loving each other despite their flaws, perhaps even because of them. But ultimately it's about unshakeable loyalty, the family they made with each other, one more important and profound than the families they were born to.

"Also," he continued, "Sylus is arguably awful to Lyndella, but I can see why you find his behavior captivating." He strained the tea, considering thoughtfully. "Nothing matters to him more than her, being with her, possessing her. There's a thrill to that fantasy, that you could mean that much to someone else. In particular, that someone so difficult to literally everyone else in the world, would love you. Sylus loves only Lyndella, alone of everyone in the world, which makes her the center of his entire universe. That's powerful."

He brought her the mug, holding it rotated so she could grasp the handle. "Careful—it's hot. But it's also at optimal steeping time, so try to drink it quickly. You can sit there."

She nearly protested that it was his chair, but also every other possible surface sported books and papers, so she sat. And sipped. Processing Cillian's rather astounding assessment of the saga. "I mostly thought it was sexy," she admitted. "And romantic."

Cillian sat down in front of her on a low table, facing her, a half-smile on his lips. "No, you didn't. I'll accept that you thought those things, sure—and it is sexy and romantic—but I bet I'm right and you just don't want to admit it. That's fine." He cocked his head at the ding of a bell. "There's the kolaches warmed up. You'll eat one."

"You sure are bossy all of a sudden," she griped.

He pointed at the book as he went to the kitchen nook.

"You like bossy."

"Not to live with," she retorted, but had to swallow a smile.

"Well, now, that's another conversation entirely. And it's early days to consider such a big step." He grinned when she scowled, annoyed at how he'd twisted her words, and returned with a steaming, fragrant kolache on a plate.

"Kolaches, *again?*" she mock-complained.

"You know you want one." He waved the plate under her nose. "Don't be stubborn."

"There's the pot calling the kettle black."

"Don't be stubborn for the wrong reasons then."

She took the plate. "I *did* eat dinner, as even you acknowledged."

"Yes, but that was coming up on ten hours ago. It's been a long night. And Healer Jonathan specifically said you needed nourishment after that healing session."

Unable to muster an argument, she took the plate and bit into the succulent roll. It tasted even better than it smelled, the fluffy pastry melting in her mouth like buttered sunshine, the spicy sausage within a perfect flavor match, somehow more nourishing than anything she could remember eating in forever. Before she knew it, she'd gobbled down the whole thing, dabbing up the crumbs with a fingertip so as not to miss a morsel.

"It was really good," she said belatedly, looking up to find Cillian watching her with an odd expression on his face.

"I'll get you another," he said, his voice slightly hoarse, taking the empty plate from her. "Drink the rest of your tea first."

Obediently, she took up the mug, now cooled enough to be pleasantly warm to wrap her fingers around, and drank, watching Cillian move with efficient grace around his little kitchen. It was oddly intimate, even homey, being in his golden-lit rooms in the small hours of the morning, with most of Convocation Academy asleep. Almost as if they were the only people in the world. *Which makes her the center of his entire universe. That's powerful.* Blushing for no good reason, Alise drank down the rest of the tea, ready when Cillian brought a second kolache and resumed his same seat on the table.

"You don't need to watch me. I will eat it."

"Oh, I know you will," he replied lightly. "I've seduced you now. It's simply a pleasure to watch you eat."

She nearly choked on a bite and had to take her time chewing.

"You don't allow yourself much pleasure, do you?" Cillian asked, then held up a hand. "A redundant question. You would no doubt argue, but I have observed the truth for myself."

"There hasn't been a lot of room in my life for frivolity lately," she answered anyway.

"Interesting, that you consider simple pleasure frivolous, but we can debate that another time. What I want to know is what Healer Jonathan meant by telling you that whatever Gordon Hanneil suggested to you wasn't your shame."

Here it was. She couldn't meet his gently inquiring gaze, grateful that she'd finished the kolache and couldn't choke on it. "I don't know either. Did he say that?"

"Alise." There was a world of reproach in the one word.

She clutched the plate in desperate grip. "I'm exhausted and need to sleep."

Cillian gave her such a long look that she thought he might refuse, but he released a weary breath and stood, easing the plate from her death grip. "Very well. I wish that you trusted me though."

"I trust you," she ground out.

"Then tell me. Let me be a friend."

"You'll be angry if you know."

Cillian regarded her mildly. "Oh, Alise. I realize you're in your head a great deal, but surely you can't be *that* obtuse." He gazed down at the plate in his hands, then abruptly hurled it against the wall where it shattered dramatically. Cillian looked from it to her. "I am already angry, darling."

CILLIAN GAZED BACK at Alise, who gaped at him in apparent shock. Not that he blamed her. Had he ever done anything like that in his life? No. Anyone who knew him would be stunned. He didn't quite understand it himself—but he also squelched the urge to apologize. It had been his plate to keep or break as he pleased. If he wanted to throw it against the wall, that was his cursed prerogative.

Alise tipped her head and narrowed her sharp, black eyes. "I can't believe you accuse me of being in my own head. You're the one who's always daydreaming."

"Yes, but at least I am daydreaming about *you*," he retorted, still too caught up in the swell of anger to think better of the admission. But then, all along, he'd had a distressing tendency to blurt out his every thought around Alise. And she already knew of his feelings for her, if only because that fucker Gordon had used them against her.

"I apologize for that, Cillian," she said quietly. "And I'll accept the charge. I am guilty of being oblivious to all the world." She let out a long breath and combed her fingers through her short, glossy hair. "I don't want you angry on my behalf."

"Why not?" He was genuinely curious and, in this interstitial bubble of time between night and dawn, he thought she might tell him. "I don't think my doing this bothered you." He gestured vaguely at the shattered pieces of ceramic, taking a step that direction to pick them up.

"Allow me," Alise said, a waft of her magic blowing past him like a warm, rose-scented afternoon breeze. A bevy of earth elementals answered her call, coalescing around the detritus, eagerly consuming it. "And no, your brief, mild show of temper hardly would attract a glance at House Elal. My papa was infamous for his rages, all the worse when he was quietly furious. We all learned to tiptoe around him." She looked briefly, profoundly unhappy, staring off at some memory. "Well, except for Nic. She always enjoyed his very best attention, until she manifested as a familiar, that is."

"I'm sorry," he told her, wishing he could comfort her in some other way.

Her gaze focused on him again. "Nothing to be sorry for,"

she replied briskly. "I envied her all that time, sure. Probably I gave into jealousy when I shouldn't have, since Nic suffered far more than I ever did. I could wish that Papa had loved me like he loved her, but at least that means he had nothing to take away from me. He punished Nic, hurt her deeply, by withdrawing his regard. He can't do that to me."

Couldn't he? Cillian wondered, but didn't say aloud. Piers Elal had a hook deeper into Alise's heart than she realized, he thought. Hopefully he wouldn't ever choose to use it. "Time enough to speak of these things tomorrow. The bed is through there." He pointed, even though it was obvious. "You need to sleep and I'm keeping you up."

He should have known better than to press her right now. It just gnawed at him, the need to know what Hanneil had said to terrify her, to do something about it. How could he begin to help her if he didn't know?

Thing was, he suspected he did know.

"No." Alise shook her head. "First of all, I'll take the couch." She held up a hand, jaw sharp with determination. "I won't put you out of your bed, Cillian. Second, let's finish this conversation, so it's not hanging over me."

A pang of guilt shot through him. This pressure came from him, from *his* needing to know. And what would he do once she told him? He couldn't fight a wizard of Gordon Hanneil's psychic might. But he could listen, and he knew from bitter experience—he'd at least learned that from the Szarina debacle—that telling someone of a painful thing lessened its sway over you. "Let's sit," he said, gesturing to the couch so they could sit together, then belatedly realizing he'd stacked it with books. "One moment."

"You don't have to…"

"Well, I will have to at some point, if I'm to sleep here."

She didn't reply, rather pointedly not renewing the argument over who would sleep where. He restacked the books without much regard for their previous order, though he kept a mental tab on the current organization, so he could revisit, then plumped the crushed cushions of the couch until they looked, if not entirely welcoming, at least not so forbidding.

Turning back to Alise, he found her eyeing him and the couch with a wry expression. "Do I even want to know how long that piece of furniture has functioned as a bookshelf instead of a couch?" she asked.

"Probably not," he admitted, unable to quite recall the last time anyone had sat there. "I don't entertain visitors often, so…" He shrugged, helpless in the face of his own foibles.

Alise sat gingerly, adjusting her narrow bottom, then frowning. "I don't think anyone should sleep on this thing. Or rather, attempt it, as I don't believe sleep would be possible."

"I can sleep in my reading chair." Sitting beside her, he had to acknowledge the truth of her observation. The cushions were packed hard as rocks. No amount of fluffing could save them. Oh well. "I sometimes fall asleep there anyway."

"Why doesn't that surprise me?" She twisted her fingers together, eyes darting away from his gaze. "I don't know quite where to start."

"At the beginning," he replied promptly. "Here, this will help." He scooted into the corner of the couch, half-reclining, and laying an arm along the back. "Lean against me."

She looked dubious, but complied, edging herself hesitantly against his hip, then lying stiff as a slim board against him, tense enough to spring up at a moment's notice. "Like this?"

"Yes, except relax. And maybe no spirit bottle," he suggested as it ground against his leg uncomfortably. "Surely nearby is good enough?"

"Sorry," she muttered, sitting up to extract the thing from her pocket and set it on a pile of books. He really needed to clear some space.

When she laid back down, he lifted the hand from the back of the couch to stroke her silky hair, going carefully, coaxing her into settling that busy head into the nook of his shoulder. "Better. Now tell me. Start with where you first encountered Gordon Hanneil."

She nodded, then began. "There's not that much to tell, really. Nothing actually happened, it was all suggestion." She told the tale in fits and starts, staring up at the ceiling while he caressed her hair, petting and calming her. When she haltingly repeated the vile threats to assault her sexually, she began trembling. The fury coursed through him cold as chilled mercury, thick and viscous in his veins, but he held himself still, not allowing the tension riding him to leak through to disturb her. Alise wept a little, a few tears sliding down her cheeks to settle on his shirt and soak through, where they dampened his skin with her fear and sorrow.

She wound down soon after, correct that it wasn't a long tale, just a horrifying one. At last emptied of the unbearable tension, Alise lay lax against him, her breathing deepening into sleep. He should move. Get up and get her into the bed. But he found that he couldn't lift even the hand resting over her forehead, her light body a delicious weight he couldn't bear to shift. Feeling his own heavy eyelids lowering, he instructed himself to move. To no avail.

$$\sim 16 \sim$$

Alise drifted up through lazy billows of sleep, a sense of renewal and wellbeing suffusing her. Such a perfect, delicious way to wake up, feeling rested, restored, and ready to take on the new day. She opened her eyes and studied the unfamiliar ceiling, the old plaster threaded with cracks in a blue-gray light. She'd been in a lot of different places lately, so she'd become accustomed to taking a moment to equilibrate upon waking, to remember if she was at House Phel or Convocation Academy, and then which room she'd most recently occupied.

Wherever it was, the bed was hard as a rock. No, not a bed—a couch. Cillian's couch.

"Ah, she's awake," Cillian said brightly, his Harahel accent lyrical as birdsong. Not that there was any birdsong, as it appeared to be late afternoon, the winter sky solidly overcast and threatening snow. "I made you soup."

She sat up, aware suddenly of the stiffness in her body, the down-soft quilt she'd noticed the night before spilling into her lap. She'd fallen asleep while talking. On top of Cillian. At some point he'd extracted himself from under her—remarkably without waking her up—then covered her with the quilt. She didn't know how to feel about that, but the emotions swirled gently, warm and sweet.

"Go ahead and use the bathing chamber while I dish this up," Cillian called. "I imagine you'd like to."

"I would—thanks."

When she returned, a steaming bowl of soup awaited her on the low table before the couch, which she realized had been entirely cleared of all but her spirit bottle. Bending over the bowl, she sniffed. Tomato soup with herbs. "When did you make soup?"

"I woke up a few hours ago and didn't want to leave you alone, so I made myself useful," Cillian answered from the kitchen. "Would you like a grilled cheese sandwich, too?"

Alise swallowed her reflexive refusal. A grilled cheese sandwich sounded amazing and she rationalized to herself that Cillian would just persist, so she might as well give in. "Yes, please." She swallowed a spoonful of soup, creamy, rich, and tasting of a summer garden. Perfect for a winter afternoon.

"*How* did you make soup?" it occurred to her to ask.

"Really you can make anything with a couple of fire elementals and some ingenuity," he answered, a smile in his voice. "I know Convocation Academy feeds us as well as they can, but cooking for a thousand people poses certain restrictions. I like my own cooking better. And working with my hands gives me time and peace to think." His voice broke just a little at the end and Alise knew instantly what he'd been mulling over.

Working with his hands—like whoever had made the quilt over her lap. "Who made this quilt?" she asked.

"My grandmother Harahel," he answered unperturbed by the apparent change of subject. He appeared before her, holding out a tray with a golden-crisp sandwich oozing pale cheese on plate. Not a plate that matched the one he'd broken. In truth, none of his dishes matched, a bit of randomness she found endearing. With a deft maneuver, Cillian palmed her half-full bowl of soup, slipped it onto the tray next to the sandwich, and handed her the whole thing. "Feel free to dip," he said with a cheery smile that belied his earlier tone. "That's the best way."

"Aren't you going to eat?"

"Already did." He'd gone back to the kitchen, puttering around.

"I'm sorry I fell asleep on you," she said, wanting to address that particular elephant in the room, anyway.

"I fell asleep, too. As my aching back can attest, you are correct that my couch is no good for sleeping."

"I'm sorry." Stricken, she stared at the sandwich, the soup, the quilt he'd covered her with. He was a lovely, caring person and she was… utterly selfish.

"That's twice you apologized for something you didn't have to be sorry for even once. Don't you like your sandwich? You haven't even tried it. With or without dunking."

He sounded so disappointed she nearly laughed. Biting into the sandwich, she groaned at the buttery richness, the savory cheese in creamy contrast to the perfectly crisped bread. Deciding to take his advice, she dunked the next bite, finding the tart-sweetness of the tomato soup the perfect complement. "Dark arts this is delicious," she said when she could.

"I'm glad." Cillian set a mug of tea on the table before her, then settled into his reading chair, cradling a mug of his own.

She sniffed the steam from her tea, suspicious. "More sleepy tea?"

"Regular herbal tea," he corrected.

"I prefer coffee."

"I'm aware. I'm also aware that it's already afternoon and you don't need to be drinking coffee at this time of day."

"Yes, Maman," she quipped, but he only sipped his tea, unbothered.

"You would like my grandmother Harahel," he said, returning to the earlier conversational topic without a beat, ignoring the remaining elephants still milling invisibly about the room. "She can tell you the author and title of any book ever written, from even a muddied or flat incorrect plot summary and a vague description of the cover, and she can cook a five-course meal for a dozen people on a moment's notice."

"And she quilts," Alise noted.

"Yes. All kinds of needlework, plus she gardens. She grew the herbs you taste in the soup. She dries and sends to me, out of concern that I won't eat well in the wasteland of Convocation Center."

"Funny—I've never heard of anyone regarding Convocation Center as a wasteland. Rather the reverse." Everyone wanted to be in Convocation Center, with all its delights and entertainments. It was called the center for a reason.

Cillian gave her a droll look. "It depends on one's perspective, yes? Where you place your priorities, what your values are. My family understands my need to be here, to work in the Convocation archives, but they also think I'm a bit daft. After all, House Harahel has an extensive library—in some aspects, more complete than here—plus beautiful countryside, excellent food, stimulating company, and a refreshing dearth of corrupt politics."

Put that way, she could see the point. "I would never describe House Elal that way. Any of those ways."

"No? I've heard Elal is a dramatic landscape, though I've never been, and the house itself an architectural marvel."

She supposed both things were true. "Dramatic is probably a good word for it, with the Knifeblade Mountains visible from anywhere in Elal—you always know where west is—and then there's the long, rocky coastline. The house itself, however, is in a fairly flat valley, in the bend of a river and 'architectural marvel' gives it too much credit. It's a monstrosity of styles, created by generations of arrogant Elals more determined to put their stamp on it than behave in a rational manner."

Cillian laughed, surprising her, since she hadn't intended that to be funny. "You have an affection for it though. I can hear it in your voice."

She considered that, finishing her sandwich and using the crusts to sop up the dregs of soup from the bowl. "Maybe," she allowed. "My maman had exquisite taste and she loved us. She made our lives good and—" She broke off, unable to continue, coughing on some of the crumbs.

"Grieving is hard," Cillian said with sympathy. "That alone would be enough for you to handle on top of finishing coursework for graduation. Now you have everything else to deal with, too."

Summoned by Cillian's words, one of the elephants, called Overdue Projects, bounced up to loom invisibly over her shoulder. She made the elephant named Matricide stay hidden in the corner, where it glared at her balefully. "Speaking of which," she said decisively, "I need to go get some work done."

"Today is a rest day."

"No rest for the wicked—or the terminally late on fifty-seven assignments."

"Your professors have been notified of the extenuating circumstances by Healer Jonathan, who explicitly told you not to work today. You meet with Morghana Seraphiel first thing in the morning. I have a meeting with Provost Uriel, which I'll go to after I escort you to Morghana. In the meanwhile, you're staying here where it's safe. To *rest*."

"Am I a captive then?" She'd meant the question to come out with sharp derision, but didn't quite get it there. Instead, she sounded... wistful? Surely not.

"Like Sylus holding Lyndella prisoner until she admitted she wanted him as much as he craved her," Cillian said teasingly, tapping the book beside him.

A new tension settled between them, sexual and fraught. Cillian was no Sylus, but then neither was Alise anything like sweet and yielding Lyndella. Unwillingly, she remembered yesterday's kiss, how hot and hungry it had been. From the heat in Cillian's black gaze, he was thinking of it, too.

"Cillian..." She trailed off, not certain what to say.

He cleared his throat and looked away. "I apologize. That

was an inappropriate remark."

"I think we've moved past inappropriate," she commented drily. Might as well summon the elephant called Our Relationship to the fore. Out the windows, it had begun to snow thickly, the afternoon sky darkening with early dusk, and the fire elemental flickering brightly in the tiny fireplace made the room warm and cozy. Alise realized she didn't *want* to leave. She wanted to stay. With Cillian. "I think we should talk about what this is between us."

"Oh. Ah. I see," he stammered, actually blushing. "Would you like another sandwich first? There's more soup."

Deflecting with busying himself. Turning things around so he was feeding her instead of talking about what he wanted. *Craved.* The word resonated in her mind. "No, thank you. I'm good for now. Stop avoiding this conversation."

"You're one to talk," he replied, "as you're avoiding discussing any number of things."

"Fine." She rolled her eyes. "How about this? I agree to stay here until tomorrow morning, without further protest, and I'll allow you to escort me to see Professor Seraphiel. I'll discuss anything you wish, but *only* after we talk about our relationship."

"I see. That's reasonable." Instead of putting his tea on the side table, he leaned down to set it on the floor, where it would pose no danger to his books. He crossed his legs, folding his hands over his knee almost primly. His elevated foot bobbed, revealing his nerves. "I think we should agree that we are friends and colleagues only, that we shall put my inappropriate feelings and advances aside. I'm fully aware that there can be nothing of a, er, romantic nature between us and I will ensure that you never again feel pressure from me, from, ah, that direction. As it were."

Suppressing a smile at how formal Cillian had become in his discomfort, Alise nodded gravely, pretending to consider. "I understand what you're saying, but I have a different solution. I think we should have a love affair."

Cillian's mouth fell open and he goggled at her in a decidedly disconcerted fashion. "I—You—But, I and you, we *can't*."

"Why not? I want to. And you want to—unless you've changed your mind?"

"I, no. That is. The provost said…"

"Provost Uriel is an admirable woman and an excellent administrator of Convocation Academy, but as she reminded me recently, just as the high houses do not command her, she does not command the high houses. At the risk of sounding arrogant, I am still the daughter and heir-apparent to the lord of High House Elal and sister to the lady of House Phel. I call as my friends the lord and lady of High House El-Adrel. You are a well-regarded scion of High House Harahel. What we do is our own business."

"Alise…" Cillian raked a hand through his curls, setting them into more disarray than usual. He retrieved his tea and gulped it like another man might take a bracing draught of brandy. "I care about you, obviously, and it's too late for me to pretend that I don't, um, desire you." He blushed more deeply, avoiding her gaze. "But you are so very beautiful and powerful. There can be no future for us."

"We can't have a future because you… like me too much?"

"No, no, that is. Ach, I'm doing this badly. I know full well that you are not meant for me. You have a brilliant future ahead of you and I'm a Harahel librarian. I can't be part of your life."

What life, what brilliant future? Alise nearly snorted aloud at that, but decided that was an argument that would go nowhere. "Even if that's so, and I don't agree, why can't we have now?"

"Because it would be better to spare ourselves the pain that parting would inevitably bring."

"Would it be inevitable though?"

"You argue like a politician," he retorted wryly.

"Probably too true. I may not have been my father's favorite, but one can't grow up in House Elal and not absorb political thinking. Still, my point is that we've started as friends. Why do you assume we wouldn't stay friends?"

"Let me amend my previous statement," he said quietly. "I think I need to spare *myself* that pain, which will be inevitable, no matter how amicably we part."

She still wanted to argue the inevitability of their parting, but Alise had an admittedly difficult time picturing any future for herself. "Isn't the thought of never pursuing this—" she waved a hand back and forth between them "—painful also?"

He briefly closed his eyes. "Of course it is. But we know *this* will end." He imitated her gesture with more vigor, then dashed his hand to the side, slopping the remnants of the tea. She evoked a water elemental to soak it up and he pointed. "See? You do that so easily."

"So because I have magic to clean up messes, you think our

relationship is automatically doomed?" Now she was getting annoyed.

"I didn't say any such thing," he retorted with heat. "We are both wizards. Wizards don't have relationships with each other."

"Why not? There's no rule that says that."

"It's commonly understood! Especially for wizards of your echelon. You'll need a familiar."

"You don't have one."

"Because there's no such thing as a library emergency. We don't need extra power. You will."

"Maybe I don't *want* a familiar. In fact, I know I don't."

"You'll change your mind," he said grimly.

She stared at him for a second, deeply offended. "I'll accept a certain amount of badgering from you," she said coolly, "because I know it comes from a place of you wanting to take care of me and protect me. But do not presume to tell me my own mind."

"And there she is. Lady Elal in the making."

Whoa. That hurt far more than she'd expected Cillian could wound her. She almost couldn't catch her breath following that unexpected blow. "Pardon me," she said, standing and deliberately folding the quilt. "I understand what you mean now about us only causing each other pain. I'll go now."

"You agreed you would stay."

"I think that agreement is moot now. Consider it a decision from on high." She lifted her nose and waved a hand in haughty dismissal, then snatched up the bottle of spirits from the table and pocketed it. "One can't trust an Elal to keep their word, after all." She headed for the door.

"I didn't mean it that way. Curse it, Alise. Don't you walk out that door."

She walked faster.

He caught up easily, seizing her arm.

"Let me go," she said, not looking at him.

"Be mad at me. I deserve it. But it's not safe for you to be out there alone. Don't put yourself at risk because I'm a fucking idiot."

"You're not an idiot," she corrected, softening. "But that was dramatically unfair of you to say."

"It was. I apologize. I was… upset. And I have issues. Please don't go."

She stared stonily at the wall. "On two conditions."

"Done."

Nearly laughing at his immediate capitulation, she dared a glance at him—and found his face very close to hers. Her amusement flamed into desire. Swallowing against her suddenly dry mouth, she said, "I like gingerbread. Can you make that?"

"I make excellent gingerbread," he answered with a relieved smile. "I can do that. What's the other condition?"

"Kiss me."

~ 17 ~

CILLIAN FROZE, HIS mouth so close to Alise's upturned lips, already so tempting, even without the glittering challenge in her luminous eyes. He wanted to kiss her, of course, had thought of little else, but the ghost of Szarina hung in the air between them like one of Alise's cloaking spirits. *None of us needs another Szarina incident.* "Alise…" he said, voice faint.

Disappointed irritation snapped into her gaze. "Fine. If it's too much to ask, forget it." She yanked out of his grip and lunged for the door.

Growling with a frustration that was an echo of hers, he leapt before her, preventing her from reaching her exit, and somehow ended up with her pushed against the wall. She stared at him in shock, eyes wide and dark. With his hands on her slim waist, he became keenly aware of the thrumming of her nerves, her narrow ribs flaring with hard, fast breaths, her heart pounding in a rhythm to match his own. "Are you sure?" he breathed, his lips already lowering to her tempting mouth, wanting, needing.

"Yes. You are the one hesitating." She slid her hands up his chest, making him shudder. How many times had he fantasized about her touching him exactly this way? Tipping her head to the side, her lips curved into a sensual, challenging smile, and she dug her short nails lightly into his skin through his shirt. "You know you want to."

He did. Abandoning all good sense, he loosed his restraint and closed the brief distance, pulling her hard against him and relishing her gasp of surprised desire, along with the delicious feel of her slight body, so delicate and yet blossoming with magic. A contrast there, between the birdlike bones of her petite frame and the robust power of the magic contained there. It billowed around and through him, roses in brilliant shades of scarlet and crimson and a bloodred nearly black, bursting into bloom, sunshine dancing over his skin and permeating his bones.

Kissing her, holding her, felt like embracing the font of life. Like a hot summer afternoon, she infiltrated him, illuminating the dusty corridors of his scholar's mind and magic. He felt as if he, himself, might burgeon into someone hotter, more vibrant, charismatic, and full of shimmering life. In Alise's arms, it seemed, he could become anyone at all.

Slowing, realizing he could relax, that no one would happen upon them, not like before with the frenzied, forbidden rush of the stolen kiss in the library, certain in the knowledge that she wanted this too, he allowed himself to savor her. Alise melted against him, braced by the wall behind her, pulling him ever closer with clinging, urgent hands.

"Cillian…" she murmured against his lips, her breath a sweet sighing.

"Yes," he answered, as if she'd asked a question. And perhaps she had. Her body fit just so against him, her curves and lines aligning with him, as if they'd been crafted precisely for one another, for this.

Drawing away just bit, Alise cupped his cheek and gazed up at him, her depthless eyes showing her shining, loving soul. They shimmered with trust, he realized.

"Can I tell you something?" she asked on a hushed breath.

"You can tell me anything," he answered promptly.

"Do you know what frightened me most about Gordon Hanneil's threats?" She searched his face, a wary hesitation in hers.

For her, he refused the immediate anger, wouldn't allow the tension that wanted to flood his muscles. He'd obviously never been a fighter, always the boy with his nose in a book, so the raw, raging impulse to find Gordon Hanneil and beat him to a bloody pulp with his fists alarmed and shocked Cillian. He didn't know how he'd accomplish it, but he could envision the moment. Not to murder him, but to punish and disable. Gordon Hanneil would face Convocation justice. As would House Hanneil. Cillian would see to it.

But for her, he set all that aside and stayed loose, embracing the woman he loved more than all the world, giving her what she needed. "What?" he asked, just as softly. Whatever haunted her, he would listen. He could give her that much.

"That… Well, if he'd made good on his threat, to twist my mind against me, and …" She stopped, chewing her lip, hesitating over the words.

"You don't have to say it aloud," he told her, understanding. "I know what you mean."

She nodded in relief. "That he would have been my first. Sex. You know. Pretty much first everything. And I didn't want that."

"It wouldn't have been sex. What he threatened you with was violence and violation."

She smiled, slightly, fingers caressing his cheek. "You know what I mean. Physical intimacy."

"Yes." He suspected he knew where she was going with this. And he didn't know what his answer would be. Should be. Caught between his longing and his caution, the only thing he could say was her name. Her beloved, lyrical, and lovely name. "Alise…"

"I want it to be you," she said simply, easing out from between him and the wall, taking his hand and leading him toward the bedroom.

"I thought your demands included only gingerbread and a kiss," he joked weakly, still profoundly torn, his body eager, his heart overflowing, and his mind whispering urgent cautions. This was a bad idea. The wrong thing to do. Except he couldn't quite remember why.

Alise glanced back over her shoulder at his poor joke, and paused, a slight frown of concern marring her clear forehead, drawing a line between her winged black brows. "I'd imagined the rest would follow on to the kiss-request. Do you not want to? Not want… me?"

"Oh, darling." Still holding her hand, he eased closer, folding the distance he'd allowed to stretch between them. "I want you like I want air. Have done since the first time I laid eyes on you, since I first sensed the sweet bloom of your magic. But I worry."

"You wouldn't be you if you didn't worry," she observed solemnly, but with a glint of humor dancing in her black eyes.

"Fair," he admitted. "Still, I have good reason. I need you to listen."

"Tell me." She turned to face him, listening with gratifying attention.

"I fear this is a reaction on your part," he explained, cautious of eliciting her ire again. Or hurting her, accidentally making her feel rejected. "You didn't want this from me before. Any of it. You barely thought of me as a friend, let alone as a lover. I'm concerned that your very real and understandable terror of what could have happened is driving you to take drastic action. That this isn't something that you'd want, that you would ask from me, if you hadn't been terrorized and traumatized."

She waited a beat, making sure he'd finished, he realized. Then dipped her chin in acknowledgment. "I understand why you'd think that. And I can't really argue otherwise. I don't know why I didn't fully see you before—except that it was as if I had been asleep. Those things I thought about before all this happened, that I believed were *so very* important, none of them matter now. You're right: I didn't see you as a lover. I held you at arm's length as a friend because…"

"Because?" he prompted, when she didn't finish.

She gave a little self-conscious shrug. "Because I liked you. Too much. And it worried me."

"Oh, my darling." He combed his fingers into her silky hair, his heart swelling when she tipped her cheek into his palm. "Whyever would that worry you? I'm harmless."

"Maybe that's why," she said, a raw vulnerability in her face as she gazed at him. No walls around her heart now. "I've all my life been around dangerous people. I know how to ward against that, how to perform the political dance, how to strive for power and supremacy. What I don't know is how to be… I don't even know what word I want. Normal? Human, maybe. How to be someone besides the heir to a high house, a powerful something someday whose job it will be to rule and crush the people beneath me."

His heart literally ached for her—or something in the vicinity of his chest did. "That's not a requirement of the job," he told her gently. "You can head a high house without doing that, being that."

She snorted. "Show me one."

"Nic and Gabriel. Jadren and Seliah. Lady Harahel."

"Outcasts, iconoclasts, and scholars," she replied, but not unkindly. "Still, your point is taken. And mine is that I don't know why I didn't see you, except that I didn't see anything except for a difficult and narrow road ahead of me." She laid her free hand over his heart. "But I see you now, and I want you, Cillian. I want you to make love to me and show me how. You are experienced, yes?"

"Yes," he got out past his newly thundering heart which seemed to have jogged up in his chest to lodge at the base of his throat. He set aside the memories of Szarina that threatened to flood him and taint this far more precious moment with Alise. He refused to let her memory ruin this. "Are you sure?"

Her lips quirked in wry amusement. "Are you going to make me say it three times to seal the charm?"

"It would help, yes."

"I'm sure. I'm sure. I'm sure."

"I think there's some extras in there."

"Really, really sure." Stepping away, she tugged at his hand, and he followed her willingly this time, though not without trepidation. It had been a while, after all.

"I might not be very good at it," he felt he should say. Total honesty and all that. Mitigate her expectations. "I'm quite a bit rusty."

The smile she flashed him held a dazzling affection. "I'm sure it's like redirecting an air elemental powering a carriage. Once you learn, you never forget."

"I was never terribly good at that," he muttered, coming to a halt beside the bed, facing her. At least he habitually kept his room clean and his bed made. A stack of books on the bedside table, yes, and the stained-glass shade on the reading lamp had tilted askew at some point. Funny that he hadn't noticed it before.

"Like reading, then," she amended with a knowing smile.

"I can't remember a time I couldn't read," he agreed. As opposed to those first few fumbling attempts with Szarina, who'd mocked his clumsiness and ignorance. *Don't think about her,* he instructed himself fiercely. *She has no place in this bed.*

"Well then, this will be the same." Alise went to unbutton her shirt.

"Wait. Let me do that."

Curious, she dropped her hands, watching him with those

wide, dark eyes.

"First things first," he told her, giving her a kiss that he'd meant to be brief, but turned lingering. Would kissing her ever feel like not a transgression, not something stolen and furtive and all the more precious for that? Not yet. Reluctantly pulling back, he dropped to his knees and extracted the spirit bottle from the pocket at the side of her leg. Handing it up to her, he smiled at her chagrined expression. "Tomorrow you deal with this, too, right?"

"If everyone will stop scheduling me to do other stuff." She set the bottle atop the stack of books on the table, absently straightening the shade at the same time. Then she caught his expression. "Yes, yes, yes. I'll prioritize it."

"Good girl," he told her, and she shivered a little, giving him a tremulous smile.

"You're still down there," she observed.

"Indeed." He slid her shoes off and her bare feet were trim, even dainty, with small, rosy toes that seemed ridiculously adorable to him. He wanted to kiss each one, but that could wait. Encircling her small ankles with his hands, he stroked his palms up her calves as high as her pants legs allowed, then transferred his touch to the outside of her thighs, smoothing upward over the subtle flare of her hips. Finding the bare skin of her waist under the baggy shirt, he caressed inward, marveling at the silky softness of her skin. Reaching the fastening of her pants, he looked up, aware of the nervous hitch in her breathing.

"Still good to go?" he asked her.

She nodded, a bit jerkily and set hands on his shoulders. "I didn't expect to be so nervous."

"It would be surprising if you weren't." Unfastening the ties, he eased the pants down, exposing her slim thighs beneath the long hem of the shirt. So unbelievably lovely. "Step out," he whispered, bagging the pants around her ankles and waiting for her to get clear. Once she did, he tossed the pants aside and slowly stood, dragging light fingers along the silky skin of her thighs, loving the way she trembled, and how her liquid dark eyes gazed at him with utter trust and vulnerability. He toyed with the hem of her shirt, lifting it a little, tantalizing them both, while he studied her face. "Still okay to keep going?"

"You don't have to keep asking," she answered with a tinge of that imperious irritation he perversely loved.

"I think I do. I'm still not fully convinced this isn't a reaction to all that's happened."

With a huff of exasperation, she grabbed the hem of her shirt, yanking it from his grasp, and pulling it off over her head in one movement. "There," she declared, planting her fists on her hips. "Is that decisive enough?"

He didn't respond immediately, too dazzled by the sight of her in the sheer white tank and blush-pink lacy panties. Her deep rose nipples thrust taut against the nearly transparent silky fabric, tipping her delicate breasts with frankly erotic effect. And the lace clinging to her narrow hips, just covering the black hair at her pubis, revealing the smooth, tawny skin of her flat belly… He nearly dropped to his knees again to better press kisses to that sweetly alluring expanse, an impulse difficult to resist with his legs going weak from the overwhelming blend of passion and tenderness. He wanted to ravish her and tend to her in equal measures, the warring needs stretching him on the tenterhooks of desire.

"Cillian?"

The sound of his name penetrated his stupor and he belatedly raised his gaze to her face, which looked wryly amused. It seemed that might not have been the first time she tried to get his attention. At least, the rational, mental variety. He cleared his throat. "I'm sorry, but you are so fucking beautiful. I'm looking at you and…"

Her expression softened, though the amusement remained. "Why are you sorry?"

"Um." He had to think. Shook his head. "Not sorry that you're so gorgeous, but that I'm apparently struck stupid by the sight of you. I didn't expect the lingerie."

She grimaced, looking down at herself. "Blame Nic."

"I believe I'll have to send her a thank you note. Perhaps a gift."

Alise laughed, eliciting a smile from him, too, which helped diffuse the tension and nerves. "I'm torn between telling you not to even consider it and wanting to be there to see her face."

"I think Nic would maybe understand what's between us."

She sobered. "I'm not sure *I* understand what's between us."

"Is that all right?"

She considered that gravely. His Alise, never one to leap to an answer or decision. "Yes," she said, nodding to confirm it. "I think… I think I'm willing to find out."

It was hardly a declaration of love, but her words struck his heart as if they were. The warmth and happiness welled up, becoming a smile that felt radiant—and that she returned, at first hesitantly, then with confidence.

He held out his hands to her. "Then let's find out."

~ 18 ~

A LISE PUT HER hands in Cillian's, the nerves still thrumming through her, but on a different frequency, changing pitch from trepidation into excitement. Standing before him, nearly naked, in the truly scandalous underwear Nic had insisted she take when her own grew ragged from too many washings—and which she'd frankly forgotten she was wearing—Alise felt new inside her skin.

Maybe it was the avid way Cillian stared at her, going off into a reverent waking dream, but she actually felt... pretty. Beautiful, even, when Cillian said so with that raw frankness, his desire sharpening his magic. As she'd told him, Alise usually "saw" magic, and Cillian's appeared to her most of the time as a quiet aura, shifting in grayscale, sometimes more black or more white, but always organized. It changed in character now as he took her in, cataloguing her body with potent admiration. And when he touched her...

Well, the tactile sensation of his magic had nothing quiet about it. It surged like the feel of ocean waves. Alise had gone to the coast with her parents one time, accompanying her papa on a summer excursion to evaluate some Elal shipyards, and she'd played in the surf while he worked, Maman absorbed with holding Nander's hand and keeping him in the shallows. Nic must have been off at Convocation Academy already. It had been a rare bit of independence for Alise and she'd swum out, discovering how to go with the swells instead of fighting them, learning to recognize when they would curl and start to break—and how to swim just ahead of them until they caught her like a hand and sent her sailing back to the shore.

Cillian's magic felt like that, both gentle and powerful, a deep swell carrying her, with a cresting force welling up, ready to take potential to crashing reality. Not at all what she'd expected from a librarian. Hidden depths.

He guided their clasped hands to his shirt, encouraging her to undo the buttons, and she did so with building curiosity. One by one, she slipped the buttons free—no fancy Ophiel garment for him—spreading the lapels as she worked. His breathing quickened, but he stood patiently while she performed the simple task, revealing his lean chest, a sprinkling of silky black hairs in loose spirals on his pale skin as if they'd been inked on by a scribe. She traced her fingertips along them, touching the velvet of his nipples, glancing up when he drew in a hiss of breath. "Did I hurt you?"

"No." He breathed a laugh, his hands in loose fists at his sides. "It's arousing."

"Oh." She actually blushed, which seemed silly, given that she stood there in her revealing underthings, touching his bare chest. Speaking frankly of arousal made the blood heat her cheeks and she had to look away.

Cillian tipped a finger under her chin, lifting her gaze to his. "Everything good?"

"Yes," she whispered. "It's just a lot."

"We can stop at any point. Just say so."

She nodded, his finger still on her chin, but she didn't *want* to stop. A large, practical part of her wanted this over and done with, so that Gordon Hanneil couldn't rob her of that first time, and that same practical part knew if she articulated those thoughts to Cillian, he'd balk again. Resolute, she pushed the shirt off his shoulders, then dropped her hands to unfasten his pants, all the while holding Cillian's gaze. "I don't want to stop."

His fingers tightened on her chin, a spasm of need that thrilled her, and when he dropped his lips to hers to take her mouth in a long, drugging kiss, those waves of his magic dragged her under water. Ancient and deep, his magic felt like thousands of minds, like diligent study and the love of words. Debates and thoughts and descriptions and the weighty feel of books in the hand and crisp pages as they turned. Never would Alise have called such things erotic and yet, with Cillian's mouth on hers, his hand on her waist sliding slowly up her ribs, nothing had felt more sensually stimulating.

When his hand cupped her breast, she gasped into his mouth, and his lips curved into a smile against hers. "So sensitive," he murmured. "So fucking sexy."

She couldn't say why hearing the normally reserved and polite Cillian curse made her more aroused, but the words rocketed through her and a moaning, pleading sound escaped her. His pants had fallen down and she clung to his naked hips, seeking more of his mouth, kissing him greedily.

"Yes, love. We'll take care of you, easy now." He trailed

kisses along her jaw and down her throat, sliding the straps of her chemise down her arms, dragging the silk over her already taut and aching nipples until they sprang free. Cillian cupped both breasts in gentle hands, though his magic swelled like a sea in an approaching storm, and he brushed her nipples with his thumbs so she trembled and shuddered, whimpering, and he slowly kissed her collarbones, and the space between her breasts, a tantalizing seduction that drove every thought and worry from her mind. Over his bent head, she dreamily watched out the window as the snowflakes emerged from the soft gray overcast, manifesting from nothing to take sparkling shape, swirling with their companions to thicken in a lacy fall.

Cillian murmured his affection, his reverent admiration, along with gentle reassurance, another blizzard, but of words, some elegant, some filthy. He kissed her nipples, drawing them with sweet succor into his hot mouth, then sucking hard and chuckling wickedly when she yipped, her hands now burrowed hard into his curls.

"I adore you," he said, withdrawing and lifting the chemise over her head before tossing it aside, his hands immediately returning to her breasts, fondling her sensitized nipples so she squirmed helplessly. "You have me thoroughly enchanted. Intoxicated. Kissing your skin is like drinking the headiest of red wines." He dropped kisses to her nipples, drawing on them as if he drank and she writhed and sighed at the exquisite sensations and the delicious words he gave her. Not just a scholar, but a poet, in thought and deed and touch. "Your nipples are dark as bloodred roses and a thousand times sweeter." He inhaled deeply, humming deep in his throat. "I could breathe you in forever. I need to taste you. May I?"

"You already are."

He laughed again, a dark sound of sensual amusement. "Oh, darling. No, I've barely begun." Kissing his way down her belly, he sank to his knees, slipping fingers under the lace of her barely-there panties. Then, shocking her, he placed a kiss directly on her mons, breathing hot, moist breath over her pussy.

"Oh," she gasped in pleasure and realization.

"Yes." He eased her panties down her thighs, inhaling again as if he couldn't get enough. "Delicious." Kissing her there again, this time with his mouth directly on her, he slipped the tip of his tongue into the cleft between her nether lips, with lightning results.

She convulsed, a strangled cry escaping her. His hair bit into her fingers, she held on so tightly. "Cillian!" she gasped.

"Oh, yes, darling," he said with satisfaction. "You taste as delightful as I imagined you would. I need more. Step out." Sliding her panties all the way down, he held them for her to kick out of as he'd done with her pants. "Good girl."

Why those words melted her, she didn't know—and she'd never want anyone else to know how they worked on her—but she loved hearing it on some core level beyond reason.

Grasping her thighs, steadying her, Cillian backed her toward the bed. "Sit, sweetheart," he coaxed. "Also, you can relax your death grip on my hair."

"Oh! Sorry," she muttered, having forgotten in her dazed desire.

"Don't be sorry," he replied, a wicked grin she'd never

seen on his face before. "Feel free to pull all you like—and you're going to want to—I just don't want you to fall over."

"I wouldn't fall over," she protested, slightly offended.

"You were swaying, dizzily."

"It wasn't that extreme."

"It will be," he promised with dark sensuality, placing his hands on her knees. "Spread."

Flushing, both self-conscious and aroused, she eased her thighs apart, allowing him to open her even wider to his wizard-black gaze. "So fucking gorgeous," he breathed. "Lie back if you need to."

"Why would I—" She broke off on an undignified squeal as he licked her nether mouth from bottom to top. The sensation shot through her, heating her to the melting point and buffeting her with the waves of his magic. Her head swam as he ministered to her, licking and sucking, making sounds like he did when eating one of his hot, fresh cinnamon rolls. That image sent her even further over the top. Unable to hold still, she squirmed under his teasing kisses and caresses, making a guttural sound when he slid a finger into her passage, pressing deep within her.

She climaxed then, a thousand times more intensely than when she made herself come. This was Cillian, his dark curls and exquisite face between her thighs, feasting on her with such erotic abandon that she lost all control, her thoughts scattered to the winds, a blizzard now of black and crimson. Distantly, she heard her sobbing cries of pleasure. Her head swam and she realized she had indeed fallen back, her fingers clawing the sheets as she bucked her hips in the helpless throes of what he brought her.

And he didn't stop there, instead looping her knees over his shoulders and feasting more, thrusting additional fingers inside her to add a deep, welling drive to the sharper sensations evoked by his scraping teeth and clever tongue. The additional contact gave her a keener, more overwhelming sense of his magic and she caught the wave of it, surfing ever higher and faster, until she crashed, tumbling head over heels into release.

With a wordless sound of delight, Cillian kissed his way up her body, pausing to lavish attention on her breasts, then laid himself beside her, smoothing a hand over her quivering belly and propping his head on the other. She rolled her head to look at him, her eyes not quite focusing.

"Still in there?" he asked with a smile, very much the cat who'd been in the cream. Recalling exactly what he'd been lapping up with such enthusiasm, she blushed. "Ah, I see you are." He bent to kiss her and she tasted salt on his lips, more echoes of the ocean. Still in a sensual dream, she imagined his magic and her body had somehow blended to make the elixir.

"Mmm. Delicious," she murmured.

"Yes, you are." He gave her one more lingering kiss. "I should get started on that gingerbread for you."

She grabbed hold of him before he could move away. "Wait. I know that's not all."

His brows climbed. "We don't have to do *everything* the first night."

But what if it's the only night? She knew better than to speak that fatalistic thought aloud to sunny-minded Cillian, with his lovely family and his head in the pages of a book. "I want to have sex," she told him decisively.

"I feel I should inform you that this is all sex," he replied with a quirk of a smile.

"Don't be pedantic. I want you inside me." She enjoyed how his black on black pupils dilated with renewed arousal. "Or I can go down on you," she added, feeling bold in the delight of taking him by surprise. "Return the favor."

"Darling Alise," he said, his voice hoarse, and he combed his fingers into her short hair, "you know it's not an exchange of favors, yes?"

"A figure of speech."

"Yes and no. I want you to understand that what we just did, I did out of desire, not to put credit into some kind of karmic savings so I can withdraw similar acts from you. Lovemaking, sex—this is for us to share. It should not be transactional."

There was a bitterness behind his earnest words that made her wonder. "Did something happen to you, to give you such strong opinions about sex becoming transactional?"

He shook his head, not in negation, but brushing off the question. "That's not a story I want in bed with us. My point is that it's very important to me that everything you do with and for me comes from a place of consent, not from obligation."

"Cillian." She laid a hand on his bare chest, unable to resist stroking the fine, silky hairs. "I don't feel any obligation. I just really want to give you pleasure also. I'd be more assertive, but I don't know what to do." Unexpected emotion swamped her. She didn't like being the naïve, awkward one. If only she were older, more experienced, and could employ some exotic, seductive skills on him, startle and please him as he had her. Feeling a bit self-conscious, she pressed a kiss to his chest, then took a chance and kissed his velvety, pink nipple. He shuddered, his fingers clenching in her hair, close to the scalp. The shockingly erotic sensation made her melt against him.

He pressed his lips to the top of her head, muttering something she didn't catch, then released her hair and dragged her up for a devastating kiss. She clung to the kiss, to him, like a drowning woman. He slid his hand down the curve of her hip, making a sound when she eagerly spread her legs for him.

"So wet for me," he said on a shuddering sigh, then turned on his back, drawing her with him. "Straddle me. That way you can control it, in case it hurts."

She'd been shy to look at him too closely before, but now she gingerly took hold of his cock, marveling at the feel of it, so very different from her own body. Her knees on either side of his narrow hips, she carefully explored his member, surprised at the softness of the skin of his shaft, the tip even more velvety than his nipples. Cillian lay still, eyes closed, pained lines creasing his face. Halting her exploration in concern, she asked, "Am I hurting you?"

He cracked open one eye. "Yes, you're killing me, but that's no reason to stop." At her hesitation, he trailed reassuring fingers along her hip. "This is my every fantasy come true, darling Alise, and I'm doing my best to ensure it doesn't end too soon for you. And for me," he added, with a hint of a smile. "However, allow me to encourage you to move on, if you're determined on this." He lifted both hands to her breasts, teasing and lightly pinching her nipples, renewing the flame of need that hadn't abated despite everything so far.

She squirmed, breath growing short, her pussy aching with it. "Cillian," she panted.

"I only stop when I'm inside you."

Having quite a bit of trouble concentrating, she positioned the head of his cock at her entrance, sliding down a bit so he stretched her. His hands on her breasts stilled and they both let out a long, sighing groan of mutual desire.

"You feel so good," he muttered, eyes closed again. "Please don't stop."

She had zero intention of stopping, though her tissues complained a little. The sting was nothing compared to the craving, and she wriggled, lowering herself more. Cillian dropped his hands to her thighs, holding her, his face once more a rictus that looked like agony but that shimmered with erotic pleasure. Watching every nuance of his expression, with him looking so beautiful with his nearly black curls spread on the pillow, his lips flushed from their kisses and play, she slowly lowered herself until he was sheathed to the hilt inside her. That last bit of contact sent bolts of pleasure through her. Having his flesh so intimately against hers came as a revelation. More than ever, she was beyond grateful she'd chosen him to be the one. It didn't bear thinking how it would be with someone else, especially in violation.

A wave of tenderness washed over her, partly his quiet magic, partly her own gratitude and deep affection for this beautiful boy filling her so perfectly, completing her so deliciously. Slowly, Cillian opened his eyes, rubbing his palms up and down her thighs.

"That can be enough, he said, gaze roving her face with concern.

"Oh no, it isn't," she replied on a breath of a laugh. Moving judiciously at first, then with more vigor, she rode him, amazed by the bone-melting sensations flowing all through her, mirrored and enhanced in him. Their magic interweaving, commingling with profound intimacy.

The orgasm took her hard, her spine arching of its own accord, a cry escaping her as she threw her head back, utterly entranced and catapulted. Cillian grasped her hips, vising his hands on her and holding her in place as he drove upward, following her with frenzied, deep thrusts that extended the waves of completion carrying her to his familiar shore.

She collapsed over him, purged and limp, dimly aware that he stroked her back with long, affectionate caresses, his love words a gentle susurrus in her ear. The thought ran through her mind, though never clearly enough to reach her lips, that this, being with him, being so connected to him… there might never be enough.

~ 19 ~

ALISE AWOKE SOMETIME later, the room dim, the sky out the window a winter painting of slate gray, snowflakes swirling in the meager light shining from the window. Most of that light came through the open door to the living area, golden from the lamps and the little fireplace where the fire elemental danced, gradually devouring the wood chips fed to it.

The rich aroma of gingerbread flowed in also, and she smiled, touched that Cillian took her whim so seriously. Her stomach rumbled with interest, too. Slipping out from under the covers he'd clearly pulled over her, she stretched, feeling the delicious ache in every part of her body, then went naked to the window and gazed out.

Convocation Academy lay still under the snow, golden lights shining out from various windows illuminating the pristine cloak. Alise had never borne much affection for the school, but in this moment the old turrets and towers, the stone wings and boxy courtyards, looked almost romantic. It was simply a structure—saturated with magic, yes—but neither good nor bad in and of itself. The people housed within made their choices, pursued their dreams and schemes, plotted to win or merely to survive. They were the ones to decide on their paths. The school simply taught them what they needed to know.

More than anything else, Alise needed those skills. She could accomplish nothing without understanding her own abilities. Deciding what to do with them could come later. The grief over Maman's senseless death, and Alise's culpability in that, would never fully leave her. But somehow, in that brilliantly intimate time with Cillian, something inside her had settled. Not healed over, not now nor anytime soon, but she felt less raw. No longer so unmoored, like a ship in full sail with no crew or rudder, plunging through storm after storm, emerging from each battering a bit more ragged than before.

No, it would be up to her to learn to steer this ship, to trim the sails, and take the measure of the wind and waves. Somewhere along the journey, she'd abdicated that responsibility, what she owed to herself.

"I thought I felt you stir," Cillian said from the doorway, a lean silhouette with wild curls. "Everything all right?"

"More than all right." She went to him with a smile, feeling sensual and replete with relaxed abandon. Winding her arms around his neck, she kissed him, long and lingeringly, loving how his hands drifted over her body, as if savoring her, one hand palming her bottom and the other between her shoulder blades, holding her close to him.

Cillian had donned a soft robe, made of a felted material she didn't recognize, and it rubbed tantalizingly against her nude body. When he drew back from the kiss, he grinned at her sound of protest and resisted her efforts to recapture him.

"No, darling Alise," he said with real amusement. "I am impervious to your wiles until you're properly fed."

"Feeding me is all you think about."

"Not *all*." His grin became a leer as his gaze swept her body. "Still, keeping you alive and well enough to handle the many stones being hurled in your direction is a priority for me. There's fresh gingerbread," he added with a purr of enticement.

"So I smell," she replied, trying to sound grudging, but her stomach chose that moment to growl in audible demand. She clapped a hand to it, groaning theatrically. "I swear, all I do around you is eat and sleep."

"Not all," he repeated with a salacious grin, ducking when she swatted him. "You need both and I'm happy to facilitate that." He tipped up her chin and gave her a sweet, chaste kiss. "Be a good girl and we can see about more of *this* later. I left pajamas for you on the end of the bed there." Taking her shoulders, he turned her to point her that way, then gave her bottom a pat. "You know where the bathing facilities are. Take your time. I'll dish up dinner when you're ready."

"Dinner?" she called after him as he left the room. "I thought I was having fresh gingerbread!"

"You'll have a proper meal, first," he called back. "Then dessert, *if* you behave."

It was absurd to be charmed by him saying such things to her, but a silly smile stretched her cheeks and she rolled her eyes at herself. Apparently she'd lost all sense along with her virginity.

ALISE EMERGED FROM Cillian's bedroom wearing his old pajamas. Or, it might have been more precise to say they were wearing her, as she was nearly swallowed up by them. And he wasn't all that big of a guy. She looked like one of his sisters' porcelain dolls: delicately lovely, lustrous eyes dominating her heart-shaped face, and wearing the clothes from an entirely different doll. She'd rolled up the fleece bottoms at the ankles, where they hovered in fat rolls above her slender feet. The sight of her adorable pink toes did something to him.

She gave him a wry look, flapping her arms in the baggy top. He noticed she had the spirit bottle in one hand. Keeping it close. He supposed that was the best solution for the moment. "I feel like I'm wearing a tent," Alise informed him.

"Have you ever *been* in a tent?" he asked curiously. He liked to sleep out in the hills in a tent, but that didn't seem like something a daughter of Lord Elal would do.

She lifted her nose. "I don't have to have slept in one to know what it is. Or what it feels like to be draped in one," she added. "My clothes seem to have disappeared."

"I gave them to the cleaning imps. They'll be done soon. Besides, I thought you'd be more comfortable in pajamas. It's getting cold out there."

"I can get the fire elemental to increase the heat, if you want?"

"That would be excellent." The old building tended to be

drafty, the generous heat provided by the elementals dispersing rapidly, especially when it got windy, as this night promised to be. He was lucky to have the little fireplace, but his sole fire elemental could only do so much. Or, it seemed. Turned out the creature hadn't been doing as much as it could, after all. While he dished up their supper, he observed with interest as Alise crouched before the flickering elemental a faint scent of roses in the air as she spoke to it in low tones, sounding not unlike someone speaking to a pet cat.

When she rose to her feet again, the fire elemental had doubled in size, dancing with increased vigor over the wood chips.

"What did you do?" he asked, carrying their bowls to the small dining table he almost never used. "I thought fire elementals were one size and strength."

"The kind already tamed and bound for household use are," she answered. "That's part of House Elal product standardization. I didn't even realize you had a dining table. I thought this was a desk or bookshelf," she teased.

He loved her humor, especially since she so rarely let it emerge. "I picked some things up, to accommodate an actual human being here."

"Don't you count as an actual human?"

"Not at all," he answered in his most serious voice. "I'm book-adjacent and serve their whims."

She laughed, a low, sensual sound. Setting the bowls down, he leaned over to kiss her, delighted to have her there, relaxed and happy. She gave him a curious smile. "What was that for?"

"Just saying hi."

She blushed lightly. "Hi."

"Go ahead and sit. Start eating. I'll grab the bread."

"This looks really lovely. And like hours of work."

He brought the basket of warm bread back to the table and sat opposite her. "You slept several hours."

"And you didn't."

"Unlike other people at this table, I regularly get sufficient sleep, so no, I did not take a nap." Instead he'd started the breads, made the stew and put it on simmer, then picked up the apartment so it would be more orderly, all the while comforted to know Alise was in the little bedroom, the scent of her drowsy magic comforting as a glass of warmed wine.

"Ha ha." She dipped her spoon into the bowl, moving pieces around. "What am I eating?"

"Beef stew, with mushrooms."

She took a bite and closed her eyes in an expression of such utter bliss that his cock stirred with renewed hunger for her. "This is delicious. Way better than anything the dining hall serves."

"Now you know why I like to cook for myself."

"Except when you're lurking in the dining hall in order to spy on me."

"To look out for you," he corrected easily. "Now that I can feed you myself, I won't worry so much."

"As previously noted, you worry *too* much."

She needed someone to be concerned about her, but he decided that wouldn't be a productive conversation. "Tell me more about what you did with the fire elemental."

"Changing the subject?"

"Absolutely." He offered her the bread basket, waiting for her to take a slice, then helped himself and swirled it in the thick sauce of the stew. Taking a sopping bite, he rolled the flavor on his tongue. Quite good, he decided. The mushrooms added a nice richness, and the red wine he'd used in the sauté reminded him of Alise's flavor.

"You like to dip stuff," Alise observed, watching him.

"I do. I love the contrast of crunchiness and creaminess." Demonstrating, he popped a bit of dripping crust in his mouth and chewed. He'd gotten the crust on the bread just right, too. "Perfect." And so was she. Alise looked exactly right sitting at his table, her magic softening the air, turning winter to rose-laden summer.

She tipped her head. "You're surprisingly sensual for someone so in his head."

"Why is that surprising? There's no conflict between thinking and feeling. I can do both."

"Yes, you can. Do you really want to know more about the fire elemental?"

"Very much."

"Why?"

"I'm curious." Also, he wanted to know everything about her. He particularly liked how her face lit up when she talked about her magic-working. She was deeply conflicted about it, too—and he wasn't sure why—but at least this aspect of her talents brought her joy and Alise didn't have nearly enough of that.

"Hmm." She sounded unconvinced, but kept going. "I

gave the fire elemental more magic, for one. As I was saying before, the production line wizards employed by House Elal summon the elementals, then bind them according to a standardized protocol. That process includes a packet of magic along with a set of instructions. The elementals can use a favored material to supplement that magic—like earth elementals eating dirt—but they can only 'charge' to a certain point. The excess goes nowhere. Otherwise, we'd end up with earth elementals growing to enormous size and power in the sewage pits. And no one wants *that!*"

He loved this side of her and mock shuddered. "A daunting image—and also something I'd never thought about."

She shrugged a little, forking up some beef and chewing. "Why would you? This kind of thing falls under the realm of house arcania, establishing a consistent product line. Of course, the process of standardizing elementals for household use happened centuries ago, crafted by my Elal ancestors, and only tweaked since then. Why fix what isn't broken?"

"Why, indeed?"

She smirked at his reply. "A commonality to high houses, I believe, clinging to tradition. Anyway, these elementals being the size and shape they are has been consistent for not only our entire lives, but our parents' lives and grandparents' and before. So it's natural to accept that as the default without examination."

"I don't much like to think of myself as having accepted something as a fundamental truth without having examined it," he admitted.

She gazed at him thoughtfully. "No, you wouldn't. But

look where your curiosity has led you: examination of the banal." She grinned impishly. "So, because I have Elal blood, it's relatively easy for me to tinker with the default settings on an Elal product. I simply adjusted the metrics that had been binding the fire elemental to the standard size and heat output, fed it some extra magic to compensate for the increases, and promised it some gingerbread as a treat."

That gave him pause. "A fire elemental can consume more than wood or oil?"

"Oh yes. They particularly like anything with heat elements, like spices."

"Like ginger."

She pointed a bread crust at him. "Exactly."

"So, will it eventually revert to standard?"

"Yours?" She shook her head. "No, it will stay this way, unless you want me to reset it. Or you could get some other Elal wizard to do it."

"You are the only Elal wizard I want mucking with my elementals."

She fluttered her lashes. "Such a romantic."

Only for you, he nearly said, but restrained the words.

"Anyway, I'm talking too much," she said.

She rarely spoke so freely, it was true, which meant he didn't want her to stop. "I asked," he pointed out simply. "And I'm delighted to keep my improved fire elemental."

"Good." Her lips curved in a satisfied smile, her dark gaze warm, and he savored seeing her in such a relaxed mood. He even allowed himself a bit of self-congratulation at having helped get her there. "More stew? Or are you ready for the gingerbread you commanded me to make?"

She groaned patting her concave stomach as if that demonstrated anything. "If I eat any more stew, I won't have room for gingerbread."

"That's a decision then." He stood and gathered their empty plates.

"I can help with that," she said, starting to rise.

"No need. Sit and relax."

"I feel like that's all I've been doing," she grumbled.

"For once in your life," he agreed. "You'll need to practice more before you get a good feel for it."

"I just don't want you to have to wait on me."

"Take care of you," he corrected. "Which I like to do, so you're pleasing me by allowing it."

She was quiet and he glanced at her, finding that she was frowning at him. "That seems backward," she explained, catching his look.

"You've been through a traumatic experience." He said it as calmly as he could, stacking the empty plates in the bin for the earth elementals to scour, controlling the immediate swell of rage as best he could. "I couldn't help you before, but I can do this much."

"I didn't expect you to help me before," she said quietly.

Ah, well, if that didn't only make him angrier. "I know." *Because you didn't trust me,* he didn't say. *Because you don't think I'm capable. Because you don't need me like I need you.* He didn't say any of it, though. Instead he focused on slicing the gingerbread.

The next moment, the scent of roses thickened and she slid

slender arms around him from behind. "I'm sorry. I didn't mean to upset you."

He set down the knife he'd been gripping too hard and laid his hands over hers, aware she pressed her cheek between his shoulder blades—and that this was the first truly spontaneous gesture of affection she'd shown him. Tempted to deny it, to brush it off, he reconsidered. If they had any future with each other—unlikely, but regardless—he should give her emotional honesty. "I understand why you didn't. I also think it wasn't only the geas or the threats that kept you silent."

She didn't say anything for a while, but she also didn't move away. "I'm used to being on my own," she finally said, sounding bleak enough that he wanted to kick himself for making her sad when she'd been so happy just moments before.

Turning, he faced her and leaned against the counter, drawing her close and cupping her head against his chest. He kissed her sleek hair, fragrant with the scent of her magic. "You don't have to be."

She tipped her chin up, searching his face. "I think I'm maybe not good at asking for help."

"Have you ever asked for help and been refused?"

A laugh escaped, bitter-edged. "Piers Elal believes firmly that only the weak rely on anyone but themselves."

"Oh, darling." He smoothed comforting hands down her back. "It's not true."

She smiled a little, but it didn't reach her eyes where doubt lingered.

"How about some gingerbread with brandy sauce?" he

suggested, rather than pushing her further into unhappiness.

"That sounds amazing," she admitted, then narrowed her eyes at him. "But I feel it's important to clarify that I didn't 'command' you make it."

"Very nearly." He chucked her under her adorably pointed chin. "All high-house lady ordering her minions about."

"Cillian!" She looked outraged but also contained a laugh. "That is so unfair."

"Don't fret, my lady," he continued, setting her back from him so he could check the consistency of the brandy sauce. "I'm a very happy minion."

~ 20 ~

T HE GINGERBREAD WAS, of course, exquisitely good—and the brandy sauce launched it into the realm of paradisial. Alise devoured it all, despite her already full stomach. While she ate, she mused over the full rotation in her relationship with Cillian and how she wanted to handle that.

Cillian was quiet, too, either similarly occupied with eating or giving her room to think. Probably the latter, knowing him. It seemed that, regardless of her best intentions, he had been drawn into her particular vortex of doom and would not be dissuaded from hanging on. So be it. She couldn't fight everyone and everything, particularly not the gently tenacious Cillian.

"So," she began, scraping up the last bits of the dessert and focusing on that, not Cillian, but fully aware she had his instant attention, "in the morning you'll escort me to Professor Seraphiel and go to see the provost about Gordon Hanneil. Once I'm done with Professor Seraphiel, I'll see Professor Cixin about the spirit bottle." And still not go to her other classes or make inroads on her passively increasing workload. She suppressed a sigh for that.

"Sounds like a good plan," he replied evenly, not pointing

out that they'd already covered this. Saying nothing more, he waited her out.

She sighed mentally for his obdurate nature. "Fine. And then we can see about a trip to House Harahel and finishing what we started."

"Good," he replied instantly. "I'll arrange it with the provost."

"If you *can*."

"Oh, I'll make a persuasive argument, no fear. The provost assigned you this independent study for a reason, and appointed me to assist for the same reason. House Uriel can't openly move against House Hanneil, but I have no doubt that they closely monitor Hanneil's activities. They have to suspect Hanneil in the actions against House Phel; Provost Uriel's tacit support of your investigation is proof of it. In addition, Uriel has traditionally seen themselves as the bulwark between Hanneil and their ongoing attempts to conquer the Convocation. Once the provost learns about Gordon Hanneil's attempts to quell you, she'll want the evidence of their perfidy even more, and that corroborating evidence can only be obtained in the House Harahel archives."

"I don't think it's entirely accurate to say the information can be obtained only in the House Harahel archives," Alise replied, looking up at him, her plate scraped as clean as it could be, and finding him preparing to argue. "Oh, don't look at me like that. I said I'd go, didn't I? And I am agreeing to go because I think we will find valuable information there. My point is that I don't think Gordon Hanneil would be slithering through these hallways, issuing vile threats, and risking Convocation censure if there wasn't *something* to be found in the archives right here."

"I had the same thought," Cillian agreed, relaxing again. "I've been contemplating the problem and I think I'm close to a solution. Library magic might not be as potent as yours, but it has its uses. I've got some ideas for a few things I can try."

"I wish you wouldn't do that," she said, continuing when he raised an inquiring brow. "You denigrate your magic, calling your wizardry low level and comparing it to mine unfavorably."

He regarded her a moment, looking taken aback. "I just want you to know that I don't have delusions about us. I *am* a low-level wizard, practicing a kind of magic with limited, very niche applications. And I'm at peace with that. I'm happy with my life."

"Are you though?" she persisted.

"Yes." But he sounded defensive, looking away to finish his own dessert.

"Because you don't talk like someone who's perfectly happy with their life."

He met her gaze again, black eyes no longer soft but glittering with irritation. "And you know *how* many people who are perfectly happy with their lives, to know how they speak about it?"

"Fine." She rose, picking up her plate. "Don't confide in me then." She whirled around on the few short steps to the kitchen. "But it's not fair, you going on about me asking for help and telling you my secrets when you don't trust me with yours."

"Have you told me everything then?" he returned.

"I don't have to tell you *everything*. We're not talking about me."

"Indeed you don't have to tell me anything at all, but you also don't get to rail at me for not laying my bleeding heart on the table for you to dissect with your sharp tongue."

Arrested, hurt, she gaped at him a moment, then took her plate into the kitchen. Tempted to hurl it into the cleaning bin, she instead set it carefully aside, extracted the clean plates from lunch, and found their proper place in the cupboard.

"I apologize," Cillian said, picking up the plate she'd set aside and handing it to her along with his own to put in the cleaning box.

"No need," she replied lightly, telling herself she wasn't hurt, restraining the urge to wail that she'd thought he *liked* her. "I do have a sharp tongue. Nic has a sharp tongue. Our papa's is like a double-headed axe. You're not saying anything I don't know about myself."

"Don't clean up," he said as she began adding the dirty pots to the bin. "I can do that."

"You cooked; I can do the dishes. A much easier task." Unable to resist, she silently enhanced the boxed earth elementals that came with the cleaning bin.

He sighed, boosted himself up to sit on the counter, and watched her work. "I *am* happy with my life—or I was until I met you."

Oh, ouch. Several bitter reproaches rushed to her tongue, including pointing out that he had pursued her, not the other way around. But, for once, she decided to say nothing rather than run the risk of speaking sharply. *You're welcome,* she thought wryly.

"I can't—" Cillian started to say, then broke off. "I'm having a hard time shaking the feeling that I'm not good enough for you. That we don't really have a future. Lady Elal and the poor scholar."

"I keep telling you. I'm not likely to ever be Lady Elal."

"But you'll still be you: brilliant, powerful, at the heart of everything happening. You're at the center of this brewing storm."

How odd that he used those exact words. The echo penetrated her cloud of sadness and hurt. "Why do you say that, put exactly that way?"

"No reason in particular. Just an observation. Why?"

She glanced over her shoulder at him to find him watching her with that keen intelligence. Might as well tell him everything, whether or not he disliked her sharp tongue. Or maybe because he did dislike that about her. What did she have to lose if hearing this annoyed him further? Wiping her hands, she leaned on the opposite counter. "House Hanneil wasn't the only one to send a messenger, and a warning."

His tension sharpened in the air between them, the slice of his inquisitive magic palpable. Not invasive—he wouldn't do that to her—but the sense of him wanting, *needing* to know was clear. "Tell me," he said shortly.

This part would take careful dancing, as she still had no intention of telling him about her ability to sever the wizard–familiar bond, nor about murdering her own mother. She would never speak to *anyone* about that. The fewer people who knew the better. Besides, she didn't think she could bear the look in Cillian's eyes if she told him the monstrous truth about herself.

"A House Ariel wizard visited me and warned me that they had information that they had received word of... tampering with the wizard–familiar bond."

Cillian waited, clearly restraining a dozen questions—and probably a tart criticism for her withholding that information until then. He raised his brows when she didn't say more. "Did this messenger have anything else to impart?"

"Nothing of import. She didn't say why she'd come to *me*, except to issue vague threats related to Iliana being at House Phel and strongly implying that someone there knew about the bond-severing."

"Is it true—have there been wizard–familiar bonds severed?" Cillian asked, catching and holding her gaze.

"Yes." She sighed, not seeing a way around this. "Two: between Maman and Papa, and between Healer Asa and his familiar Laryn."

He whistled, long and low, considering. "*Does* someone there know about it?"

Alise shrugged, turning away. "I can't imagine who. She seemed to think that, because the bond was severed between Maman and Papa, I would know something about it. But obviously, I don't."

"Is that obvious?" he asked quietly.

"What would I know?" She did her best to sound innocently perplexed. "I haven't graduated yet, so I don't have the information on how the bonding enchantment is created in the first place. Wait, do you know?"

Cillian cocked his head and raised his brows, indicating that he did, but that he couldn't speak of it due to the geas that accompanied the information. "What *do* you know about how the bond was severed between your parents?" he asked. "And between Asa and Laryn for that matter. It can't be coincidence that both unprecedented severings occurred at House Phel."

She should have known the inquisitive, observant librarian wouldn't have missed that pattern. They'd been careless. And she should never have taken him to House Phel in the first place. If she'd left him by the side of the road to House Harahel, so many complications would have been avoided. She also wouldn't be there at that moment, her body lax and sore from his lovemaking. So difficult to balance the positives and negatives.

"I really don't know anything. Who could perform such a trick? I didn't even know it was possible."

"You're deflecting. I can see it in your face and smell it in your magic. You can trust me, Alise. You have to know I wouldn't harm anyone you love, which includes all of House Phel."

With palpable relief, she realized he didn't suspect her. "You think it was Gabriel?"

He shrugged thoughtfully. "The evidence certainly adds up." He ticked the points off on his fingers. "Gabriel Phel never attended Convocation Academy, which gives him a rather enviable intellectual freedom when considering what can and can't be done with wizardry. He therefore never graduated, which means he has a flexible concept of the wizard–familiar bond."

In lieu of speaking words he could not, Cillian raised his brows significantly. "Lord Phel is also an idealist, an iconoclast who openly struggles with the entire system of wizard–familiar bonding and the second-class citizenship the practice confers upon familiars. Not that I disagree. He's significantly invested in Nic's happiness and would love to kill your father. He'd have been motivated to please his wife and to injure Elal. Finally, his combination of moon and water magic hasn't been seen in the Convocation since the previous iteration of House Phel collapsed, metaphorically and literally, so we don't know what kind of capability it confers."

He frowned, looking perplexed, speaking more slowly as he thought it through. "The flaw in this logic is there's no reason to believe the wizard–familiar bond is created by Gabriel Phel's brand of magic and every reason to assume it's a subset of psychic wizardry." Cillian considered her, his agile mind perceiving far too much. "Which would explain House Ariel's concern, given that historical records hint that their techniques in psychically binding animals to their purposes may have contributed to the early experiments that resulted in the implementation of wizard–familiar bonding. It would also explain Hanneil and Uriel's interest in *you*."

"In me?" she nearly squeaked. "I don't follow."

"I think you do. I think you follow far too well." He hopped off the counter in a surprisingly quick and sinuous move, caging her against the counter she'd unwisely trapped herself against. "Look at me, Alise," he commanded softly, steel beneath the velvet, waiting until she reluctantly complied. He framed her face in his hands. "No lies. No evasions. Tell me what happened. You owe me the truth."

"I owe you nothing," she hissed, trying to wrench her face from his hands.

He held on, strength in his determination. Alise could have repelled him easily, but she couldn't bring herself to do it. As awful as him discovering the monstrous truth would be, some part of her wept in relief at not having to carry it alone any longer.

"Allow me to rephrase," he said. "This is a secret so potent it could destroy you and I'm not going to stand by and allow that to happen. *This*, I think, is at the heart of what's been eating at you. I've watched you work your wizardry, felt the ebb and flow of your magic as you manipulated those spirit bonds in the archives. You figured out how to sever the wizard–familiar bond, didn't you? *You* are the one who did it."

Abruptly she burst into tears, the sobs wrenching out of her in agonizing convulsions of grief. "I'm sorry," she sobbed. "I'm sorry I'm sorry I'm sorry."

Her head spun. The room darkened, and she found herself being carried into Cillian's bedroom. Cradled against him, she lay in the bed that smelled of him and resonated with their intertwined magics, grating out the apologies that would never be enough while he soothed her and spoke words she couldn't hear in a chanting rhythm of surcease.

~ 21 ~

C ILLIAN HELD ALISE as she broke open with a profound grief he'd never had guessed lurked within the cool, collected and often inscrutable wizard-woman. He'd been chipping away at her, deliberately working at getting her to confide in him, employing every trick he could think of to seduce, cajole and, yes, even bully his way through her reflexive defenses.

He hadn't expected this immense grief. Nor that she'd be, in the end, so fragile when she gave up the walls she'd been hiding behind. Guilt assailed him that he'd done this to her, but he set it aside. She shouldn't have had to bear this burden alone. If this is what it took to get her to open up to him, then so be it.

He only hoped that she wouldn't hate him for it.

At last those ugly, horrible sobs weakened, diminished, then faded away altogether. They lay there together in near silence, broken only by her occasional sniffles. She also gradually tensed as she recovered her senses, the wine-red, rose-red, crimson scent of her magic intensifying as her formidable intelligence reasserted herself.

Figuring he'd better strike now, in this interstitial moment between the utter devastation of her grief and the moment she'd recovered enough to begin rebuilding those usually unassailable walls, he spoke. "Tell me the story," he said in a quiet, gentle voice, "from the beginning."

She stirred restlessly, quite as he'd expected, and he firmed his embrace. "There's no wriggling away from this," he informed her. "The proverbial cat is out of the bag, so you may as well arm me with the information I need."

"I can't decide if I hate you or…" She trailed off, not willing or able to finish it, much as his heart longed to hear the possible alternative.

"You don't hate me. You hate being vulnerable."

"Is that why you trapped me here?" Her voice had a can-tankerous note, but he knew her sharp tongue well—and, to tell the truth, had become perversely fond of being flayed by it—and her heart wasn't in the accusation.

"*Wrapped* you here," he corrected, "in my arms, my blan-kets, and my silence. I suspect I may end up saying this to you all our lives, but you can trust me, darling Alise."

"All our lives?" She snorted, her face pale in the shadows as she pulled back to look at him in the dim light filtering from the other room. "And here just moments ago you were going on about not fitting into my life or this grand future you imagine for me as Lady Elal. Though now you should understand the main reason why that can never be."

He didn't tell her about his fantasies, how he imagined being her friend and advisor, no matter how high she rose. That he couldn't be her lover forever went without saying. Only Alise being at this nadir of her life prevented her from seeing that as clearly as he did. But he would savor being her lover as long as it lasted. He'd store up every moment, every touch and scent and flavor and whispered word, even the sharp ones she spoke in anger. And he would do his best by her, to help her through this, so that when she inevitably left him and moved on with her life, she'd think of him fondly. Perhaps receive those visits he dreamed might persist throughout their days, if only she recognized his value to her.

"Tell me the story," he said again, "from the beginning."

She sighed, but he sensed her capitulation. "This will sound like an excuse, but it was all Nic's idea."

Cillian thought wryly to himself that he wasn't at all surprised. Even when she'd been a promising uncat, all but universally acclaimed as a wizard and the next head of House Elal, Lady Veronica Elal had been a force to be reckoned with. He kept quiet, however, hoping receptive silence would keep Alise talking.

"It began with Laryn," she continued on a long breath. "She betrayed Nic to the Sammaels, you know. Or perhaps you don't. Gabriel had been psychically injured in the effort to rehabilitate Seliah and was unconscious for days and days. Laryn told Sergio Sammael and he, assuming Gabriel would die, abducted Nic to his house so he could force her to bond with him as his familiar. This is maybe going into the weeds too much. Anyway, once Gabriel had rescued Nic, they faced the problem of how to deal with Laryn. Asa, as her wizard, felt deeply betrayed, but she also carried their baby, got during their Betrothal Trials. No one wanted to execute Laryn as she deserved."

"So Nic hit upon the idea that you could sever the wizard–familiar bond and free Asa of his connection and obligation to Laryn."

"Yes, in part. She thought to offer the option to Laryn as an alternative to execution, because it would allow me to practice for what she most wanted me to do."

"Free your mother from her wizard, your father."

"Exactly." She shoved her hair back from her face, the inky silk of it falling through her shadowy fingers. "They found Maman in the tower where Nic had been imprisoned, left behind when Papa fled. Maman wasn't herself, possibly from being kept in alternate form for so long—as punishment for helping Nic escape her wedding—or because of the attenuation of the wizard–familiar bond."

"So, Nic came up with the arguably innovative and fascinating idea of severing that bond in an attempt to save your mother's life." It really *was* a clever solution. The Convocation texts were filled with tales of the tragic effects of the wizard–familiar bond attenuation, both nonfiction and fiction, including—notably—*The Saga of Sylus and Lyndella*. The familiar inevitably wasted away and perished. Cillian hadn't gotten to that part of Sylus and Lyndella's tragic tale, as Lyndella's death in her wizard's arms as he rescued her too late to save her obviously came near the end, but that famous fictional familiar's epic passing was often referenced in that context.

"Innovative and clever, yes, except that now we know why no one does it. The technique didn't work." Grief and, worse, self-recrimination haunted her voice. "It truly is impossible."

"Not to be pedantic," he said, hugging her close to give what comfort he could, "but clearly the technique *did* work and is possible. You successfully severed the wizard–familiar bond between two couples. That's an amazing achievement."

"You and I must have different definitions of the word 'success,'" she replied sourly. "Laryn became listless and decidedly unhealthy. And Maman… she died." Alise's voice broke entirely. "I did that. I murdered my own mother, who I loved dearly. *Not* a rousing success."

Cillian debated with himself on what to say to her. He hated that she'd been carrying this burden alone—and would love to have a chat with Lady Phel about she and Gabriel sending Alise off to cope with this bleeding wound by herself, without any support—but the logical flaws were apparent to him and might help her. "May I offer a different interpretation?"

"Cillian…" she said on a long sigh. "You don't have to try to make me feel better. I know what I did. I'm coping with that."

"While I would love to make you feel better, I think I have a valid set of logical arguments here, but I understand that now might not be the right time."

She made a snuffling sound that he finally realized was a laugh. Shallow and watery, but definite amusement. "Only you."

He wasn't sure whether to take umbrage at that. Still, she sounded less broken and that heartened him. "Listen, you're talking about an experimental technique with a dataset of two points. One of those points—not to be unfeeling about your maman, but regarding the situation with a level of objectivity—was a person already in peril. She'd been non-responsive since her rescue, had spent far too long in her alternate form, and seemed unlikely to survive as she was. Yes? Or you wouldn't have tried a desperation move to attempt to save her."

"True," Alise agreed reluctantly. "But Laryn—"

"Right. Data point number two. A woman who was pregnant, disgraced, feeling the intense displeasure of her bonded wizard. No matter the status of their relationship, she sounds like someone already deeply unhappy to the point of apathy. Was she in robust health and spirits before you performed the severing?"

"Well, she was imprisoned in her rooms and barely eating."

"I'm gonna call that a no."

"Fair." Alise sounded somewhat less despondent, which was definitely encouraging.

"Finally, every good experiment testing a new technique requires a control and you had none."

"I don't know how you'd control for that."

"Offhand? I don't either, but I can say with confidence that this was a flawed experiment."

"It wasn't an experiment so much as—what did you call it?—a desperation move."

"Exactly." He squeezed her lightly, aware of her birdlike bones and resilient spirit. "You can't draw conclusions from that. You tried something desperate to help your mother, with the best of intentions, and it tragically didn't save her life. But," he said, talking over her when she tried to interrupt, "bear with me a moment, please, because this is important. The outcome could have, very likely *would* have, been exactly the same, with or without your attempt to save her."

Alise was quiet for a long time. "I feel like you're making excuses for me," she finally said.

"Was Nic upset with you—did she blame you for your mother's death?"

She twisted to look up at him, though he figured she couldn't see more of his expression than he could hers. "Of course not!"

"Because Nic is so even tempered, forgiving, never expects much of anyone." He nodded knowingly, just in case Alise missed the sarcasm.

"Right." Alise snorted at the image of fiery, strong-minded Nic being any of those things, then she sighed. "I know what you're doing. Nic told me it wasn't my fault, but…"

"But you decided to blame yourself anyway. And nearly tore yourself apart in the process."

"I have to hold myself accountable," she said quietly. "I don't want to become a monster. I don't want to be my father."

"Oh, darling Alise. You couldn't be. It's not in you. Your heart is too big."

"You have a worryingly skewed perspective of me," she said wryly. "What about my sharp tongue?"

"Sharp tongue, soft heart," he intoned. "That's what my people say."

She snort-giggled. "They do not."

"You'll see when you come to House Harahel. In the meanwhile, what are you doing to hone this skill you discovered?"

She levered up onto one elbow, a darker shadow looming over him. "Are you crazy? Nothing! First of all, if word of this possibility gets out, it will upend the Convocation, probably start a war between houses. And second, there is no way I'm going near doing anything like that ever again."

He waited, but she had nothing more, silently vibrating in challenge. "Allow me to rebut then. First of all, word clearly *has* gotten out or House Ariel wouldn't have sent that message, specifically to you. They know something. Maybe not all of it, but they suspect and—more saliently—they suspect *you*. You're in danger, Alise, and you can't wield denial as a blunt force weapon in hopes that the threat will go away. That goes for your second point, as well: you might wish you could undo the past, but you can't. This is an ability you have. Do you really want to wait until you're feeling desperate enough, again, to try a skill you never spent time honing and perfecting?"

"I just won't do it," she answered sullenly, after a significant pause.

"Not even to save someone's life? To save Seliah's life? Or Nic's?"

"You don't know it would come to that!"

"Neither of us knows that it won't, either."

A low growl emanated from her and she landed the meat of her fist in the center of his chest, making him grunt, mostly in surprise. "You are impossible to argue with," she complained.

"I love you, too," he said, quickly pulling her down into a kiss to cover the impulsive words. He'd promised himself he wouldn't pressure her. She resisted only a moment, flattening her hand on his chest and releasing a little mew of pleasure. So sweet, his Alise, her tongue caressing his, soft and sensual, not sharp at all.

They divested themselves and each other of their clothes, taking their time and sharing long, lingering kisses and caresses in the process. The mood had turned between them, somber with the release of Alise's intense grief, joyful in their shared intimacy. In the muted darkness, with the snow muffling all sound from outside, he slid into the welcoming embrace of her body with the final and finite sense of coming home at last.

~ 22 ~

FORTIFIED BY ONE of Cillian's homemade cinnamon rolls, on top of a full breakfast, Alise nearly rolled her way through the busy halls on her way to Professor Morghana Seraphiel's office. She wisely restrained any complaints about her overly full belly, lest she elicit another lecture from him on the necessity of *blah blah blah*.

He was so adorable. And her body sang from her toes to her giddy heart from his devoted attention, in bed and out. She wouldn't want to have to swear to it, but she suspected this effervescent sensation was actual happiness. Maybe even love.

They didn't hold hands, of course. They still hadn't discussed how to handle their new affair, not in so many words. Over breakfast, Alise had tiptoed around bringing up the topic, meeting with Cillian's cheerfully steadfast refusal to take up the conversational bait. She'd been left with no choice but to broach the question baldly. Call her a coward, she'd been too at peace eating his delicious food and enjoying the casual affection he showered upon on her at every opportunity. She didn't want to ruin things, especially since that seemed to be one of her particular talents.

So, they walked along, occasionally brushing against each

other when more boisterous students or determined faculty crowded them. The bottle of spirits bumped against her thigh and several more scouted ahead, making sure no one lurked, watching for her. She'd thought Cillian might be annoyed when she suggested that having a couple of scouts to spy out her path might be helpful, since he seemed so bent on protecting her personally, but he'd happily agreed. He still insisted on escorting her, in part to make sure she had backup—and as a witness—should anything occur, but also to show Alise the way to the dark arts wing, as she'd never had occasion to go there in the vast labyrinth that was Convocation Academy.

She'd rather imagined a gothic tower or a dismal dungeon. Instead, Cillian guided her to a glass-ceilinged hall with earth instead of stones for the floor. At her puzzled look, he gestured to the view of the heavily overcast sky. The glass must have been enchanted to shed snow, as none lay piled on that part of the roof as it did on the other crenellations. "The dark arts wizards need access to earth and sky," he said, as if that explained anything.

Alise nodded sagely, having no clue why that would be the case. They reached Professor Seraphiel's office, Cillian knocking with the back of his knuckles on the half-ajar door.

"Come in," Professor Seraphiel called in a silky voice, the first time Alise had heard her speak in all the times she'd glimpsed the woman in the archives. "Archivist Harahel," she commented as they stepped in, surveying them both with interest. "We missed you on your usual shift last night."

Alise started guiltily, having been so absorbed in her own

woes that she'd clean forgotten that the rest day would have ended at the onset of Cillian's night shift. He gave her a half-smile and a slight head-shake. "I had other duties," he said to Professor Seraphiel. "I trust you received notice of our visit?"

"I wouldn't be here in my office, still awake, instead of in my bed, would I, if not?" She turned wizard-black eyes on Alise. Morghana Seraphiel looked the quintessential dark arts master, with her corpse-pale skin, skeletal frame, and sleek cap of iron-gray hair. Incongruously, her feet were bare and dirt-encrusted, her long, bone-white toes digging into the soil beneath her chair. Snowy light poured in from the wall of windows and arched atrium-style roof. An enchanted waterfall sheeted down one of the interior walls, while the other was occupied by a large fireplace with a real fire burning wood, not an elemental.

"I don't recall having you in any of my classes, Alise Elal," Professor Seraphiel said.

"My father wished otherwise," Alise replied politely, not correcting the professor on her preferred house affiliation.

The steely wizard-woman snorted indelicately. "Piers Elal can kiss my narrow ass. He always was jealous of House Seraphiel—and acquisitive. We know about his espionage and the attempts to steal some of our proprietary techniques. Ah, I see you're genuinely surprised by that. I can easily read that in your thoughts. You'll want to work on both your transparent expressions and your psychic shielding if you want to be Lady Elal."

"With all due respect, Professor, I don't want that."

"No? Then you're either a fool or smarter than you look.

Which is it?"

Alise opened her mouth to answer and realized she'd been trapped into picking one of two unwelcome and untrue, options. "Bitter," she replied instead.

"Interesting. Bitter I can work with. Archivist Harahel, why are you still standing here? I won't eat the girl and surely you have better things to do."

"Nothing better to do, by any stretch, but duty calls," Cillian agreed cheerfully, giving the wizard a little bow. He cast a quick look at Alise, something in his expression telling her he'd like to kiss her goodbye, along with his deliberate step back, as if he didn't trust himself not to. "Be good for the nice professor," he told her with a wink. "And be careful."

"Also interesting," Professor Seraphiel said, watching Cillian leave. "The famously unattainable beautiful librarian boy falls at last. About time he got over Szarina, but does Tandiya know?"

It took Alise a moment to put together that Tandiya was Provost Uriel's given name. She had no idea who Szarina might be, except that perhaps that was the name of the person Cillian hadn't wanted to allow into their bed by discussing her. "It's not the provost's business. I'm an adult," she answered stiffly, "and doing nothing wrong."

The wizard snorted again, tapping blunt, gray-enameled nails on her desk. "Correction: you're a student at this academy and not a very good one at that."

"I've had extenuating circumstances," Alise said, wrestling her immediate ire.

"Not interested. Life is an extenuating circumstance. You

either handle your shit so you can get done what you need and want to accomplish, or you succumb to every little thing. Which do you plan to do, Alise Elal?"

"I claim House Phel as my affiliation now," Alise replied, stung enough to say so.

"How whimsical of you. Does Daddy know?"

"Lord Elal and I are not on speaking terms at the moment."

"I'll just bet you're not. Still you're an Elal whether you wish to claim that particular albatross or not. It seems I am graced with the opportunity to teach you something more useful to do with your wizardry than twiddling about with ghosties. Shall I teach you how to summon a demon? Far more potent than any of your typical non-corporeals."

Alise wasn't quite sure what to make of this rather bizarre interview. "I was given to understand that Healer Jonathan Refoel sent a referral for me to learn psychic defenses from you."

The wizard tapped her nails in a staccato of boredom, making a face as she did. "So dull. Baby steps. It's a disgrace that Convocation students aren't taught such elementary techniques as a rule. Why do you suppose that is, Alise Elal?"

Alise wanted to answer that she had zero control over Convocation Academy curriculum or policy, but she caught the canny gleam in the woman's gaze. A test then? "Because of the potential for abuse."

"Indeed. The dark arts are regarded with such superstition that all in the Convocation swear by us even as they avoid us. If not for House Seraphiel's historic place and considerable influence within the Convocation, I and my colleagues would have been eliminated from the academy entirely. As it is, high houses are allowed to excuse their students from coursework in the dark arts, as did your own dear papa."

"He is hardly dear to me," Alise pointed out, increasingly intrigued by the cantankerous woman.

"Well, that answers the question of whether you're a fool. Tell me, why do you need to learn these psychic defenses Healer Jonathan recommends? House Hanneil up to their old tricks, I suppose."

Alise didn't know whether to confirm, deny, or plead ignorance. But something about the Seraphiel wizard's frankness disarmed her. And the compulsion had been removed. She owed Gordon Hanneil nothing. So she told Morghana Seraphiel everything that had occurred with Gordon, grateful that she'd spent enough of her grief and terror in the telling already that she could keep relatively composed during the recitation. The dark arts professor listened with attentive interest, working her bare toes in the loamy soil beneath her chair thoughtfully.

"Take off your boots," she ordered once Alise had finished her summary. "Don't look at me like I'm barmy, girl. You're here to learn; I'm here to teach. Logic implies that you would do as I say, yes?"

All right, though it struck her as a bizarre ask, Alise complied, sitting in a rickety corner chair to pull off her boots and socks, then standing again before the professor. Her feet sank into the soil, which held a surprising amount of warmth and moisture. It felt strange, but also oddly grounding and familiar, as if she'd recaptured a moment from childhood, except that her own childhood had never held such opportunities.

If anyone had asked her to imagine what a lesson in the dark arts would be like, she would not have said anything close to this. She had truly expected considerably more bubbling cauldrons and sulfur, a thought that made her smile.

"Earth and sky," Professor Seraphiel said, as if answering a question. "Water. Flame." She pointed in turn to the trickling waterfall and the fireplace. "The dark arts have more in common with ancient forms of witchcraft than modern wizardry likes to acknowledge."

"I didn't realize," Alise murmured.

"Not with a hole in your education, you wouldn't. But you are experienced with elementals, so you should understand. The numinous is grounded by the elements of our physical world. Psychic manipulation is a magic that relies upon controlling the mental energy of another. Just as you harness the incorporeal to your will, so does an unscrupulous wizard, such as the Hanneils have perfected over centuries, attempt to bind and tame *you*. You are, after all, simply a sophisticated spirit gifted with a corporeal form."

Alise had never thought of herself as a spirit with a body, and the idea gave her a sense of dislocation, as if the world had jumped to the left and suddenly presented itself from a different angle. Her head swam woozily.

"Toes. Dirt," the wizard woman instructed, pointing at Alise's feet.

Obediently, she dug in her toes, finding that sense of rightness and realness returning.

"Gives you a different perspective, doesn't it, on all your spirit binding and taming? As you do unto others, so can be done unto you. It's worth remembering. Sometimes I think those of us in houses that trade in variations of psychic magic—Seraphiel, Uriel, Elal, Sammael, Ariel, and even Refoel—retain our ancient enmity for Hanneil not so much from hatred of the perverted control they've attempted over the centuries, but out of envy that they do what we scruple not to."

Alise gaped at her. Morghana Seraphiel waved that away. "A philosophical discussion for another day. Tell me, given your extensive experience in harnessing spirits to your will—think of the most evolved and complex spirit you've bound—what weapons does it possess to resist you co-opting its free will?"

She didn't like to think of herself as a Gordon-type, terrorizing others and tethering them to her will in the same way she'd been tormented. The dark arts professor watched her knowingly. "Now you begin to understand why everyone is chary of the dark arts. We embrace a different perspective that many find... unsettling. Answer my question if you wish to learn, young Elal."

Alise bent her mind to the riddle. How *did* spirits attempt to resist her? "Any number of ways," she answered slowly, as she thought it through. "Evasion, first. If they can't be found, they can't be caught."

"Good. What else?"

"I'm not sure how to describe it, but a kind of ... slipperiness? They wriggle through my mental grasp like water through my fingers."

"Excellent. Remember that. And if they cannot evade or elude?"

"They fight. They use strength, matching their power against mine. Depending on what I have available, they sometimes succeed. I don't always have enough magic to outlast them or quickly overpower them."

Professor Seraphiel nodded. "You're not a complete idiot, so that's helpful. Which of these weapons do you think you could employ to resist a similar attempt to control your thoughts?"

Trick question. "All of them, depending."

"It's too late for evasion. House Hanneil knows who and where you are. Can you elude the next attempt?"

Alise considered that, aware she'd furrowed her brow, thinking of that second encounter with odious Gordon. "I might. I could be like water, like air, like sand through a sieve, though it would take practice."

"And practice we will," the professor replied with satisfaction. "That is your first and best line of defense. To outlast and outpower—well, that would take more resources than you possess at this time. So we will focus on teaching you to be elusive."

"I thought I'd be learning shields," Alise admitted, "but I understand now how this approach makes more sense."

"Shields are a martial metaphor. They imply a static defense that can be circumnavigated or broken. You will learn to be like the spirits you tame, like the spirit you *are*, everywhere and nowhere. You cannot be broken because you cannot be fixed into place."

Alise found herself smiling. "I like the sound of that."

Morghana snorted, but a hint of a mirroring smile softened her stern face. "Of course you do. All Elals are slippery. You shall learn to be more so than most."

THEY DRILLED FOR several hours until Alise satisfied the dark arts professor that she could successfully elude any number of attempts at psychic control—including several truly terrifying attacks from the Seraphiel wizard herself.

Soaked in sweat, Alise found herself on hands and knees, digging all fingers and toes into the grounding soil.

"Barely escaped me on that one," Professor Seraphiel informed her, "but the good news for you is that was an extremely difficult attack to handle. There are full Seraphiel wizards who couldn't have done so well. You have a real talent. Are you sure you don't want to study the dark arts?"

"At this point," Alise panted, then found it within herself to climb to her feet again, particularly bolstered by the rare words of praise from the wizard, "I'm wondering why everyone *doesn't* study the dark arts."

Morghana Seraphiel laughed softly. "Now you know why everyone fears and avoids us."

Giving the professor a rueful smile, Alise nodded, accepting the towel Morghana handed her, using real water to wash the dirt from her hands and feet as instructed, returning both to the soil floor before neatly folding the towel. Considering whether this was wise and also that it could be her only opportunity, she said, "May I ask a question, Professor Seraphiel?"

"You might as well take advantage of my undivided attention to make up for the years of education in the dark arts you missed." She raised her steely brows into forks at Alise's hesitation. "Well?" She prompted. "Ask. If I am able, I will answer."

"Have you ever heard of someone being able to sever the wizard–familiar bond?" Alise asked, in more of a rush than she'd intended, or that was probably wise.

The forks inverted into a frown, the Seraphiel wizard gazing at her with baleful interest. "That would be a revolutionary feat of wizardry," she said slowly, displaying the caution Alise had failed to. "Why do you ask?"

Alise shrugged, trying to be nonchalant and no doubt failing miserably. "Just rumors. You know how students gossip."

"Indeed, I do." She studied Alise a long moment. "Tell me something, Alise Elal. Why *is* House Hanneil so interested in you?"

Alise widened her eyes in false innocence. "I have no idea."

"You really must become a better dissembler," the professor noted in disgust. "Lying is an art like any other."

"A dark art?" Alise retorted impudently, more confident now that she saw through Morghana's brusque manner.

"Quite the opposite. The dark arts are about uncomfortable truths. There's no room for denial or self-deception when dealing with demons. Are you going to answer my question?"

"Is it important that you have that answer?"

"Cagily handled. You will do well as Lady Elal."

"As I said previously, I have no interest in heading House Elal."

"Would you leave that role to your idiot of a brother? I must say your honest look of surprise serves you better than your attempts to feign ignorance. Of course I know of Fernando Elal. There are many of us who make it our business to anticipate who might next head influential Convocation houses and affect our lives and businesses. A fool can do far more damage than the most malicious intellect. You can bargain with evil. Speaking of which, my regards to Lord Phel in appreciation for him removing that nitwit Sammael heir from existence."

Alise could only process that with considerable astonishment, unsure where to begin.

"Never mind," Morghana Seraphiel waved a hand. "I've flummoxed your beliefs and expectations enough for one day. To answer your question, I could say yes, it's important for me to know why Hanneil is so interested in you, but it would be a lie to no purpose. I have my own suspicions and it will be entertaining to see if I prove to be correct. Still, tell your people at House Phel that House Seraphiel stands ready to assist. Now away with you. I'm excessively wearied."

With that dismissal, Alise didn't feel she could ask what Morghana meant by that tantalizing message.

~ 23 ~

"**I** THOUGHT," SAID Provost Uriel, before saying anything else, "that I expressly and clearly told you to stay away from Alise Phel."

So this is how it would go, Cillian thought with resignation. It had been futile to hope that the provost somehow wouldn't find out, wouldn't read in him all that had transpired between Alise and him, how their relationship had changed. As he *hoped* it had changed, anyway. He had the definite sense of both holding something precious gently enough not to break it, firmly enough not to lose it through carelessness, and being braced for it to fly away from him no matter what he did.

"Her magic is distinctly intertwined with yours," the provost added, "so don't bother to deny it. You put the Szarina incident behind you and I thought learned your lesson from that unpleasantness. *Why* did you have to complicate an already wickedly fraught situation?"

"The situation is more fraught than you know, Provost Uriel," he said instead of answering. He and Alise were both adults, both consenting. The Szarina incident was the worst thing he'd ever done and everyone knew it. He refused to let that taint the best thing that had ever happened to him and he wouldn't be pushed into defending or explaining. "We have a Hanneil spy in our midst and, I believe, an imminent civil war."

Provost Uriel stared at him a long moment, closed her eyes briefly as if in pain, then pointed at him to sit. Striding to her door, she called to Priyan to clear her schedule for the next hour. Instead of returning to sit behind her desk, she angled the chair beside Cillian to face him companionably and invoked a silencing shield with a twirl of a finger. "Tell me everything."

IT TOOK MORE than the hour she'd cleared, as Tandiya Uriel might be more autocratic than some people liked, but she was also thorough and so intensive in her questioning that Cillian regretted not having Alise present. He could not, for instance, tell the provost the name of the Ariel wizard who'd visited Alise. That lapse was exacerbated by his need to dance around Alise's involvement in severing the wizard–familiar bond.

Nothing like trying to lie by omission around a powerful psychic wizard skilled at ferreting out the truth. Tandiya studied him with a vaguely disappointed expression, though much of it might have been the trouble increasingly clouding her brow as she listened. Her magic nudged him, not an invasion of his thoughts—anathema to anyone of House Uriel's proud principles—but delivering an impulse to speak more, to spill any of his several secrets, including an abrupt and unwelcome urge to talk about Szarina, which he never felt under normal circumstances.

He narrowed his gaze at the provost. "Stop that."

"Then tell me whatever it is you're withholding."

"No. It's not mine to tell."

She sighed with extravagant weariness and dropped her head into her hand, braced by the elbow on the arm of her chair. "Alise Elal. The bane of my existence. I should never have readmitted her to Convocation Academy."

"She prefers Phel now."

"I'm aware. That makes her no less of an Elal. She might struggle against her fate, but it will chase her down regardless. Some people attract trouble and she is one of them."

"It's not her fault. Allowing her to complete her education isn't what's causing all of this."

"No, but she's the one who woke the bear and brought it here on her tail," the provost retorted. "I don't like it. Hanneil espionage and high houses jockeying for political position in my hallowed halls. I don't like it one bit," she repeated, glaring at Cillian as if he'd somehow allowed it all to happen.

"It's not as if any of us do," he replied in mild rebuke, making her sigh again in exasperation.

Launching herself from the chair, Provost Tandiya Uriel prowled to the windows ringing her tower office, gazing out with her hands folded behind her back. Pressing her fisted hands to her lower spine, she arched backwards, groaning at the stretch. "I'm getting too old for this," she remarked.

"Nonsense, Provost," Cillian said. "You will live forever."

Tandiya Uriel had been provost of Convocation Academy his entire life. The prospect of someone else helming the august institution alarmed him on a foundational level.

She turned and gave him a wry twist of lips that wasn't a smile. In the harsh winter light of the windows, her skin looked papery thin, the map of fine wrinkles apparent. "No one lives forever, young Harahel," she replied, not unkindly. "It's the one thing each of us can be sure of. However," she continued briskly, "today is not that day for me. Not quite. I will handle the problem of this imposter who managed to be hired under fraudulent circumstances. You will remove young Wizard Alise from my academy with all speed. Take her on your field trip to House Harahel. And for the dark arts' sake, get me some real evidence, please. If we're going to deal with House Hanneil once and for all—as should have been done back when they first took down House Phel, which I curse my ancestors for allowing—then we need documentation to convince the majority of Convocation high houses to take the risk moving against Hanneil."

So many questions swarmed through Cillian's mind that he didn't know which to lead with. "Then you believe that House Hanneil engineered the fall of House Phel?"

She snorted. "Of course. Everybody knows that."

"No," he said slowly, "I don't think everybody does."

"Anyone who was paying attention when it happened does. House Uriel knows. I'm surprised House Harahel doesn't. Surely at least one of your eager historians wrote it down."

He would certainly be asking questions on his visit home.

"What about the other enemies of House Phel, like Sammael and Elal?"

"What about them? They're simple scavengers and opportunists emboldened by Hanneil's machinations. They'll fall into line when faced with the might of the allied houses of the Convocation. They won't *like* it, but they'll do as Uriel tells them. Especially if they want to keep their lucrative high-house contracts."

Cillian mused to himself over the commonly accepted wisdom that Elal was the most powerful house in the Convocation, when it was apparently Uriel, but obviously didn't say so. "You mention the risk of taking on House Hanneil. Surely if all the wizards and familiars of all the high houses stand together, Hanneil will not be able to prevail?"

Provost Uriel raised her brows, pressing her lips into a line. "First off, we won't get everyone. There will always be those who seek to ride the coattails of those lunging for absolute power, thinking they themselves will enjoy same. They are fools to believe that. House Hanneil, if they attain the power they crave, will destroy or assimilate their former allies in time. There is no room for anyone else on the throne of an empire. The other houses are wise in their cowardice, perhaps. There is no guarantee that we can defeat Hanneil. The unprincipled control of thoughts is a powerful weapon, and insidious in its operation. There are few defenses against it."

"The dark arts," Cillian offered, wondering how Alise was doing under Morghana Seraphiel's tutelage.

"The dark arts, yes," Tandiya acknowledged with a tone of resignation more than enthusiasm. "Though those operate on an individual basis and not all can learn those skills. I anticipate that Alise will be able to, but she is unusual in many ways, even uniquely suited to that sort of wizardry. There had been discussions early in Alise's academic career regarding adding the dark arts to her curriculum. No doubt Morghana will be able to give her useful tools this morning. I know everything that occurs in my academy," she added at Cillian's start of surprise.

He bit his tongue on the retort that she hadn't known about Gordon Hanneil.

"Most everything," she amended, "and I intend to correct my recent failure to notice what I should have. At any rate, worrying about these things is my problem not yours. Remind me what you *are* to be worrying about?"

"Documentation of Hanneil's conspiracy against House Phel."

"Good boy," the provost said with a twinkle of amusement.

"Provost, I think that Gordon Hanneil wouldn't have tried so hard to stop Alise's search of the archives here if there wasn't something to find."

"I'm not an idiot, Cillian Harahel. I understand the implications. I have understood all along, which is why I assigned the task to Alise Elal to begin with and you to supervise, given your own unique abilities. Did you think I made those decisions randomly?"

"No, Provost Uriel," Cillian answered, chastened by her arch tone.

"What I want to know is, aside from the interference with

Wizard Alise's research, why haven't *you* discovered the missing records, or whatever it is under my roof that Hanneil fears will be so damming?"

"I don't know." His considerable frustration with his failure made his face heat.

"I certainly hope it's not a result of you being distracted by your fascination with your lovely new lover."

And they were back to the beginning of this conversation. "Our relationship is mutual," he told her, "and we are—"

"Yes, yes, I know," she interrupted. "Consenting adults, therefore I can't stop you. I won't attempt to and, after this, I won't offer my advice. But, Archivist, you are an intelligent wizard. You've never struck me as someone who deludes himself about his station in life and what that allows you to aspire to. I don't mean this unkindly." She actually produced a sympathetic smile and, in that moment, reminded him of his grandmother—who would probably proffer the exact same advice. Possibly in even more stringent terms. "Szarina was a different matter and ill-advised, but Alise Elal? You have to know that it cannot last and likely will end badly, and that you will be the one to take the most damage."

"I'm aware, Provost," he replied, speaking around the ache in his chest. "You are saying nothing I haven't said to myself. I know I handled Szarina badly, but I'm older and wiser now."

"Oh, Cillian." She dropped a hand on his shoulder, squeezing lightly, sympathy in the gesture. "You didn't handle Szarina badly. *She* handled *you* badly. Alise is a very different wizard, but I fear the outcome for you will be much the same."

"I have my eyes open," he said, standing up so he wouldn't

be obviously shaking off her hand. "I should get busy with the several tasks you've laid out for me. If I may be excused, Provost?"

"Go, go." She waved him away. "In all my years of leading this academy, you'd think I would have learned by now that unsolicited advice is almost always unwanted advice."

"Unwanted advice doesn't mean unvalued," he replied gravely.

She answered with a quirk of a smile, then resumed her usual stern expression. "Begone. I have much to do, as do you. Get me that proof, Wizard Harahel."

~ 24 ~

ALISE ENDED UP seeing Professor Cixin at the end of the day, as he didn't have office hours until then. Thus, she was able to attend her afternoon classes and make some inroads on the backlog of work. The nape of her neck prickled with awareness, her senses alert for the appearance of Gordon Hanneil—ready to practice her new defensive skills—but she never so much as glimpsed the proctor.

Gradually, she relaxed enough to concentrate on her work. Maybe the efficient Provost Uriel had already had Gordon arrested. A comforting thought.

Later, she left Professor Cixin's office hours unburdened of both the bottle of spirits and residual guilt over missing the make-up lab work she'd recklessly promised days before. Oh, the venerated Professor of Noncorporeal Entities had not been at all pleased with her effort to secure the gaggle of spirits in the bottle, calling her work amateurish, sloppy, and heedless of the potential consequences.

But he'd also used the words "bold" and "innovative," so Alise felt reasonably good about her wizardry. Plus she'd learned some interesting techniques for putting a bonded spirit into stasis using a one-time enchantment that would not continue to drain her magic. True to form, Professor Cixin had required that Alise perform the actual magic working, under his close supervision, with the upside that he declared the lesson sufficient to compensate for the one she'd bungled. Alise received the definite impression that Cixin was doing her a favor, but she wasn't too proud to take it. And the reprieve allowed her to procrastinate ever so slightly on working on bond-severing. She'd get there, she really would. But she'd done a lot that day and weariness had set in, a vague headache forming behind her eyes.

That was the downside of all she'd learned. Between the intensive tutelage from Professor Cixin and Professor Seraphiel, she needed her magic reservoirs refilled, which meant finding Brinda. She didn't care to play the supplicant, but Alise also knew that she'd suffer far more from the people in her life—namely, Cillian—if she let her magic run low again. That meant seeking out Brinda. Fortunately, she had something to offer the Chur familiar. Alise had received a missive from Nic.

The Ratsiel courier had been waiting for her outside of Professor Cixin's office, lightly landing on her shoulder as she emerged, and digging in imperious talons indicating the urgency of the message. House Phel had paid top coin to send an expensive, enchanted for privacy, private missive from the outside to a student. Those lengths seemed over the top for Nic to share her "secrets" of having a short Betrothal Trials period, so Alise hoped for some news from home.

Home. Funny how House Phel had become that in such a short time.

She couldn't yet go back to her own room, not until she was certain Gordon Hanneil had been contained and hopefully eliminated. She also wasn't truly comfortable going to Cillian's apartments. He probably wasn't there anyway and it would take time to recode the Iblis lock to admit her also. He'd mentioned it in passing, but she had kind of dodged replying since it felt like a big step. *Bigger than taking him as your first lover, knowing he's in love with you?* a snide internal voice whispered, but she ignored it. Still, all of that meant she needed to find somewhere else to read her letter from home.

Settling herself into one of the deep window seats of the long arcade that led to the dining hall, Alise put her back to the corner and coaxed the little courier off her shoulder. Using a bit of wizardry, she verified her identity, unlocked the missive, and let the courier perch on her upraised knee. It had been tasked to receive her reply, which hopefully she'd have time to write.

Eagerly, she began reading Nic's elegant script.

Dearest Alise,

How good to hear from you—although with questions regarding my betrothal trials??

Not at all what I expected. I hope that you are not contemplating such a step, at your tender age, though it would be entirely your business if you do. And I know you'll likely want a bonded familiar at some point. I certainly understand you wanting that bond along with the intimacy of a sexual relationship. And children, of course. I just...

Well, I am restraining myself from telling you all of my

thoughts on the matter, a heroic effort I very much hope you appreciate.

Alise laughed softly, imagining Nic's impatient head toss as she wrote that. Also, oops. In her efforts to inquire discreetly, Alise had inadvertently given Nic the wrong impression. She'd have to correct that. Funny that Nic would think Alise had any interest in locating a male familiar to test fertility with when the only person she wanted was... Not a familiar. Firmly setting thoughts of Cillian aside as not relevant to the moment, Alise continued reading.

To answer your questions, there is no way to shortcut the Betrothal Trials. Ignore any rumors you might hear regarding fertility enchantments and so forth. Not only are they impossible in the first place, they're terribly illegal and strictly forbidden by the Convocation, to the point of voiding even an established bonding.

There was that logical question: why would the Convocation bother to strictly forbid something that wouldn't work anyway? Nic might be trying to tell her something there. Hmm.

Beyond that, the only advice I can give a familiar for surviving the Betrothal Trials is: endure. The experience is in no way romantic. It's not easy. I'm going to say I wouldn't advise it? Yes, it turned out well for me, but only through happenstance—and the fortunate appearance of a certain obdurate wizard. That was a lucky lightning strike that no one should or can rely upon.

Before Gabriel arrived… well, it was awful. I kept that to myself, to spare Maman, though I think she knew more than I realized at the time. The thing is, you think that you're complying because you agree to the trials. I asked for it! To please Papa, which was misguided in retrospect, obviously, but also because I viewed the trials as my sole avenue to have some influence over who my wizard would be. The ability to use my right of summary dismissal to eliminate suitors I didn't want gave me the illusion of control, but I relinquished a far more critical level of choice in doing so. I didn't think it would matter to me so much, letting those men have me, attempt to impregnate me, but… it did. It hurt me inside in ways I can't describe.

Alise choked back a little dry sob at Nic's confession, especially poignant from someone who so rarely spoke of her feelings. Or acknowledged them, really. Alise supposed they'd both been relentlessly trained by their father to pretend they didn't *have* emotions. The intimacy of this reveal was the reason Nic had sent the message so securely. Alise marveled that the so very proud Nic had written this down at all.

My point is, please tell your "friend"—assuming there truly is one—that the Betrothal Trials are more damaging than liberating. Like so many of the rules and traditions surrounding familiars, the trials pretend to give us choice while operating to further destroy our free will. Had I been sequestered in that tower much longer, had Gabriel not come along to change my entire world, I'd have succumbed to both despair and the overwhelming need to escape that monthly and harrowing night with my suitors. I would have agreed to anything, to anyone, to any level of treatment to escape the extended torture of boredom punctuated by rape.

Because that's what it is, no matter how they dress it up as informed consent.

But now I fear I've written too much. I didn't intend to become so impassioned on the topic. Now I'll need some arcanium time with Gabriel to purge the emotions this stirred up. Hopefully that doesn't shock you.

Alise hadn't been shocked until Nic added that line—and she still wasn't because she didn't really understand. Like the arcaniums of all wizards, the House Phel arcanium stored magic that Gabriel and Nic generated together, serving as a dedicated reservoir for Gabriel to employ for more complex feats of wizardry requiring greater amounts of magic, like fending off an assault by their enemies. She didn't know what Nic meant, exactly, but it was clearly sexual and perhaps more than that in some way? Regardless, she didn't need to know.

The long and short of it (more long than short!) is that the Betrothal Trials are not something I'd recommend to anyone. Tell your "friend" to use that as a last resort. It's no way to begin a life together. Tell them to take any other available path. That's my very best advice.

Enough on that. I hope you're doing well. Your missive was chary on details or any real information. If you're concealing troubles, well… Know that you don't have to stay there. I realized I pushed you into returning to the academy, so you could graduate and to cauterize certain conversations, and there were good reasons for that, but not at the expense of your health and happiness, not at the expense of you. Gabriel will set the courier to await your reply, which will also be sealed and private.

If you say for us to come get you, we will. No questions asked. Our mutually loathed progenitor has been making noises I don't like. I have a bad feeling, so please tell me if there is anything to be concerned about there with you. Gabriel says that the pregnancy is affecting me emotionally, possibly because I nearly stabbed him with a fork when he wondered out loud if I shouldn't have gone into labor already, even though Asa says everything is fine and we have a visiting wizard from House Gaia here now to take over as a maternity specialist, who also says everything is fine. I am heartily sick of lugging around a belly ten times the size of my own head. Another strike against the Betrothal Trials! Even if you "succeed," you're having a baby at the same time you're trying to sort your own life and…

*And I just made this about me and it's not. I'm fine. The baby is fine. Gabriel will be fine if he figures out how to keep his stupid mouth shut. *sigh* Anyway, what's the point of being Lady Phel if I can't throw around my (now quite considerable) weight?*

Just tell me true: should we come get you?

All my love, reply right away or I'll explode (maybe literally)
Your sister

Alise read the letter over again, savoring every word, especially Nic's offer to come and get her. If this note had come only two days before, she'd have been beyond tempted to send back a scream for help, for rescue, despite her resolve to see it through to graduation.

Now… She didn't want to go. She actually *wanted* to meet Professor Seraphiel for another exhausting lesson in the morning. She'd promised Professor Cixin that she'd practice some new exercises and, instead of feeling crushed by the tasks looming over her, she found she'd been looking forward to the challenge.

Maybe, just maybe, she could figure out more about the bond severing and why it had gone wrong. That prospect gave her a surprising sense of relief and freedom, like clear water washing away the mud of regret and dread. Maman would never have wanted her to be feeling this way. Her mother suddenly came alive again in Alise's mind, not as she'd been during the course, and at the end, of that horrible, long, agonizing decline, but as she'd been before. Full of elegance and pride, no matter what she faced. Maman would never have approved of Alise wallowing in grief and guilt.

If you think you accidentally killed me working your wizardry, Maman's voice rang crisp and clear in Alise's mind, *then it's incumbent on you to learn to do better. Guilt never got anyone anywhere but depressed and ineffective. I expect more of my brilliant daughter.*

Alise smiled, albeit sadly, Nic's words on the page blurring together with Maman's voice in her head, a deep, abiding affection for them both filling her. She wasn't alone and never had been.

"What do you have there, Wizard Alise?" Brinda Chur bounced onto the window cushion, peering at the Ratsiel courier tenaciously clinging to Alise's knee, and perhaps trying to get a glimpse of the letter Alise immediately folded out of sight as she quickly invoked a silencing shield around them. The familiar grinned cheekily. "A letter from House Phel? I knew you'd be able to help me. What did Lady Phel say?" Brinda rubbed her hands together in anticipatory glee. "I'm so ready for her sage advice."

Alise gazed back at Brinda in some dismay, unwilling to tarnish this bright enthusiasm with Nic's dark cautions. Except that the experience of the Betrothal Trials would do far worse to the earnest, sweet-natured girl. Fortunately, Brinda mistook Alise's hesitation, flushing and clapping a hand over her mouth.

"What am I doing? I apologize for my atrocious manners. Here." She held out a hand. "Take as much magic as you like. With yesterday being Rest Day, I have a lot. I saved it for you," she added, almost shyly. "Because I appreciate you helping me, so much."

"Oh, that's not necessary," Alise protested, not firmly at all.

"Nonsense. This is our bargain and I can see you're low again. Drink up!"

Not particularly loving the vampiric analogy for taking a familiar's magic, Alise reminded herself not to be unrealistic about this nature of their transaction. Brinda Chur certainly wasn't. Alise transferred enough to refill her reserves and then some, which thankfully left Brinda not at all drained.

"Thank you," she said, offering a warm smile. "Your magic is truly as bright as you promised."

"House Chur is the best!" Brinda crowed, happily. She

pointed at the missive, the House Phel crest of a moon over water evident. "Now gimme." Brinda mitigated the impertinent demand with a wriggle and flutter of lashes.

Internally, Alise groaned. "I asked my sister…"

"Yes, and? And?"

Nothing for it but to be honest. "I didn't say who'd asked me, but she told me to tell my friend not to do the Betrothal Trials if she, that is, you could possibly avoid it."

Brinda's anticipatory expression faded, her brow furrowing in what looked more like petulance than puzzlement. "She did not."

"She did," Alise insisted. "She said it was a terrible experience for her and that even the most dismal-sounding option is better than putting yourself through it."

"But she won," Brinda said, as if explaining it to Alise.

Alise shook her head, fingering the heavy stationery of Nic's letter. "The Betrothal Trials isn't something you 'win.' She calls it something you endure."

Brinda's face set in mutinous lines. "I'm going to win! I'm going to snag the best possible wizard to be my master and have a brilliant life. Your sister is just jealous because she ended up with a black sheep of a Phel."

Well, that took a turn fast, Alise thought to herself, but then, she'd known Brinda wouldn't take this news well. And she was young, not experienced at moderating her reactions. "My sister is very happy with her life at House Phel, and with Gabriel Phel," Alise told her with gentle insistence. "This advice does not come from a place of jealousy—again, I didn't say who was asking—but from a place of genuine sympathy and concern."

Brinda sulked a moment longer, arms crossed over her bosom. "Well, did she at least say what she used to conceive so quickly?"

Alise allowed herself a moment to assimilate the shift, and what that portended. "There isn't anything. You know the Betrothal Trials rules forbid any kind of fertility enchantment, if any exist, which they don't. A Refoel healer will unlock your fertility, but then it's up to nature and compatibility."

"Oh, come on," Brinda scoffed, leaning in closer, dropping her voice to a confidential whisper, despite the silencing shield. "Everybody knows there are certain spells we can use to ensure the wizard we want is the one to succeed. The proof is right there—why would the Convocation forbid something unless it was possible?"

As Alise had had that exact thought, she could hardly argue. "I have no idea. I just know that I've never heard of such a spell and neither has Nic." She waved the missive in demonstration. "That Gabriel Phel was the one was pure luck, and compatibility, which is what the trials test for to begin with."

"Everyone knows that's not true," Brinda practically hissed. "If Nic didn't use something—and who could blame her as no one would deliberately choose to be 'lady' of that half-drowned manse in a backwater swamp of nowhere—then Lord Phel did. Everyone knows he's a rebel, not even academy trained, disrespectful of his betters, and desperate to be admitted to polite society. Of course he'd be exactly the sort to employ an interdicted potion of some sort, to hedge his bets, to cheat. I want to know what it was. If you don't give me what I want, what House Chur wants, then I will expose the truth."

Appalled, Alise didn't know what to say, words of response dry and useless in her mouth. Gone was the silly, bouncy familiar, replaced by a malevolent, cunning enemy. "There's no truth to expose," Alise managed to say, proud of the evenness of her tone. "If you had proof of this nonsense, then you'd already have this fictious spell you're seeking."

Brinda narrowed her pretty hazel eyes, now glittering with malice. "We don't need proof."

"One house can't set Convocation policy," Alise replied tightly. "Not without legal process."

Scoffing, Brinda waved that away. "Words have power and if something is said often enough, people will believe it, with or without legalities. The reputation of House Chur is ancient and impeccable, whereas everyone knows that House *Fell* is populated by the Convocation's rejects. The family is a disgraced and decrepit line that should never have been resurrected. The proper houses of the Convocation only allowed the temporary and probationary status of Phel out of pity and so that they would quickly learn they had no place in our world. That they've held on, like some sort of vermin-ridden parasite, is unthinkable, an insult to polite society. One negative word from House Chur and they'll have that charter revoked faster than this!"

Brinda snapped her fingers, her smile vicious. "And then where will your precious sister be? Passed around and sold to the highest bidder."

Completely aghast, Alise couldn't summon a response,

which satisfied Brinda, thinking she'd won this round. Assuming her pleasing personality again, Brinda dimpled at her. "Get me that spell and all will be fine."

"I—I'll try." Alise added the stammer deliberately, swallowing hard and trying to look pitiful. "But I'm afraid it doesn't exist."

"Oh, it does. Everyone says so."

Alise was heartily tired of Brinda's calling upon the supreme "everyone knows" to express her opinions, but she contained herself.

"You'd better *hope* it exists," Brinda added in a falsely sweet voice, "or face the consequences."

Alise simply nodded.

"That's better. We do have a deal, after all." Brinda adjusted the ruffles on her colorful skirt in satisfaction. "Everyone is talking about you and Archivist Cillian Harahel," she confided brightly. "A nice bit of arm candy for you, though obviously it can't go anywhere. He's pretty enough, but a word to the wise, he's a social climber. Enjoy him, but don't fall for him. You don't always demonstrate the best judgement, after all."

Stung into defending Cillian, Alise still chose her words carefully, figuring whatever she said would be all over Convocation Academy in another hour. Or less. "Wizards have the luxury of being able to enjoy each other without making it into a lifelong partnership," she replied airily, not at above needling Brinda on the sore subject.

Indeed, Brinda flushed in anger. "Well, you know the levels he stooped to for Szarina."

That name again. Unfortunately, Alise was too startled to

cover her reaction.

"Oh! You *don't* know," Brinda cooed. "I had it all from my older sisters. The academy tried to keep it quiet, but of course people talk, especially when the story is so, well, *distressing*." She waited, almost coyly, for Alise's questions, making a moue of disappointment when Alise didn't say or do anything.

Alise was, in truth, torn. Really, she should ask Cillian for the story, but he'd balked at telling her, so Brinda's gossip might give her at least a few answers, as long as she took the information relayed with a generous helping of salt.

"Szarina Sammael," Brinda said in a musing tone, dangling the bait with glee. "I hear she was astonishingly beautiful. Rivers of white-blonde hair. She defied convention when she manifested as a wizard, refusing to cut it, and no one blamed her. It's not as if anyone would have mistaken *her* for a familiar." Brinda seemed oblivious in that moment to her own lowly status as a familiar, lost in a reverie of admiration. "I never saw her, myself, of course, but my older sisters say she was ethereal, the most beautiful woman they ever saw. And a Sammael, too, which confers natural elegance and poise. Breeding will tell."

Alise nearly lost the battle not to roll her eyes.

"For whatever reason," Brinda continued with obvious relish, "Szarina decided to dally with Cillian Harahel. No one knew why, except that he was always pretty. Well, and easily led, poor bookish boy. He'd already manifested as a wizard, so everyone knew Szarina couldn't be thinking to train him up as her familiar, but she wrapped him around her little finger. From what I understand, he became essentially her lap dog, following her everywhere, fetching and carrying for her, *baking* for her." Brinda tittered knowingly behind her hand. "No one knows if he imagined that she'd elevate him to House Sammael, but they even attended the Winter's Ball together. She bought him a suit for it and everything."

Alise had glimpsed an Ophiel suit in Cillian's closet, carefully sealed in the distinctive garment bag, out of place amidst the inexpensive, low-key clothing he normally preferred. She hadn't wanted to snoop, so she hadn't looked closely, but she wondered now. Was it a remembrance of the lost Szarina? The beautiful wizard so astonishing in every way that Cillian hesitated to allow even the least mention of her name into their bed, lest… what? Alise struggled with a wave of insecurity, wondering if perhaps Cillian had worried that evoking the glorious Szarina—even her name was fabulous—would make Alise pale by comparison. Alise undoubtedly came up short in any point by point comparison, but that Cillian likely also thought so hurt more than it should.

"What happened?" Alise asked through numb lips. She didn't really *want* to know, but she seemed to be unable to resist finding out.

"What you'd expect," Brinda answered with glee, fully in her element. "It turned out that Cillian had been helping Szarina *cheat*." She whispered the word with fabricated horror, as if saying it full voice would be too distasteful. "Not only with her out-of-class work, but using his wizardry to obtain the answers to exams for her. It was only when her work in practicums came up so far short of her stellar exam grades and other work that the faculty put two and two together. Provost

Uriel *expelled* Szarina and sent her home to House Sammael in disgrace. So horrible." Brinda actually wriggled in delight.

"But Cillian wasn't expelled?" Obviously not, as he'd not only graduated from Convocation Academy, but was hired to a staff position there, albeit a lowly one. Was the night shift a punishment?

"No!" Brenda answered, sounding impossibly shocked. "No one knows how he escaped equivalent justice, but everyone knows that's why House Harahel and Sammael have been feuding. I suppose him being relegated to Convocation Archives for the rest of his unimpressive career is punishment enough."

"Hmm." Except Alise knew Cillian loved his job. "What happened to Szarina?"

Brinda shrugged with negligent ease. "Who knows? House Sammael is hardly going to trot out a disgraced scion for social functions. Well, I must get ready for dinner." She patted Alise's hand. "I'm so glad we've become friends. Let me know when you have that information for me." With a jaunty wink, Brinda exited the bubble of silence, leaving Alise alone inside it.

Quickly, Alise penned a reply to Nic. Short, but to the point.

> *Thank you for your wonderful letter and for sharing with me. I love and admire you so much. Don't worry about me. I'm fine and Cillian Harahel is watching out for me. I'll write more soon. All my love, your sister.*

Before she could change her mind, she gave the missive to the tenacious little courier and sent it on its way back to Nic.

Alise would figure out how to appease Brinda's insistent questions without bothering her very pregnant sister, who had much more important things to worry about.

Alise sat there a moment longer, savoring the rare moment of peace and quiet, then dispelled the silencing field, allowing in the tumult of people traveling through the hallways. For once, the noise gave her comfort.

~ 25 ~

Beginning to feel the effects of his upended sleep schedule and knowing he wouldn't be able to tackle the major magic working he had in mind without a bit of rest, Cillian was able to squeeze in a decent nap before heading to his shift in the archives a few hours early.

If all went as planned, he could execute this refined search before his work day started. It meant missing dinner, but he felt confident Alise would eat in the dining hall and he'd scarfed some leftovers at his place. The sleep had helped and he felt energized with renewed determination.

This was something he could control. The Szarina thing had spiraled out of his grasp with astonishing speed—if he'd *ever* had any control in that relationship—but this was different, even if it was technically helping Alise. It did not, however, count as white-knighting. Doing this research was part of his job, delineated as urgent by the provost herself and was something he could do well, if only he applied himself. About time he concentrated on that task.

The whole situation with Gordon Hanneil had distracted him, which he ruefully had to concede to himself had been the intention of House Hanneil, to derail this research. Rage still clouded his thoughts now at what they'd done and tried to do Alise, and he needed to set that aside to formulate this magic working clearly. And trust that Provost Uriel would handle the situation.

Cillian waved to the librarian on duty, then proceeded directly to his private nook in the archives. On the way, he mentally reviewed his plan for this entirely new working and his own magic reserves. Ruefully, he acknowledged that he might not have enough power for the magnitude of what he had in mind—and no familiar to supplement his magic. *There's no such a thing as a library emergency*, he'd told Alise. It just figured he faced the equivalent of one now.

He deliberated on acquiring sufficient magic. Maybe he could ask Marah or one of the other for-hire familiars employed by the academy for such purposes. But that might tip off anyone spying on him that he was up to something unusual. While he mused over that, Cillian sketched out the basics of his plan. This would be a multi-layered approach. He could employ some of his standard techniques for indexing information and some of his tricks for locating texts related to vague descriptions from patrons, but he needed to supplement that with ways to search for hidden and deliberately obscured information.

There were only so many methods for hiding texts in the archives, which had been explicitly designed to make stored materials findable. Occasionally, however, faculty members asked to make certain valuable and potentially dangerous texts difficult to find except by those approved to handle them. The Archivists Council had compromised with a work-around that allowed carefully selected works to be placed in a space that could be accessed only by those in possession of a password that activated a trigger to reveal those texts. The enchantment had to be of the sort that could be operated by anyone, even mundanes with no magical ability, to preserve the availability of the archives to all Convocation citizens. The documents were also still listed in the commonly used indexes, for the same reason. Functionally, that meant the librarians could find the hidden texts, but most people lacked the appropriate skillset.

The most closely guarded secret regarding the Convocation Archives was that, huge as the physical space was that housed the centuries' worth of collected texts, the archivists also employed library magic to allow a far greater volume of work to occupy that space than was physically possible. This proprietary magic—provided by House Harahel, of course—operated invisibly to most patrons, even highly gifted wizards. It helped that the ambient magic of the ancient building, saturated with centuries' of wizardry, created enough background "noise" that even the most sensitive put down the sense of space and time dilation to that, especially in the deepest parts of the archives.

Also, the stacks had been designed to add to the sense of disorientation. It didn't take much—amplified shadows, a bit of optical illusion built into the construction of the shelves, giving them a looming quality. The archives lacked timepieces that gave cues on the passage of time. To preserve the materials from the ravages of natural light, there were already no windows.

Most people who ventured deep into the archives ascribed the sense of lost time to becoming absorbed in their search, which wasn't far from the truth.

One reason Cillian had paid close attention to Alise's explorations of the deep archives—at least in the beginning and that hadn't been solely a rationalization to excuse his interest in her movements—w as to ensure she emerged safely again without having lost too much time. All of the House Harahel librarians took on that responsibility as part of their sacred duty to house and Convocation. No one wanted some hapless student, or absentminded professor, to become lost in the stacks for an extended period of time.

Cillian had been mulling the seemingly vanished materials regarding House Phel, along with House Hanneil's urgent need to stop Alise's search, for quite some time. Only one answer made sense: someone had to have found a way to use the archives' unique characteristics to hide materials from even him and the other, far more experienced archivists. Did that mean another Harahel wizard had done so? His sinking stomach indicated there could be no other explanation, which was also why he'd dragged his feet for so long on pursuing this particular avenue until he'd exhausted every other possibility. Some things you just didn't want to know.

Also, penetrating this deception required a level of psychic sleuthing that went beyond his normal skills. "But not my abilities," he muttered to himself, though the lack of magic amplification made the challenge even more daunting. "I can do this."

"Can do what?" Alise asked. She gave him an impish smile

at having startled him. "You must have been lost in thought. That's the first time I've been able to sneak up on you, and I wasn't even using a cloaking spirit."

"Shouldn't you be at dinner?" he asked, unbending from his scribbled diagram and stretching. He had been concentrating a while.

She raised a brow. "It's long past. Now I *know* you're preoccupied if you forgot about spying on me to make sure I was adequately fed and—before you ask—yes, I ate in the dining hall, even though the snacks you gave me could feed a small family for a week."

"What time is it?"

"About half an hour before your shift starts. I figured I'd find you here. How did it go with Provost Uriel?"

"Well. She's handling it. You've had no further incidents?"

"None." Alise shook her head, blue-black feathers of hair shimmering around her face. "What are you pumping yourself up to do?"

He debated with himself for only a moment. "Some of this is proprietary Harahel information, so I'm walking a line here in what I can and can't tell you. I have an idea for how and where I might look for those missing records."

"That's brilliant." She smiled broadly, eyes shining in a way that made him feel like a true hero of the old tales.

"I've never done anything like it before. It's kind of… next level."

"Next level librarian wizardry. I love it. If anyone can do it, you can."

Her sincere faith in him was staggering. "The problem is, I

may not have enough magic. I was trying to think of a familiar, or a few, I could borrow magic from without raising suspicion. Would your friend, Brinda Chur, help me, do you think?"

Alise instantly chilled, in expression and in magic, the scent of roses going frosty. "She is no friend of mine, nor of yours. Now's not the time. I'll tell you the story later, but fair warning."

"Too bad." He wanted to ask more, but Alise was right that this wasn't the time.

"However," she added more brightly, "I just filled up on magic from Brinda, fortunately before our distressing conversation that I'll tell you all about later, so I can give you plenty."

He stared at her a moment, feeling as if he'd missed a step. "But you're a wizard."

"I'm aware of that," she replied in that grave manner she used when she was amused by him.

"I need a familiar," he clarified, frowning when she laughed.

"Wizards can give each other magic," she told him. "There's nothing stopping us. They do it at House Phel more and more. It's just not typically 'done' in the Convocation because wizards are competitive and jealous of their power, and thus not interested in helping other wizards. They're also eager to exploit familiars who really have little to no ability to object."

She was right, he realized, rather astonished that this hadn't occurred to him. "But you need your magic," he protested, though he was happy to see she had indeed filled up, glowing with transmuted fire and sunlight.

"This is important," she reminded him. "Very high on our list of priorities. Besides, during our, ah, intimacy, our magic already blended some. This should feel quite natural."

He loved that she blushed, her astonishing eyes skittering briefly away. "Our *intimacy*?" he echoed, teasing her.

"You know what I mean, Cillian Harahel," she replied sternly, then bent to kiss him, all too briefly, before proffering her hand. "I'll maintain skin contact, so take as much as you need as you work. Let's get this done."

Charmed, grateful, so dazzlingly in love with her, he changed their hand clasp so their fingers interlaced, and bent his attention to his diagram. Alise angled her head to look at what he'd drawn, but didn't comment. He doubted his arcane scribbles—an abstract representation of how the hidden stacks felt to his wizard senses—would make any sense to her. And she was conscientious about his house proprietary information, granting him both the courtesy of not inquiring and the quiet he needed to concentrate.

He began with basic librarian wizardry, performing a search that he'd executed so many times now that it had become practically rote, seeking references to House Phel. He'd long-since modified his indexing with the techniques he used to search for items that patrons described vaguely or, on more than one occasion, flat out incorrectly. Another Harahel invention taught in-house, this fancy bit of magic operated almost with its own kind of intelligence, seeking what might be close to the search term, but not precisely it. Cillian had no idea how it actually worked, but it yielded amazing results, able to collect information not consciously remembered.

During his brief visit to House Phel, Cillian had chatted briefly with Gabriel about the restoration of the manse and how the process had taken on a life of its own, drawing on some sort of ancestral Phel memory of how the house had been before it sank into the swamps. Cillian had been fascinated, thinking of the search spell and suspecting a similar magic operated there, with it drawing on information from elsewhere.

Tempted to try his standard search one more time, just because he still couldn't believe every previous attempt had turned up exactly nothing—which had never happened to him before and still annoyed him no end—he resisted, figuring it would be a waste of magic to confirm what he already knew. Instead, with the special search mentally prepared, he left it poised while he took on the next, very experimental step. Meticulously sliding his wizardry into the folded parts of the stacks, he identified the hidden, coded ones. It took a while, as there were a number of them that had been created over time, for different groups and different purposes. He'd searched them all before, more than once, so he again resisted looking just 0one more time.

Instead, once he'd catalogued them all, he lined them up in a mental queue, drawing on some of Alise's magic to bolster his. It reminded him a bit of how she'd described mentally holding a multitude of incorporeal entities. The folded spaces didn't like to be identified and tended to slide away given the least bit of inattention. The magic from Alise, as heady as potent red wine, improved his concentration immensely.

It felt very different, drawing from a wizard rather than a

familiar, though it did help that their sexual intimacy had allowed for some interweaving of their magical natures already, as Alise had so astutely discerned. Still, the flow from her had a more… deliberate feel than it would from a familiar. Rather than feeling as if he drank from a passive container, Alise's magic pushed into him and he had to be careful not to metaphorically choke on it. If they ever planned to do this again—and why would they? Library emergencies came along once in a lifetime—they'd have to practice.

Making sure he maintained a pin of concentration on the correct number of verified hidden archives, Cillian launched an entirely new search for something that *should* exist but didn't to all normal appearances. This was the tricky bit as it was very difficult to look for a null value. If his theory proved correct that this was how the Hanneil conspirators had hidden the House Phel archives, they would have disguised the fold carefully—and very likely with the specific intention of foiling Harahel indexing techniques. Otherwise, the senior archivists responsible for the regular cataloguing and maintenance of the collection would have noticed a discrepancy long before this.

That search took more time, and even more magic, rendering him excessively grateful for Alise's offer and her steadfast flow of magic. Now that he'd become more used to it, he found he liked the way she injected magic into him as he needed. She seemed to intuitively know when he required a boost, somehow tracking the waxing and waning of his wizardry. Possibly she could sense his efforts, the feeling of her in the back of his mind a strong and reassuring presence. Without her, he would have flagged long since. Limitations, perhaps, the conspirators had counted on.

As it was, he very nearly missed it. In fact, he *did* miss it, mentally passing over the blip disguised as an irregularity in the ambient magic.

He only caught the scent of it in hindsight, realizing that the slight bump faintly radiated an odor that reminded him of House Hanneil. Their magic didn't truly smell rank, but he disliked them enough that he perceived their brand of psychic magic that way. In passing, he wondered if Lord Elal would smell sweet like his daughters' magic or unpleasant, given how much Cillian loathed the man. Nander Elal, the youngest of the bunch, didn't ever frequent the archives, so Cillian didn't have that basis for comparison.

These idle musings rolled through the back of his mind, ungoverned, as he wrestled the multiple tasks of having his multilayered, experimental search poised at the ready while he kept a mental eye on that infinitesimal inconsistency in the ambient magic, and as he extended an indexing probe to unlock what he hoped was a hidden archive. The more he was able to hold it still for examination—though it felt as slippery as separating an egg yolk from the white without breaking either—the greater his certainty. It *felt* like the same construction as the other hidden archives, which unfortunately meant Harahel magic, but he'd think about that later.

Naturally, he didn't have the password. That would be equally hidden away, if not more so. He did, however, have a thorough knowledge of the Harahel methodology for creating the "lock" an enchantment would fit into. He didn't need the password when he could open the archive from within the indexing that kept it folded and inaccessible.

He hoped.

"Here we go," he breathed, hoping Alise would understand. He didn't dare divert his concentration long enough to check with her that she was all right. Getting this finished would do more to spare Alise's reserves than anything else.

Using one of his proprietary Harahel indexing magics, he sank his concentration into the folded archive. Essentially what made these archives inaccessible to standard searching was a sort of reverse-indexing. Rather than cataloging the contents of a section of the archives, this magic inverted the metadata tags, turning the information inside out and rendering it nonsensical. If he could just find the right thread to pull…

There.

Inside his head—and somewhere in the depths of Convocation Archives—the stacks that had been folded away reentered their shared reality. Quickly, he scanned the contents. So much material on House Phel, going back centuries. Really, it had been a sloppy shortcut to hide so much of it. It would have been wiser, and less obvious, to have hidden only the texts with whatever incriminating information worried them so.

But then, the deception had worked, so who was he to criticize? Also, it could be that *all* of the documentation threatened the conspirators. The surge of triumph at his success began to disintegrate around the edges as he realized what a monumental task going through all of that material would be, even with focused library magic.

Carefully extracting his wizardry from the sticky folds of the index, he met Alise's concerned gaze.

"You look unhappy," she remarked. "It didn't work?"

"Oh, it worked all right." He let out a long sigh, abruptly aware of his exhaustion, despite the wine-warm, rose-infused sizzle of Alise's magic still coursing through him. "That's the biggest, most complex magic I've ever performed."

"That's amazing news!" she exclaimed. "Let's go see."

He held onto her hand as she tugged at him to rise. "There is a *lot*," he cautioned her. "It's going to take weeks, maybe months to go through it all."

"Then no time like the present to begin," she replied, sparkling with excitement. "At last I have something to actually research for this project."

"True." Cillian wasn't sure why he couldn't seem to share her enthusiasm. Was he simply feeling tired? Something felt off. "Though we can use the House Harahel archives for that, too."

She pressed her lips together impatiently. "Why bother to journey there when the archives we need are here?"

"Because we need the corroboration between the two sets of archives for quality control," he answered, battling his own impatience. The feeling of wrongness worked on him, aggravatingly nebulous.

"Well, sure," she replied, a line forming between her brows, "but I could go through what's here first, catalogue everything, then we can go to House Harahel to run the comparison."

"I can catalogue the collection here faster than you can," he pointed out.

Her chin firmed mulishly. "No doubt, but this is *my* independent study, as you may recall. Just because you want an excuse to visit family doesn't mean—"

"That is *not* why I want to go," he interrupted, a bit more stung than he should be, given that he had been dreaming way too much about introducing Alise to his family.

"No?" Her black-winged brows climbed. "Then why are you being so cranky all of a sudden? This isn't like you to—"

"Shh!" He clamped down on her hand, distantly aware of her squeak of pained indignation and that asking her to be quiet inside the silencing shield made no sense. But he needed to concentrate. Something about that stack he'd just unfolded.

Something very, very wrong.

~ 26 ~

A LISE BIT BACK her questions, increasingly alarmed by Cillian's distraction—and concentrated attention on something beyond her ken. As when he'd been using his wizardry to locate and extract the House Phel archives, his magic had resolved from grayscale into crisp black and white lines. They spiraled out neatly into the archives, seeming as if they formed a text she'd be able to read if only she could focus her eyes correctly.

She hadn't had occasion to participate so closely while a different kind of wizard worked their magic. Observing Cillian had really brought home how very differently their magical styles operated. As if they used the same voice, but in entirely unrelated languages.

She'd learned enough about his techniques in the last hour, to be keenly aware of how his wizardry combed through the archives, with a distant sense of pages ruffling, as it did now, but with an urgent intensity. Also, she'd never seen Cillian so tense. Really wanting to ask, but knowing better, Alise reviewed the skills Professor Seraphiel had taught her, readying herself to fight. She also summoned her warrior spirits, though she kept them invisible for the moment. Cillian complained that library magic wasn't useful for battle. Well, hers was and she would protect them both.

Though it would help to know what had so abruptly and profoundly worried Cillian. She breathed a sigh of relief when he focused on her again. Short-lived relief, as it turned out.

"I set off some sort of alarm," he said in a low, terse voice. "I'm an idiot. I should have realized that—"

"No time for that. Is someone coming? Now? Gordon?" She managed to keep her voice steady saying his name, wrestling the immediate stab of panic. She refused to let that odious slimeball cow her.

"I don't know." Cillian sounded steadier. "I can just sense the archive sending out a kind of call. Who knows who's being signaled?"

"Can you shut down the alarm?"

"Maybe… with time, I could—"

"We can't count on the luxury of time," she said, cutting him off with what she recognized as Elal ruthlessness. Papa would be proud. "What if you fold up the Phel stacks again—will that stop the alarm?"

"Possibly." He sounded dubious. "Even then it might be too late, if they've already been alerted."

"We have to take the chance. Fold up those stacks again."

"But we need that information!" He glared at her in frustration.

"And we'll get to it later," she answered, marveling at her own calm. Nice to know she didn't turn into a frightened, gibbering mess at every sign of threat. "For now, we need to protect those stacks and that information. Hide it all again—

and alter the lock so only you can access it."

"Good idea." He heaved a sigh. "I hate to ask, but…"

"My magic is your magic," she said, squeezing his hand and pouring more into him. "Work fast."

He did work more rapidly this time, knowing what he was about, seeming more confident, despite the gaffe of not thinking about the archive being tagged with an alarm. Frankly, she should have thought of that, too. They could exchange recriminations later. Cillian's magic lanced out with black and white precision, clicking efficiently. Somewhere on the periphery of her wizard's senses, she heard a vast groaning, the sort of sound you'd imagine a roomful of shelves packed with heavy tomes would make if you folded it like origami. She wasn't sure, however, if she actually heard a physical sound or if it was a synesthetic perception of Cillian's magic. Tense, she waited for it to cease.

A moment later, he sighed again, this time in relief and nodded an answer to her questioning look. "It's done and only I have the passkey."

"Great, let's move." She tugged him out of the chair, relieved that he complied this time, grateful to be able to physically release some of the fierce need to flee. Or fight. Fleeing sounded much better. "If someone *is* coming, I don't want to be here when they arrive. At least we know those stacks are secured against further tampering. No one's getting into them without you."

That was the wrong thing to say. Cillian dug in his heels. A stricken look crossed his face. "Oh no! That was a terrible idea that I coded the spell to only me. What if something happens to me? Those texts will be lost forever. I have to—"

"You have to get a hold of yourself," she told him crisply, pulling him along. "And we'll make sure nothing happens to you."

He nodded miserably, unconvinced, but at least moving. "But what if—"

This time he stopped himself on a gargle of horror. Alise couldn't blame him, as the shadows between the towering stacks resolved into the slinking forms of hunters.

The creatures had been designed to instill horror, deliberately made into monsters by the houses that combined their magic to create them. Alise had been seen hunters before, though never this close, at the siege of House Phel. In her classes, however, she'd read about the abominations in the wizard-only texts.

A conglomeration of numerous animals, shimmering with various magics, the hunters sported the long jaws of a jackal filled with rows of fangs. They moved with the loping grace of weasels, their paws tipped with hard, curved talons. They also possessed a rudimentary intelligence—some more than others—and were nearly impossible to kill. Chopping them into pieces too small to be a threat worked best, but even then they sometimes reassembled themselves.

A moot point anyway, since neither she nor Cillian wore any weapons to attack with. She'd been prepared for all that evading and eluding should Gordon Hanneil show up, not for fighting hunters hand to hand. Still, the hunters typically went after familiars, not a high-level wizard, student though she might be. She should be able to handle this.

And so, she stepped forward, putting herself between the hunters and Cillian.

"Alise," he gasped, grabbing her shoulder.

She shrugged him off with a sharp gesture and a glare. "Hide. Run. I'll handle this."

"I'm not leaving you!"

She tapped her temple. "You are the sole repository of those records." She pointed forward, the warrior spirits she'd had on hold becoming visible. "This is my forte. You keep saying so."

Turning her gaze firmly forward, she nevertheless sensed his hesitation. Then, thankfully, he slipped away. Cillian would know the labyrinth of the archives better than anyone. He would be safe, if only to ensure the preservation of the stacks he'd hidden away. Putting him out of her mind, Alise focused, drawing ruthlessly on her magic—and on a few more spirits she'd kept on hold.

The lead hunter advanced, jaws agape and dripping. Unlike the stories she'd heard of the hunters pursuing her friends, these didn't comment or give instructions. She counted five of them—and none that she'd seen peeled away after Cillian. Likely they'd been tasked to kill anyone opening those stacks, which meant whoever enchanted them to that purpose had anticipated an archivist. Not an Elal wizard.

One of her warriors leapt, swinging its ethereal sword. As she'd counted on, the hunter in its path ignored the spirit as immaterial, just like the animals that made it up would. The sword condensed just enough upon contact to sever the hunter's head from the body. The long-muzzled head tumbled to the floor with a satisfying thud, spewing black blood, the jaws snapping futilely from a point too distant to bother her. The temporary surge of triumph at that small success faded immediately as the hunter's body, of course, kept advancing on her.

Along with the other four intact hunters.

Maybe she'd been overconfident. Too late now. Using her magic to control both warriors, she also summoned a group of fire elementals, mentally apologizing to the archivists and promising that she wouldn't let the flames spread. Feeling as if she worked multiple puppets with both hands at once, she set the warriors to attacking the advancing hunters. Then she unleashed the fire elementals to burn.

The effect was startling. Along with the smell. The stench of burnt fur and slowly roasting canine flesh billowed out, followed by black oily smoke that stung her eyes. The fire elementals gleefully danced over the still advancing hunters, bright spots of flame in the greasily thickening shadows. Some elementals fell off into the gloom as the warrior spirits cleaved away limbs. It was all eerily silent, the hunters giving no sign or sound of suffering. As the flames penetrated their immortal flesh, however, the sizzle of fat and crackling skin became audible, turning her stomach.

Until an alarm wailed—some embedded enchantment to detect smoke or flame in the archives. *Well, shit.*

Quickly, Alise summoned water elementals to douse the fire, which resulted in more suffocating smoke, but hopefully preserved the materials in the nearby stacks. Cillian would never forgive her if any harm came to the archives. Recalling what little she knew about fires, she quickly summoned air elementals to disperse the smoke, to prevent that kind of damage, too, which had the side-benefit of giving her a clearer picture of the aftermath. And relieving the burning ache in her lungs she hadn't paid attention to until that moment.

Twitching, seared, and smoking chunks of hunter laid strewn across the floor, Alise's warrior spirits continuing on their assigned task of chopping them into even smaller bits. Fire elementals burned sullenly, squabbling with the water elementals. Black blood pooled everywhere. In the distance, shouts indicated the fire alarm had been heard and answered.

"Dark arts," Cillian breathed, coming up beside her. "What a mess."

She flicked him a more than irritated glance. "I told you to run and hide."

"I did the latter," he answered, unperturbed. "Then I came out when it was safe to do so. And I don't take orders from you, Lady Elal. Deal with it."

Oh, he was asking for it, he really was. Alise knotted her hands into fists. "Listen, you—"

"Better summon some earth elementals to devour the evidence," he interrupted, "unless you want to answer a lot of questions. The less notice the better at this point."

"Fine. We'll argue later."

"I look forward to that," he murmured, setting a reassuring hand on the small of her back. "But you know I'm the better debater."

Despite herself, she smiled. She had no idea how he could amuse her like this, especially under such circumstances.

Feeling a bit thin on magic—though Brinda's infusion had really lasted through a lot—Alise summoned a veritable horde of earth elementals to devour the blood, ash, and remaining twitching chunks of decimated hunter. The last did give her pause. What would those unkillable creatures do inside an elemental? She didn't know if anyone had tried that approach before. At the Siege of House Phel, Jadren El-Adrel had "healed" the hunters and returned them to their constituent animal parts. Not an option here, not without Jadren's truly unique brand of wizardry.

Still, Cillian was right that the last complication they needed at this point was to attract even more attention—especially not knowing exactly who their enemies might be. It was bad enough that they'd inadvertently alerted whoever had hidden the Phel archives to their tampering; they didn't need their blissfully ignorant colleagues developing suspicions, too. She encouraged the earth elementals to devour every trace, allowing the fire and water elementals to return to their own realms, and sent her personal cadre of spirits back into stasis.

The earth elementals snuffled over the floor, seeking any last traces of organic snacks. Footsteps approached, the glow of lanterns growing brighter in the dimly lit stacks.

"We should go," Cillian said with increased urgency. "That has to be good enough."

Using the enchantment she'd learned that very day from Professor Cixin, she put the earth elementals into an incorporeal space and sealed it. The elementals should be content enough there for a while, as they were thoroughly sated. If all went well, maybe they'd have completely digested the hunters' immortal flesh when she checked back.

Cillian was already pulling her along as she worked mentally, deftly weaving them back through the more obscure stacks, away from the commotion. Unfortunately that meant they were also moving away from the one exit from the archives.

Finished with her magical tasks, Alise dug in her heels. "We need to get *out* of here," she protested. "We're trapped in this place."

"I know that," he snapped with frustration. But he stopped, pulling her into an alcove, and drawing her into his arms. "Let's take a breath."

She did, leaning against him as they embraced. It felt good, right, and safe, no matter what happened outside their shadowy circle. "They're going to know it was us," she said after a beat, pulling back to look at him. "No one else could have done this, so we're not hiding so much as evading. And eluding," she added, thinking of Professor Seraphiel.

"Suggestions for doing so are welcome," he replied grimly. "There are good reasons for the archives to have a single exit, but that's working against us at the moment."

"I can cloak us."

"Do you have enough magic?"

Did she? She'd used a lot, but she'd been replete at the start. "I do. Plenty to get us out of here."

"All right." But he looked glum. "What worries me next is how we'll get back to those Phel texts though."

"We can think about that later."

"Can we though? What if this is our last opportunity to get at them? There's no guarantee we'll be able to get in here again. You should go and I can stay."

Alise tried to contain her exasperation. "You're just going to hide in the archives for days or weeks?"

"Whatever it takes," he answered with that stubbornly noble tilt to his chin. "I know these stacks like the back of my hand. I can hide from anyone."

"Even from more hunters?"

"Maybe there won't be any more."

That was hoping for a lot. "What will you do for food and water?"

He hesitated. "I can get by for a few days."

Cillian was being totally unreasonable, but she'd also learned to recognize when he'd entrenched on a course of action. "All right," she agreed, deliberately slumping her shoulders. "I'm sure I'll be fine without you. Gordon Hanneil won't dare come after me openly."

That worked, the agony of indecision contorted Cillian's face as he grimaced. "Dark arts," he cursed. "No, you're right. Your safety comes first. We'll just have to leave the archives and hope we can come back. Besides, I don't know how we can examine the contents without setting off the alarm again."

"We need to find a way to put the equivalent of a silencing spell around them," she mused, resuming their winding trek through the shadowy archives toward the exit. Cillian didn't correct her trajectory, so it must be more or less the right direction. "Still, any time we return to the archives, we'd run the risk of being trapped. I wish we could somehow take the documents with us."

Cillian snorted at that. "That won't happen. There's an

enchantment that prohibits removal of archived materials. Every student should know that."

She did, of course, know that. It was the topic of much griping among the student populace that only certain texts could be borrowed and taken out of the archives. For anything truly useful, they had to sit there and work on site. It could be super inconvenient. The wizard-students in particular were forever concocting work-arounds to try to sneak texts out of the archives, but even the smallest of books secreted in a pocket set off the enchantment...

An inspiration struck.

"Wait, I have an idea. Tell me—before you unlocked the Phel stacks, they didn't take up any physical space, right?"

"Well, it's an interesting conundrum. The concept of physical space is debatable," he began.

"Cillian," she said, stopping him firmly. "You can explain the conundrum to me later. Yes or no?"

His usually gentle black gaze glittered mutinously. "It's not a simple yes or no answer."

"Dark arts preserve me. Are they portable enough for you to simply bring the folded-up stacks *with* us to House Harahel for a side-by-side comparison there?"

$$\sim 27 \sim$$

CILLIAN STARED AT Alise, beyond shocked by her suggestion. "You can't remove stacks from Convocation Archives!" To his chagrin, his whisper ended in a horrified squeak.

"Can't as in shouldn't or can't as in impossible?" she persisted with relentless logic. "It seems like the enchantment triggers on the removal of physical texts."

"*Shouldn't.*" He was insistent on that point. He could not possibly do what she was suggesting. Not even for Alise could he contemplate such breach of ethics. *None of us needs another Szarina incident.*

Alise still gazed at him expectantly. He should lie to her, insist that it was impossible. Except that he likely *could* get around the enchantment. "And very nearly impossible," he finally said when it was clear that she'd wait him out, and that he couldn't find it in himself to speak the lie to her face.

"Very nearly impossible leaves room for possible," she replied gently. "So, the enchantment might be bypassed if the texts are in a non-physical state?"

"Maybe," he answered unhappily. "By someone who knows how the enchantment works."

"And who knows how the enchantment operates?"

He couldn't meet her knowing gaze, looking past the tip of her left ear. "The archivists."

"Harahel wizard-archivists?" she asked, not really a question.

"Yes," he answered on a hush, unwilling to speak the anathema too loudly. "But Alise—I couldn't possibly! It goes against every ethic that underpins my avocation and my profession. No archivist would commit so grave a crime as to remove materials from Convocation Archives."

"Not even to *save* them from evil conspirators?" she asked, wizard-black eyes wide. "People who now know the hidden archives have been discovered and will fight to recover them. Probably this time to destroy them forever," she added darkly.

Cillian knew exactly what she was doing and still couldn't fend off the horrified reaction at her suggestion. "They *wouldn't.*"

"Are you willing to take a chance on that possibility? Especially when we have something we can do to prevent it."

"You don't understand, Alise," he said slowly, willing her to listen, knowing she couldn't possibly get the extent of his fears. He should have told her about the Szarina incident before this. Now it was the entirely wrong moment. Though, even in the best of moments, he couldn't possibly explain his shame over what he'd done, nor why he'd done it. Looking back, he hardly recognized himself. He'd been so dazzled by Szarina, so eager to help her. *I know all about your white knight tendencies,* Raya's mocking voice reminded him. Yes, he'd been a fool, thinking he could save Szarina, be the hero for once.

Worse, he'd thought she'd love him for it. What a fool he'd been.

"It's true. I don't understand," Alise said. "But I want to."

Cillian took a painful breath, willing himself to explain. The words that would damn him forever in her eyes refused to come. He couldn't bear to have her look on him with the inevitable disappointment. "I just… can't," he finally got out. "I can't do something unethical like that. Not again, not even for you."

"Ah." She nodded, a sympathetic smile twisting her lovely mouth. "'Not again.' By that I assume you're referencing what happened with Szarina Sammael."

He'd expected many replies from her, but not that. Grappling with his shock, his crawling shame, he couldn't look into her face. "Who told you?" he asked, voice hoarse. And how long had she known?

"Brinda Chur." Alise nodded, wrinkling her nose as his astonished gaze flew to her compassionate one. "That's only one reason she is no friend of ours.

"But…" He had to clear his throat, seeing none of the contempt and disgust he'd dreaded. "But if you know, then…" He couldn't finish.

"I know *you*, Cillian," she said, softly but firmly. "Whatever you did, I'm sure you did for the best of reasons, if perhaps not the wisest ones."

He couldn't help smiling at her gentle teasing. "I don't know about that. I was a fool."

"Well, I want to hear the whole story—no doubt the *real* story—directly from you, but let me put it to you this way."

She gazed at him with a level of trust, of earnest faith that rocked him to the core. "Preserving those archives, analyzing how they were tampered with and why, that is your calling as an archivist. You wouldn't be doing this for me. You wouldn't even be doing it for House Phel. It's for the integrity of these archives, which belong to all Convocation citizens. Something you believe in before all else."

She was good. And he had no defense against her. Wouldn't have, even if her rationale hadn't made sense. He hadn't been able to refuse Szarina either, but he could at least count on the fact that Alise would never use and betray him. "You've presented an argument too slippery for me to counter," he allowed. "I may not be the better debater, after all."

"Elals are known to be deft politicians for a reason," she answered glibly, though her deliberately cocky attitude faltered. She worried so much about becoming like her father.

"You're using your powers for good, though," Cillian told her with firm conviction. "I only hope that history paints me that way, too."

"If anyone dares to write otherwise, we'll just alter the archives," she responded with impish glee, grinning when he choked on his shocked reaction. "Oh, come on—that was a joke. I wouldn't really."

Yes, she absolutely would. Alise possessed a different moral scale that way, one that drove her to protect the people who mattered to her, no matter the objective right or wrong. They would discuss further. For the moment... "All right, cloak us," he told her. "And I'll bring the Phel archives with me."

He was pretty sure he could do it. The hidden stacks hovered there, neatly parked where he'd mentally bookmarked them, so bringing the folded-up space with him required something of a hook, not unlike picking up a stack of books instead of leaving them on a table. A bit unwieldy, and it required some mental balancing. He worked on it while Alise summoned her cloaking spirits. Once he had a feel for the thing, he could carry the weightless burden just fine.

Holding Alise's hand—mainly to stay close within her range, though the contact with her soothingly warm and rose-scented magic helped steady him—he walked along with her toward the exit and safety.

Getting through the enchantment with his burden in tow would take more finessing. Alise was right, however, that any Harahel wizard trained by the house and who'd worked any length of time in Convocation Archives could likely pull this off. That came as a reassurance that perhaps a Harahel had *not* been involved in concealing the Phel archives. Why go to those lengths if smuggling the stacks out of the archives entirely was an option? Surely Alise wasn't the first person to think of that possibility. Yes, it hadn't occurred to him, but that was because the ethical breach was essentially unthinkable. *Leave it to a wily Elal to come up with that,* a sneaky voice suggested. He ignored the voice, knowing better than anyone how vicious and damaging and outright false such gossip could be.

Regardless, it didn't matter—yet—who'd done the expert work of hiding the Phel archives. They would investigate that later. He needed to focus on the exigencies of the moment.

In the end, however, bypassing the rather basic enchantment didn't take anything extraordinary. Without realizing it, he'd been practicing for this moment practically every day as he checked out allowed materials, ensuring that anything removed from the archives had been recorded to the person taking it, adjusting the enchantment to let them pass, reestablishing it when the materials were returned. This monumental theft came far too easy.

When they reached the door, Alise glanced at him and he nodded. They walked out unobserved—and would have been regardless, as no one was about. Likely anyone awake had gone chasing the alarms. He and Alise walked right out, taking the Phel archives with them.

And walked straight into Gordon Hanneil.

~ 28 ~

F OR A WILDLY hopeful moment, Alise thought her cloaking spirits would save them. Gordon Hanneil seemed to stare right through both Cillian and her, his wizard-black gaze narrowed menacingly on the doorway to the archives.

Then his expression cleared, a smile that could only be called triumphant lighting his face as he focused exactly on her. "Oh, Alise." He tutted sorrowfully. "You didn't imagine you could fool a psychic wizard with a stale party trick like draping yourself in ghosties, did you?"

She didn't answer, mouth dry, her panicked thoughts groping for the morning's lessons, which now eluded her with all the thorough agility she could wish she could wield to get them out of this.

Gordon heaved an irritated sigh. "Come out already. You and the besotted archivist. I grow bored with this charade and you won't like what I get up to when I'm looking for entertainment."

The cloaking spirits were draining magic she might need to battle Hanneil anyway, so Alise let them go—though she kept them close by. She would use every trick she could muster. "What do you want, Proctor?" she demanded coolly, figuring

310

she might as well take the offensive.

"Why, I want what you have," he answered easily. "What you *stole*. I know you broke into the archives that I explicitly instructed you to leave alone. I don't know how you found them." His gaze rested on Cillian, a hint of quizzical irritation in his expression, as if he hadn't thought the quiet librarian had it in him and he didn't enjoy the surprise. "But I can read in your mind that you have somehow extracted them from the Convocation Archives, which turns out to be terribly convenient for me."

"Stay out of my mind," Cillian ground out, his hand clenching hers.

Gordon dimpled. "Make me, pretty boy. Oh, boo." He mock pouted. "You can't, can you? How sad for you. One bad decision after another, all for gorgeous wizard-girls far beyond your value. You do reach high, I have to give you credit there. But one day you'll have to learn it does you no good to reach for what you can't hold on to. Give me the archive and I'll let you both go."

"We're supposed to believe that?" Alise asked, the question dripping with gratifying sarcasm. Her fear and panic had dried up during Gordon's contemptuous speech, baked away by the fire of her righteous anger. Cillian was the finest of men and she was growing heartily tired of people acting like a youthful love affair and earnest desire to help someone else counted as a massive character flaw. Maybe in the cutthroat Convocation version of ethics, it did, but not in her book.

Gordon's smarmy magic reached for her, oozing tendrils groping for a hold on her will. She'd have to thank him for indulging in that little speech as it had given her opportunity to recall her lessons in the dark arts. Grounded again, she slipped herself away from the psychic wizard's grasp, mentally eluding him with ease. Losing his pose of superiority, Gordon frowned at her, his magic lunging in an unexpected strike.

She wisped away again, tempted to give him a smug smile, but wise enough to keep looking afraid—and unaware of his attempts. "I don't think you'll let us go," she prompted, bringing his attention back to his claim.

"I don't want *you*, baby wizard," Gordon snapped. "Or your nothing of a boyfriend. I'm your window of opportunity to escape the consequences of your impulsive actions. Give me the archive and I'll go. That's all I want. But I'm warning you: push me and I'll take you to those who *do* want you and you can enjoy being my little sex-puppet on the way."

"I *can't* give the archive to you," Cillian blurted, sounding on the verge of tears. "I would if I could, but you don't have library magic. Please leave Alise alone. Don't hurt her."

Gordon turned his unwinking black gaze on Cillian. Alise got a very bad feeling. Cillian had just drawn the focused attention of the viper, thinking to protect her. His tearful plea was probably an act, and he had the best of intentions, but she still wanted to kick him.

"What fools love makes of us," Gordon said to Cillian with soft and sweetly derisive sympathy. "But thank you for the suggestion. I don't need you to give me the archive when I can simply have *you*."

Alise saw the spear of magic, like a whip made of solid oil, shooting out and burying itself in Cillian's forehead. She cried out along with Cillian's gulp of agonized shock, his hand vising on hers as he convulsed, spine arching as he writhed in place. She had no way to protect Cillian, she realized with stomach-dropping terror. Everything she'd learned had been to save herself, not someone else. It seemed deeply, ironically fitting that even in this, she was completely selfish. She couldn't nobly sacrifice herself for Cillian because she simply didn't have the ability. How apt.

"Let him go!" she shouted, rounding on Gordon.

He flicked an amused glance at her. "Let me consider that request. Hmm. No."

"I'll go with you willingly," she offered. No, pleaded.

Gordon tsked at her, turning his attention back to Cillian, who calmed now, no longer physically fighting the Hanneil wizard's psychic grip. "I admire your grandiose perception of your importance in all this, sweetheart, but you've always been a mere pawn in this game. Your relevance has come and gone—though I personally appreciate the role you played in retrieving what my employers will reward me richly for appropriating. Thank you for your service to the cause."

Cillian had fully stilled now, his hand lax in hers, his gaze dully complacent.

"What cause?" Alise demanded, stalling for time. To do what, she didn't know, but she needed to *think*. "Who are your employers?"

"Silly bean." Gordon chuckled, shaking his head. "Only in novels do people monologue about their grand schemes, and then only if they intend to kill off the audience. Your dear papa would be most displeased if I did away with you, so that can't happen. I advise you to ask him. He strikes me as the type to jerk off his ego by monologuing. Now, book boy, come along with me. Places to go, people to see."

Cillian went willingly, a blank expression on his face. Holding onto his limp hand, Alise went with him.

Gordon arched a brow at her. "Coming along? I know you're hot for me, but really your eagerness is becoming an embarrassment. Maybe when you've grown up a bit, filled out some curves, you can send me a courier. Daddy will know where to find me." He winked at her and turned, Cillian following behind like an obedient pet.

"I won't let you take him," Alise ground out, firming her grip and planting her feet, so their arms stretched out long, Cillian still trying to walk away from her.

Gordon heaved an exasperated sigh. Without warning, he threw a psychic attack at her—not an attempt at control or to subvert her will, but to harm. She could see the menace in the magic hurtling toward her and instinctively understood that it would fry her mind.

Too late to evade or elude. She could only fight with whatever power she could muster. With the limited magic remaining to her, she threw up a desperate defense, pitching her magic against the Hanneil wizard's.

He blasted right through it.

The psychic blow hit her with devastating force, sending excruciating white-hot magic all along her nerves. Distantly she recognized this as a form of illusion. He was making her think she was in pain, but her body didn't know the difference and she dropped to the floor in a rictus of agony.

Freed from her hold, Cillian walked a few more steps to Gordon's side, turning to watch her with a curiously impassive expression, as if he didn't even recognize her. Likely he didn't.

"Cillian," she begged, reaching a hand to him. "You know me. Please help me."

"He can't help anyone, sweetmeat," Gordon said. "Least of all himself."

"I can be of assistance, however." Provost Uriel stepped out of the shadows, her platinum hair a radiant beacon, her familiar Priyan a step behind her. Alise sobbed out her relief, hoping against hope.

"Provost Uriel." Gordon nearly snarled, but he also straightened his shoulders and gave her the appearance of courtesy. "I apologize that you've been disturbed, but this is routine proctor business. Nothing to concern your august attention."

With the diversion of Gordon's focus, his attack on Alise fell off and she sagged in a limp heap on the floor, too weak to move.

"I'm not sure how you can imagine that to be true, Proctor Hanneil," the provost replied, unruffled, glancing down at Alise and offering her a hand. "This looks far from routine. And with one of my archivists involved, too. Most unusual."

Alise, grateful for the assistance, struggled to her feet. Very tempted to slide behind the provost and metaphorically hide her face in the intimidating woman's skirts, Alise made herself stay by the provost, on the other side from Priyan, and face Gordon with chin high. Whatever Gordon had done to Cillian, the effect remained in place, and Alise fretted internally that the Hanneil wizard might have damaged Cillian's mind forever. His brilliant mind. It couldn't be.

"With all due respect, Provost," Gordon said, sounding anything but respectful, "I've got the situation under control. If the issue needs to be elevated to your attention, it will be."

The provost's clear, cool, crisply academic psychic magic glittered with calculation over the little scene. Alise marveled that Gordon seemed to be oblivious to the thorough and clinical assessment—and to the fact that Priyan's presence implied the provost expected to need power.

Provost Uriel smiled without humor. "I believe that the issue has already been elevated to my attention—Tarin of House Tausa," she added after a beat, emphasizing his true name. "I'm also utterly uninterested in any explanations or excuses you may offer. I've been looking for you."

Gordon hurled an attack at the provost, exactly like the one he'd used to so incapacitate Alise. With seamless grace, Priyan put a hand on his wizard's side, supplying the needed magic to her. Tandiya Uriel flicked Gordon's attack aside with enviable ease, as if it were nothing more than an annoying gnat. Gordon's flabbergasted expression mirrored Alise's own shock. She'd had no idea the administrator possessed such ability.

The provost slid her a mildly reproving look, which she then fastened on the Hanneil wizard. "What, you all think I'm Provost of Convocation Academy because I excel at sliding documents around my desk?" With Priyan staying in contact, she advanced on Gordon, who stammered incoherent fragments of protests. Alise expected him to back up, but he seemed to be rooted to the spot. Not through his own will, it turned out a moment later.

"No, indeed," Provost Uriel continued in a silky tone, laying the palm of her hand on Gordon's visibly sweating forehead. "I am in charge here because I am the one capable of upholding the sanctity of this educational institution. I am judge and executioner here. This is *my* academy and the likes of you *will not fuck* with it."

On the heels of her words, a blaze of light of blinding clarity billowed from the point of contact between the provost's hand and Gordon's forehead. The Hanneil wizard emitted a kind of pitiful squeal, and deflated, crumpling into a boneless heap on the floor. Provost Uriel gazed down at him with distinct distaste a moment longer, then turned to survey a waking, but clearly confused Cillian. She crooked a finger at Alise.

"Now, the pair of you had better explain this business of setting fire to my archives."

~ 29 ~

ALISE COMPLETELY IGNORED the provost's demand for information—and ran to Cillian instead of answering. "Are you all right?" she demanded, framing his beloved face in her hands, aware that tears coursed down her own.

Cillian blinked at her in vague recognition, but didn't answer, and Alise choked back a sob. Rounding on the provost, she reined in the worst of her temper, but couldn't hold back her own imperious nature. "You have to help him."

The provost arched her platinum brows in affront. "My dear wizardling, I don't *have* to do anything. Especially for a lower-tier faculty member, already on probation for a previous transgression, one who appears to have stolen a valuable set of archives."

"He was trying to *protect* the archives," Alise hissed, pushed past the limits of courtesy. "He only brought them out of the larger archives because I asked him to."

Provost Uriel gave her a look of very real sympathy. "Alise, I admire your devotion to your lover and your willingness to take responsibility for him. This however, is exactly the concern with Wizard Harahel. It's not the first time he violated his ethical code, and the rules of this academy, to please a pretty girl."

Alise went spine-breakingly rigid with indignation. "I know about Szarina Sammael and this is *not* the same situation."

"Isn't it?" the provost returned coolly. "Through an academic lens, viewed objectively, the details are distressingly parallel."

"That's ignoring context and nuance," Alise protested. "You're not being fair to—"

"Alise," Cillian said, his voice creaking as if he hadn't used it in a long time, "Provost Uriel is correct in her assessment."

Alise practically flew the few steps back to him. "Cillian! You're all right?"

He smiled faintly, a hint of pain in it, and put his arm around her, less in affection than an obvious need to lean on her for support. "'All right' isn't how I'd describe it, but I'm alive and in possession of my own mind."

Call her picky, but she wasn't much reassured by that.

"He needs a Refoel mind healer," Provost Uriel instructed, not without sympathy, but clearly not happy with the situation. "His mental burden is difficult enough to carry. The Hanneil attack needs immediate attention if the archivist is going to be able to continue to endure the magic drain of holding those archives. Take the archivist there immediately, Wizard Alise. After which he can go home. I'll hold Wizard Harahel's dismissal until morning."

"Until *morning?*" Alise echoed, aghast at how fast things were moving. It wasn't the question she meant to ask, but her thoughts were lagging behind her reactions.

"Yes." Provost Uriel gave her a patient stare, Priyan grimacing in sympathy. "Once Archivist Harahel is no longer employed by this institution, he cannot receive Refoel services provided by the academy. He'd have to pay out of pocket. I'm doing him a favor."

"This is *not* a favor!" Alise nearly spat. "You can't fire Cillian over this."

"I not only can do so, I must," the provost corrected. "In truth, merely firing an archivist for removing materials from Convocation Archives will be seen as a dereliction of my duty. I will be called upon to answer for my decision to be so lenient."

"*Lenient?*" Alise seemed to be incapable of doing anything but repeating key words from the provost's incomprehensible statements. "You aren't being—"

"Alise," Cillian interrupted her again, squeezing her to his side. "Provost Uriel is doing all she can for us. She's letting me leave. I can go *home.*" He gave her a significant look, and understanding dawned.

Home. Not to his faculty apartments, but home to House Harahel. With the Phel archives still in tow. Still, Cillian shouldn't lose his job over this. She faced the provost defiantly. "I'm going with him."

"That is your choice," the provost replied, adding a graceful dip of her chin in resignation. "Though I cannot guarantee that you'll be readmitted to the academy for a third time."

"I'm willing to take that chance," Alise said with dignity.

"No, Alise," Cillian protested, the vigor of his denial entirely undermined by his unsteady weaving on his feet. "You can't do this. Not for me."

"I'm not doing it for you," she returned fiercely. She wouldn't say aloud how little she cared about graduation at this point. She retained that much discretion, at least. In a world where a Uriel wizard could squash a wizard with Gordon's power, Alise could recognize she had a great deal to learn. She might need to return to the academy someday—but she didn't have to be a doormat about it. "I'm finishing what I've started," she said instead, catching and holding the provost's gaze.

She didn't think she imagined the glimmer of approval in Provost Uriel's wizard-black eyes. "Off with you then," the provost instructed, as if they said goodbye at a faculty reception. "I'll deal with this mess." Dubiously, she toed the heap that was Gordon Hanneil. Or had been.

Alise couldn't be sure if he was alive and, in truth, didn't really want to know. He would obviously never threaten them again and that's all that mattered. "Come on, Cillian," she said gently. "Let's go to the infirmary. With any luck, it will be Healer Jonathan and we won't have to do a lot of explaining."

Cillian resisted her efforts to pull him along, instead facing the provost. "Thank you, Provost," he said simply.

"You are welcome, Archivist," Provost Uriel replied.

"I'll need to clear my faculty apartments."

She waved that off. "In time. I'll have them sealed. Who knows, we may need them for evidence at some point." Amazingly enough, she winked, then ruffled Priyan's hair. The familiar smiled at her in adoration. "Now go. Oh, and both of you—please don't set fire to anything else."

~ 30 ~

ALISE WAS RIGHT and they were in luck, amazingly enough, and Healer Jonathan Refoel was indeed on duty. That seemed particularly fortuitous given the run of exceptionally bad fortune they'd been experiencing up until then. Although, Cillian had to acknowledge, Tandiya Uriel had showed up at exactly the right moment. He owed the provost a great deal, more than Alise could understand, truly.

Especially as he couldn't ever tell her.

He didn't think he ever could describe to her how it had felt to be locked inside the prison of his own mind, unable to think his own thoughts. It wasn't only that he likely wouldn't be able to get the words out—though he feared he might not be able to—but also that he didn't *want* Alise to know. He'd rather that she have no idea how profoundly that brief experience had affected him. She'd blame herself, which wasn't fair to her and would only make him feel worse.

Those few minutes of being Gordon Hanneil's utter captive had aged him decades and broke something deep inside. The one thing Cillian had always been able to rely on was his own intelligence, his ability to *think*. He would never be the hero, the beefy sword-wielder, or even a wizard worth much of anything besides sorting books. But he had always been proud of his smarts. Even at his loneliest, he'd always had his own thoughts for company.

Without that, he'd been reduced to nothing in a blink. A minor exercise of Gordon Hanneil's prodigious talents and Cillian had ceased to exist. And that was on top of Cillian's utter failure to take action against the vile man who'd hurt Alise. For all of Cillian's nursing of his anger and dreams of revenge, when the opportunity had arisen, he'd done nothing at all.

He didn't think he'd ever be able to forget that feeling. If he'd felt unworthy of Alise before, Cillian's complete failure to act in the face of that fight proved his worst fears. Not only had he failed to protect Alise; he'd been a liability.

"You'll be fine," Jonathan Refoel said, meeting and holding Cillian's gaze, seeming to be attempting to reinforce the message on several levels. He rested his lean, brown fingers against Cillian's temples, his mint-scented healing magic infusing Cillian's mind with paradoxically invigorating calm.

Behind him, Alise hovered, face pale and drawn and dark eyes huge with anxiety. He'd done that to her. "Carrying that archive is a drain on you," Jonathan continued, "but it's nothing you can't withstand. And don't worry—your secret is safe with me. The primary problem at this point is that your encounter with the psychic wizard exhausted you. I'd recommend bed rest and a few nutritious meals to rebuild your energy, but I understand from Provost Uriel that there is an urgent need for you to travel to House Harahel."

"Yes, that can't be delayed," Cillian said, forcing himself to focus on what mattered. His existential angst ranked far below getting this stolen archive to House Harahel for analysis. And it had been kind of Tandiya to withhold that he'd been summarily dismissed for the gravest of transgressions. "I'll leave immediately."

"And I'll be with him," Alise said, flashing him a stubborn glare, clearly annoyed that he'd said "I" instead of "we."

In truth, as much as he'd dreamed about bringing Alise to House Harahel, to meet his family, to see all his favorite places, now he saw those fantasies for the foolishness they were. "You should go to House Phel," he suggested, not meeting her eyes. "You'd be safe there."

"Highly debatable," she replied crisply. "And you can save your breath. I'm not letting you travel to House Harahel alone. I'll go arrange for a carriage and supplies," she told Healer Jonathan. "Can someone bring him to meet me by the griffin door in half an hour?"

"I don't need to be escorted," Cillian griped at her.

"When you can stand without leaning on someone, I'll believe that," she retorted, eyes snapping. Then she relented. "You'd insist on the same for me."

She was right, which only bothered him more. He liked being the one to take care of her. That's what he brought to the table. If he became a burden on Alise in that aspect, too, then what? He hated to imagine her staying with him out of guilt. But this wasn't the time or place for that conversation—especially with Healer Jonathan present—and he could see Alise was entrenched. There would be no arguing her out of going. Maybe, once she'd satisfied herself that he was happily ensconced in the bosom of his family, he could convince her to return to the academy. That's where she belonged.

If Alise didn't graduate because of him, he'd never forgive himself.

"I'll meet you outside in half an hour," he told her.

"In the meanwhile," Jonathan put in, "I'll continue to infuse Wizard Harahel with healing magic. That should go a long way to helping him withstand the journey."

Alise hesitated, as if tempted to say something more, then lifted her chin, nodded to them both, and left. Cillian let himself put a hand to the pocket where he carried her promise of a favor. He kept it on him all the time now, like a good-luck totem. Briefly he considered using it to protect her, to force her to separate from him. But she'd find a way around that. And something told him he might need that favor for a more extreme situation in the future.

Healer Jonathan gave Cillian an encouraging smile. "She's worried about you. That's not a bad thing."

With the healer currently rummaging through his mind—a lot of that going around lately—Cillian could hardly argue, either about Alise's concern or that he didn't like it. "I worry about her, too," he finally said.

"Sounds like a relationship with a future then," Jonathan replied, winking jovially.

Cillian knew otherwise, but wasn't about to argue that either.

HE MET ALISE outside the griffin door, one of the side entrances to the sprawling complex that was Convocation Academy, so named for the stone griffin looming on the lintel. Somehow Alise had obtained a closed elemental carriage, very expensive.

"Courtesy of House Elal," she informed him with a determined smile, though her eyes remained shadowed in the steady, but muted light of the elemental lantern she carried. "Turns out Papa forgot to take me off the permissions for our house carriage that we keep here."

Cillian hesitated at the sight of the plush interior. "Won't he be angry?"

"Like I care?" She snorted. "What Daddy doesn't know won't anger him. I already reset the air elemental pilot so no one at House Elal will detect anything. As far as they'll know, it's still sitting quietly in the garage. Hop in!"

He didn't exactly hop, but he did manage to get up the step, steadied by the aide Jonathan had sent with him. Settling himself in the soft cushions, he had to admit the luxury felt like bliss to his bruised spirit and exhausted body. The archive hung heavy over his consciousness and he only wanted to sleep, his eyelids drifting closed.

He forced them open again as Alise covered him with a furry blanket. "I don't need you fussing," he complained, aware the doors had closed and they were already gliding away from the academy.

Alise tutted at him. "Shoe pinches on the other foot, huh? Just relax. It's cold out and there's nothing wrong with cuddling." She tripped some button that raised a footrest, elevating his feet, which made him even more comfortable, curse it. Then Alise slipped under the blanket, too, snuggling against him. "See? Cozy. Are you hungry? I have a whole basket of supplies. From the dining hall, so it won't be as good as your food, but Provost Uriel arranged for all kinds of excellent food and drink."

"I just want to sleep," he answered, thinking that the shoe did indeed pinch on this foot. And he was being ungrateful. Alise affectionately curled up beside him under a deliciously warm blanket, just the two of them, alone and together. This should be his happy ending.

"Sleep then," Alise said softly, settling her head into the crook of his shoulder, and wrapping a slender arm around his waist. "Sweet dreams."

He could only hope.

Alise and Cillian's journey continues

in

STRANGE FAMILIAR

Coming January 2025

Coming July 8, 2025 from Jeffe's new pen name:

Jennifer K. Lambert

Never the Roses

TITLES BY JEFFE KENNEDY

FANTASY ROMANCES

BONDS OF MAGIC

Dark Wizard

Bright Familiar

Grey Magic

Familiar Winter Magic

(Also available in Fire of the Frost)

RENEGADES OF MAGIC

Shadow Wizard

Rogue Familiar

Twisted Magic

HEIRS OF MAGIC

The Long Night of the Crystalline Moon

(also available in *Under a Winter Sky*)

The Golden Gryphon and the Bear Prince

The Sorceress Queen and the Pirate Rogue

The Dragon's Daughter and the Winter Mage

The Storm Princess and the Raven King

The Long Night of the Radiant Star

THE FORGOTTEN EMPIRES

The Orchid Throne

The Fiery Crown

The Promised Queen

THE TWELVE KINGDOMS

Negotiation

The Mark of the Tala

The Tears of the Rose

The Talon of the Hawk

Heart's Blood

The Crown of the Queen

THE UNCHARTED REALMS

The Pages of the Mind

The Edge of the Blade

The Snows of Windroven

The Shift of the Tide

The Arrows of the Heart

The Dragons of Summer

The Fate of the Tala

The Lost Princess Returns

FACETS OF PASSION
Sapphire
Platinum
Ruby
Five Golden Rings

FALLING UNDER
Going Under
Under His Touch
Under Contract

EROTIC PARANORMAL

MASTER OF THE OPERA E-SERIAL
Master of the Opera, Act 1: Passionate Overture
Master of the Opera, Act 2: Ghost Aria
Master of the Opera, Act 3: Phantom Serenade
Master of the Opera, Act 4: Dark Interlude
Master of the Opera, Act 5: A Haunting Duet
Master of the Opera, Act 6: Crescendo
Master of the Opera

BLOOD CURRENCY
Blood Currency

BDSM FAIRYTALE ROMANCE
Petals and Thorns

Thank you for reading!

About Jeffe Kennedy

Jeffe Kennedy™ is a multi-award-winning, bestselling author of 66 published titles, primarily in epic fantasy romance. She is a Past-President of the Science Fiction and Fantasy Writers Association (SFWA). She is best known for the RITA® Award-winning *The Pages of the Mind*, the recent trilogy, *The Forgotten Empires*, and the wildly popular *Dark Wizard*. She recently signed a six-figure deal with Tor for a new romantasy series writing as Jennifer K. Lambert™, with book one, *Never the Roses*, forthcoming in hardback July 8, 2025. Jeffe lives in Santa Fe, New Mexico. She is represented by Sarah Younger of Nancy Yost Literary Agency.

Jeffe can be found online at her website: JeffeKennedy.com, on Facebook, Goodreads, BookBub, Twitter, YouTube, Instagram, and—just like all the kids these days—TikTok.

jeffekennedy.com

facebook.com/Author.Jeffe.Kennedy

twitter.com/jeffekennedy

goodreads.com/author/show/1014374.Jeffe_Kennedy

bookbub.com/profile/jeffe-kennedy

Sign up for her newsletter here.

jeffekennedy.com/sign-up-for-my-newsletter